Hounds Abound

LINDA O. JOHNSTON

BERKLEY PRIME CRIME, NEW YORK

THE BERKLEY PUBLISHING GROUP
Published by the Penguin Group
Penguin Group (USA) Inc.
375 Hudson Street, New York, New York 10014, USA

USA / Canada / UK / Ireland / Australia / New Zealand / India / South Africa / China

Penguin Books Ltd., Registered Offices: 80 Strand, London WC2R 0RL, England
For more information about the Penguin Group, visit penguin.com.

HOUNDS ABOUND

A Berkley Prime Crime Book / published by arrangement with the author

Berkley Prime Crime Books are published by The Berkley Publishing Group.
BERKLEY® PRIME CRIME and the PRIME CRIME logo are
trademarks of Penguin Group (USA) Inc.

For information, address: The Berkley Publishing Group,
a division of Penguin Group (USA) Inc.,
375 Hudson Street, New York, New York 10014.

ISBN: 978-0-425-26843-8

PUBLISHING HISTORY
Berkley Prime Crime mass-market edition / April 2012
Read Humane edition / May 2013

PRINTED IN THE UNITED STATES OF AMERICA

10 9 8 7 6 5 4 3 2 1

Cover illustration by Jennifer Taylor/Paperdog Studio.
Cover design by Rita Frangie.
Interior text design by Laura K. Corless.

This book is dedicated to all the pets out there who need good and loving homes, particularly those who are older or who have special needs.

I also want to thank, and dedicate this book to, the many, many people who care about homeless animals. I have been delighted and amazed to see how many selfless animal lovers there are, and I'm proud I've gotten to meet some of them both in person and online via blogs and Facebook. Kudos and hugs to you all.

As always, I thank and dedicate this book to my husband, Fred, who encourages me no matter what my endeavors.

Chapter 1

It's not always easy to be a pet rescuer.

I find it particularly hard when I go to a high-kill shelter to save animals in immediate danger because of lack of space. I have to pick and choose those I think are most adoptable. That almost always includes young dogs and cats in good health.

It too often excludes seniors, and those with infirmities, no matter how adorable or endangered they are. Or how sad it makes me to leave them behind.

That was one reason I was so excited about where I was headed that September day.

The other was that I was spending a while in the company of my dearest friend, Dr. Carlie Stellan, an excellent veterinarian who travels a lot thanks to the TV show she hosts on the Longevity Vision Channel, *Pet Fitness*. That makes me value our time together even more.

I'm Lauren Vancouver, director of HotRescues, a wonderful no-kill pet shelter in LA's San Fernando Valley. I love animals and would do anything I can to save as many as possible.

As a result, I was delighted about our upcoming visit.

Carlie and I had just arrived at our destination and gotten out of my car. "This must be the place," she quipped as we walked up the wide paved path toward the two-story boxy building in front of us. It resembled a huge, remodeled stable. Over the door hung a large sign that read SAVE THEM ALL SANCTUARY and was decorated with cartoonish dogs and cats.

Yes, our destination was the new animal shelter that was already nicknamed "Save'Em." We had come to Shadow Hills, in the northeast part of Los Angeles, to visit—and to make our own evaluation about whether Save'Em, which had only opened a few weeks ago, was as outstanding a facility as this kind of shelter needs to be.

As Carlie reached for the elongated handle on the glass door, it opened. "Hi!" said the smiling girl who stood inside holding the door so that we could enter. The thin teenager wore a red shirt that proclaimed she was a volunteer. "I'm Peggy. Bella's in the office. Come in." That would be Bella Frankovick, who had just opened this very special pet shelter.

Peggy led us inside. A dog came up to us immediately, though slowly—a waddling dachshund whose muzzle was gray despite the darkness of the rest of his coat. "Hi, sweetheart," I said, kneeling to pet him. The little hound waggled all over, obviously happy with the attention.

"That's Ignatz," Peggy said. "He was our first rescue, so he's kinda like our mascot."

With a final hug and a pat on Ignatz's head, I stood again. I was interested to see that the floor was of irregular tile—probably easy to clean, but also helpful in keeping an unsteady dog like Ignatz from slipping. The entryway was small and, except for the archway through which Ignatz headed, surrounded by doors.

Peggy led us to the closest door on the left—and knocked before turning the knob and opening it.

The room looked more like a parlor than an office, with comfy chairs in a burgundy and deep forest green plaid scattered all around. There was a desk, and that's where the woman who now approached had been seated, but it was small, positioned unobtrusively in a corner.

An attractive room, yes. Appropriate for a very special pet shelter? Well, maybe, if it helped to keep Bella in the right frame of mind to take the best care of all her charges.

Now that I could see her close up, Bella appeared to be near my age and Carlie's—mid-forties, which indicated she was sufficiently mature to take on the high-stress responsibilities that were now hers. That was a good thing. She was also as attractive as Carlie. My good friend is slim enough to look right at home on TV, with blond hair that skims her shoulders and well-defined facial features.

I admire her but am glad I don't have to go out of my

way to impress people with my looks—which fortunately aren't too bad anyway. I'm fairly well preserved for a forty-something woman, with a pleasant face and black hair cut into a short cap so I don't have to pay much attention to it.

Bella Frankovick was even more model-like than Carlie, with long brown hair, lovely blue eyes emphasized by perfect makeup and curved brows, and full lips that didn't appear to have the ugly plump that suggested collagen enhancement. Which was interesting, if true, since her ex-husband was a cosmetic surgeon.

I had done my research before coming here. Not that I had to do much digging. For anyone who watches just regular TV news, and not even those paparazzi-driven celebrity reality shows, it would have been hard to avoid seeing something about their difficult divorce.

"Thank you for coming," Bella said in a delightful British accent, her large smile revealing—of course—perfect teeth. She wore a denim work shirt that said SAVE THEM ALL SANCTUARY on the chest, over slimming blue jeans. She shook first my hand, then Carlie's, as we introduced ourselves. "I'd love to chat with you, but I'll bet you'd like a tour first." Her quizzical expression raised her perfect brows.

"Absolutely," I said and Carlie agreed.

As we exited the office, I let Carlie take the lead, walking beside Bella and asking questions. They'd no doubt work out a symbiotic relationship of sorts. Carlie could provide not only veterinary care but promotion of this facility, too, which could bring in both substantial donations and needy residents. Bella could provide a wonderful topic for one or more of Carlie's upcoming shows.

I had a purpose for being here that could also help Bella. I had a lot of contacts within the pet rescue community. If I liked this new facility, I'd get the word out. Between my acquaintances and me, we could help Bella keep Save'Em filled. Maybe even send potential adopters her way, but that could be difficult. The kinds of pets she was taking in were largely unadoptable—or at least less likely to be chosen over puppies and kittens and fully healthy adult animals.

"Please come this way." Bella led us into the entry area and toward the open archway through which Ignatz had disappeared.

Peggy emerged from another door. "Want me to staff the entry?" she asked Bella.

"Oh, yes, please, dear," Bella responded, her smile appearing grateful. Interesting, that despite her elite background and power here at Save'Em, she seemed like a genuinely nice person. At least so far.

As we went through the arch, we emerged into a huge, two-tiered room with an upper balcony perched above the lower floor. Each level appeared to be lined with kennels much larger than those we had at HotRescues—large enough to accommodate the staff members inside who were attending to one or more dogs.

"The people who help me here are wonderful," Bella said. "Though we're new, I've enlisted both staff and volunteers. They all go through a tremendous vetting process to ensure that they not only love animals but will do everything required to take care of them."

We stopped at the first enclosure. Inside were two senior women. They sat on plastic stools on the tile working with three dogs that seemed equally elderly for their species.

One dog appeared mostly Basset hound, another was a small golden Lab. The third had ancestry I couldn't guess but he had long and floppy ears and a relatively short muzzle.

The women teased their charges with rawhide bones and gave commands to sit, lie down, and more. The dogs obliged, acting quite lively considering how aged they looked.

"Are they as senior as they appear to be?" I asked Bella.

I didn't think I'd spoken very loudly, but even so, "Yes, for all of us," cried the nearest of the women inside the enclosure. The other one laughed as their canine charges continued to play at their feet.

"Then I applaud all of you," I said, and both Carlie and I clapped. The woman who'd spoken wore a black shirt that read SAVE'EM STAFF, and the other wore a red volunteer shirt that matched the one Peggy had on. The staff member stood, bowed, and used a treat to get one of the aging dogs to dance on his hind legs with surprising ease.

"As I said, I have a good group of people who come here to help," Bella said. "They are appreciative of the dogs who show them that getting older, for one's species, does not mean one should give up and feel sorry for oneself."

"And they show the dogs something similar," Carlie pointed out as we walked away from the enclosure. "I've learned, working with animals, that so many are highly perceptive. They may not fully understand our spoken language, but our body language can be interpreted by a lot of them. A person who's a bit stiffer than the kids who come here can still play, and I'm sure your senior dogs recognize that on some level, right?"

"Absolutely," Bella responded.

We had reached another enclosure, as large as the first, with the ubiquitous tile floor, and a big plastic-and-metal crate at the rear with towels fluffed up in its base. This kennel had only one dog in it, an apparent Rottweiler mix with sagging jowls and lots of graying fur edging the black-and-red coloration of his face.

He ran up to the fencing and nosed at it, as if he wanted us to pet him. I glanced at Bella for permission.

She nodded. "Dolph could use some attention." I went inside for a love fest of licks and hugs and nose-butting. I laughed as I played with him, enjoying every minute of it.

But I did exit after a few minutes. There were other dogs to visit, other parts of the shelter to see.

When I'd carefully latched the kennel behind me, Bella petted Dolph through the mesh gate. "Poor fellow was kept outside in his owner's yard," she said. "Lived there, I gather, for eight years, with his only shelter a drafty doghouse—until a neighbor who moved in next door had a young Lab that liked to jump. He got over the fence and attacked Dolph, who fought back and . . . well, the Lab survived but Dolph's owners dumped him at a public shelter. I hated that story—so unfair to poor Dolph—and so I took him in."

"Poor Dolph," I echoed. "Before. But he seems to be doing well now."

We continued walking through the kennel area. Save'Em's facility was as huge inside as it had looked from the exterior, clean and attractive and filled with kennel enclosures. Not all were occupied—a good thing, since I'd already decided to make my contacts at the Southern California

Rescuers Web site aware that Save'Em was open for business for special-needs pets.

And we hadn't even reached the area where the neediest were.

Before we got to the end of the kennel area, a man with glasses and a distracted look on his flushed, narrow face walked up to us, hands filled with papers. "Oh, sorry, Bella," he said. "I didn't realize you were showing people around."

"I'll stop in your office and talk to you just as soon as I can, Kip," she told him. To Carlie and me she said, "This is Kip Schaley, Save'Em's accountant and my excellent financial advisor." The smile she turned on him was warm and made his complexion redden even more.

"Hi," he said to Carlie and me. "Catch you later, Bella." He turned and strode away.

I didn't need to ask about the funding for Save'Em. From the little I'd made myself listen to on TV, I'd gathered that Bella had extracted herself from her marriage with enough money to keep her and an awful lot of needy animals in food and shelter for a long time—maybe. Apparently she and her ex were still at odds about it, though, or so the media vultures claimed.

The probability of her having sufficient funds gave us something else in common. HotRescues, the shelter where I'm head administrator, is well funded, too. Not by me, certainly. I'm a single parent with two kids. And, now, I have a wonderful dog, Zoey, as my pet-in-chief.

But I'm fortunate to run the shelter that Dante DeFrancisco started. He's the CEO of HotPets, a really successful chain of retail pet stores. He's rich. And he gives a lot back to animals.

We continued along the inside kennel area past some unoccupied enclosures, then up to the second floor, which was mostly empty. Bella next took us outside to a separate building housing aging felines in three well-furnished cat rooms. Red-shirted volunteers sat on the floor giving the kitties attention and love. These volunteers were much younger, on the whole, than the people socializing the dogs.

Then Bella said, "I've been saving the best for last."

We walked along the blacktopped path back to the main building. Bella took us in through a rear door.

There, the kennels were moderate sized, but they were plushly furnished with pillows and even more toys, along with the standard towel-filled crates. It was apparently an attempt to make the residents as comfortable as humanly possible, and I was impressed.

"Here's where our special-needs residents are housed." Bella looked at Carlie. "I particularly want your opinion, Dr. Stellan. I watch your *Pet Fitness* TV show all the time, and I was especially interested in the one not long ago where you featured that company in the eastern U.S. that manufactures prosthetics and other equipment to help make handicapped dogs and their owners' lives better. I loved it! Any suggestions you can make here . . ."

"I'd be delighted." Carlie smiled at Bella.

"And . . . well, I'd thought I had my veterinary situation here established, but I am looking for a new one, as it turns out. I would love to give your clinic a try."

"Who am I to turn down business?" Carlie's grin widened.

"For regular fees," I added, in case Bella thought Carlie would donate her skills and those of the other vets at The Fittest Pet Veterinary Clinic.

"Of course." Bella nodded her head so her long hair skimmed lower along her work shirt. "I want the best care possible, and I'm willing to pay for it."

Good. We were all in sync—and I liked Bella Frankovick. I liked her Save'Em attitude and her practicality.

I liked her, and her facility, even more when she introduced us to a few of her special-needs animals.

In a feline room along one side, there was one cat who was totally blind and another who had a spinal defect that made her back curve oddly.

One dog was deaf. Another was three-legged.

A third, a Basset hound mix, had no control over his back legs at all and just dragged them behind him.

"It's difficult to keep poor Nifty clean," Bella said, "but I've wondered whether one of those gadgets on wheels that was on your show could help him, Carlie."

"We can give it a try." Carlie looked wistful, the way she sometimes gets when seeing an animal she really wants to help but isn't sure how much good she can do.

That's one of the reasons we're such good friends. I adore her for caring so much.

She broke the spell a bit when she asked Bella, "How would you feel about my featuring Save'Em on a *Pet Fitness* show? I'd enjoy telling the world what you're doing here. I love it!"

"That makes two of us," I added. "You've got a completely different business plan here from HotRescues, and I suspect it will work wonderfully. The more you let people know about it, the more contributions will be made to help you out."

"I hope so." Bella looked down at the floor as if bashful to admit she could use the donations. "I've got some resources, but of course they are not endless, even if . . . Well, it's just so important to me to take good care of all these poor animals. Save'Em won't be able to take in every senior pet, or all those with special needs, but I'll bring in all I can. I hope to find new homes for as many as possible, especially if we can rehabilitate some of those with physical issues. If publicity helps with contributions, then I'll do what I must."

She looked quizzically at Carlie, who nodded. "We'll work out a time soon for me to come and film here."

A short while later, we walked through the door from the special-needs area back into the regular kennel facility. "We'll also work out a time in the next day or so for me to give all the residents a cursory vet check," Carlie said to Bella. "If you could e-mail me the records first, that would be helpful. I'll bring along a few of my colleagues, too. Just give me a call." She reached into the large purse she always carried and pulled a business card out of one of the pockets. "I'll be in touch anyway, once I get some things lined up for the filming ."

"Delightful." As Bella took Carlie's card, a cell phone rang. It was apparently hers. She reached into her pocket, then frowned after looking at the caller ID.

She glanced back at us. Her pretty face looked rigid, upset. "Sorry. I'd best take this."

She hurried off toward the area of the dog enclosures as Carlie and I walked slowly toward the front of the building so Bella could catch up with us.

Her voice caught up first. It was raised and filled with anger. "You son of a bitch, Miles. You'll never get me to shut down Save'Em. Do your damnedest. I'd kill you before I'd let you hurt me, or my new charges here. Believe it."

Chapter 2

"Why is it that the best pet rescuers seem to have started their calling by leaving bad marriages behind?"

Carlie was joking. Wasn't she?

We were back in my car, a Toyota Venza with all kinds of accessories to make it easier and safer to transport pets and their food and equipment. It was a crossover, not extremely large, so I relied on the HotRescues van for major pickups. But this was a great vehicle for everyday use.

We were making good time on the freeway. We still had to go south on Reseda Boulevard, but it wouldn't take much longer to reach Carlie's veterinary clinic in Northridge. I had picked her up there earlier, after dropping off a couple of owner-relinquished cats. Her fellow vets had promised to check them over while we were out critiquing Save'Em.

"At least you recognize that I'm among the best," I retorted. "It remains to be seen about Bella, although I was really impressed by what I saw. Apparently you were, too."

"She's got not only a heck of a concept, but she's putting it into effect in a great facility." Out of the corner of my eye, I saw Carlie lift her large purse from the floor. I glanced toward her. "My mind's churning about how to approach the show I'm going to do on Save'Em," she said. "Need to make notes."

I nodded. "If you tie it in with the orthotics and prosthetics company you visited before and their promise to work with you on camera to use their gadgets, it should be a real winner—especially for the animals you help. But"—I had to get my own dig in—"it's a good thing you're a celebrity and veterinarian, and not a pet shelter administrator."

"Why? Because I've never married?"

"You're the one who brought this whole thing up," I reminded her.

"You're just jealous," she said. "I have consecutive, interesting relationships." I laughed, but she was right. She always had a guy in her life, each better looking and more successful than the last. She threw herself into every relationship until things started to get boring or bad. By then, she had another man waiting.

Me? Well, right now I have a guy in my life. Sort of. I met Captain Matt Kingston of Los Angeles Animal Services at a puppy mill rescue a few months ago, and we've been seeing each other ever since.

But a while before that, I'd been in a terrible marriage that I had ended. After deciding to change my life, I'd put together an excellent business plan for a new pet shelter that was in the concept stage, submitted it to Dante DeFrancisco, and gotten hired to help start, then run, HotRescues.

But saying that I was a happily divorced woman didn't give credence to my really extraordinary first husband. My dear Kerry Vancouver had given me ten wonderful years and two wonderful children. He had died, though, from a rare form of cancer. I'd married the second time to give Tracy and Kevin a new father. He had never been that. My kids had turned out great anyway. Both were now in college.

"At least that jerk Charles is out of your life now," Carlie said. "Judging by that phone call, and what I've seen in the news, poor Bella is still trapped in the stage of things where she has to deal with her miserable ex. And she has to do it publicly. That's got to make it even worse. Good thing she's gotten a lot of money out of it—or so I've heard."

"Maybe, but with the way they're fighting, she's undoubtedly spending a lot on her lawyers." I sighed on her behalf. "Heck, Miles Frankovick is a plastic surgeon to the stars. He must have a huge income. Turning over whatever community property Bella is entitled to apparently makes him mad, but so what? He has a lot more years of face-lifts and tummy tucks to make up for it."

I turned off the freeway and onto Reseda Boulevard. We weren't far from The Fittest Pet Veterinary Clinic. Carlie had called ahead and the cats I'd brought in had checked out fine. I was just going to drop her off and pick them up.

"You'll keep me in the loop as you schedule your show at Save'Em, won't you?" I asked.

"Do you have any doubt?"

We were stopped at a light and I glanced over at her. "Nope. Just wanted to remind you."

"Fair enough. So, like I said, if I want to start a new pet shelter in a year or two, maybe I should get married first, to give myself time to get divorced."

I felt my eyes widen in surprise. "Are you seriously considering marrying Liam?" Liam Deale was her latest guy friend.

"Not at the moment with my lifestyle being so crazy. I'd be going into it certain that I would have to dump the guy someday to make sure he didn't dump me. But maybe when things settle down . . ."

"Then you *are* serious. Oh, Carlie, that's great. I want to get to know Liam better."

"So you can give me advice? Just remember, I'm the one who gives advice on national TV."

I pulled into the almost-full lot at her clinic and parked. A lady got out of a car near the entrance with two Yorkies on a leash. They looked healthy, and I assumed they were there for shots or a checkup.

"You advise about pets and pet care," I replied to Carlie. "I'm the one who can advise you about the good and bad things that come along with marriage. And I remember the bad only too well."

I got out of the car, and so did she. I love her veterinary clinic. It's a single-story box of pink stucco—very unobtrusive outside, but full of delightful amenities inside, like a park area in the middle where animals were brought out for fresh air.

As we approached the door, I gave Carlie a brief hug. "Maybe you and I can schedule dinner sometime soon and bring Matt and Liam along."

"So you're considering marrying Matt?"

I was so shocked at the question that I started laughing. "This conversation has gotten way out of hand," I said. "We're just dating."

"So it's too soon to plan a double wedding." Carlie giggled, then preceded me inside to gather up my cats.

When I returned to HotRescues, I parked in the side lot near the welcome area and called for Pete Engersol, our all-around helper, to grab one of the two cat crates to carry inside.

He joined me almost immediately. Pete is thin, a senior citizen who stays in amazingly good condition, probably in part because of all he does to keep HotRescues going. He slings bags of food, cleans up kennel areas, and acts as a general all-around handyman.

"Are they okay?" he asked as he picked up Slinker's crate.

"They're both fine," I assured him as I slid Alta's crate out of my car.

We entered through the side door to the main building. Nina Guzman, my assistant administrator, was there, staffing the welcome area behind the tall, leopard-print reception desk, and surrounded by photos of happy adopters on the bright yellow walls.

So was Zoey, my own dog—an adorable Border collie–

Australian shepherd mix. She was mostly black and white, with some merle gray thrown in. I'd adopted her recently, partly thanks to Matt Kingston's introducing her to me.

Zoey had been at HotRescues enough times to be used to the disloyalty I displayed by carrying cats around and paying attention to other dogs. She greeted me eagerly, rubbing against my leg and revving up her tail in a wag that made me smile. "Hi, Zoey," I said. "I missed you, too."

"Want me to take Alta?" Nina stood from the chair where she had been working, as usual, on the desktop computer.

"I've got her. Thanks." Telling Zoey to stay with Nina, I followed Pete through our reception building and into the yard behind it, where our rows of kennels began.

Our cat facilities used to be right there, in the building in the middle, but Dante had recently bought the property next door and fixed it up with additional kennels and a new building where we housed our kitties. The original center building had been remodeled to have a real apartment upstairs, where a member of our security staff slept each night.

As we walked by the kennels, some of the dogs barked. Hard as it always was, I ignored them, not wanting to encourage behavior that might make them less adoptable. Besides, with a cat crate in my hands I couldn't easily stop to reward them.

But I didn't ignore them completely. Not in my mind. I felt so proud, and so blessed, that all the animals we had here were adorable, healthy creatures who might, with our help, soon find forever homes.

My heart, and gratitude, went out to Bella Frankovick

once more. Her Save Them All Sanctuary was one wonderful facility.

I hoped it stayed that way.

I hadn't intentionally been eavesdropping on Bella's side of her apparent conversation with her ex. Obviously the guy was threatening her and her choices. She'd threatened back, and, having gone through something similar in the past, I could only applaud her for it.

She was probably as likely to kill Miles as I'd been to dispose of Charles—and my ex was still around somewhere, probably ruining another woman's life.

"Would you like me to post a notice on the site?" Nina asked.

I had returned to the welcome area and now leaned on the side of the leopard-print counter and looked down at her. The top I'd changed into matched hers—a blue knit HotRescues shirt. It looked better on her than on me. She was younger and curvier. But I'd decided long ago not to hold that against her. She was also a nice, caring human being who'd triumphed over an even uglier marriage than mine.

Under Carlie's latest principle, maybe Nina should have started her own pet shelter by now.

"That would be great," I told her. I'd brought up my intention of contacting Southern California Rescuers, which was a loosely knit alliance of local shelters that shared information on food bargains, adoption events, animals in trouble, and anything else of general interest to its followers. "I'll bet there'll be lot of interest in Save'Em. So many shelters have pets they thought would be adoptable who wind up staying till they're geezers too old to be placed in good homes."

My intention was not to let that happen at HotRescues, but I was pleased to have a good alternative if we ever needed it.

"I've got to go see that place," Nina said. Her light brown hair was long and loose, cut into bangs framing her face and flowing down her back as she looked up at me with her waiflike deep brown eyes. "It sounds like a castle built in a cornfield."

I laughed. "Not a bad description. I think Bella started with an old horse farm and remodeled its house and stable. She did an amazing job. Anyway, yes, please post something informative on the SoCal Rescuers site. While you're at it . . ."

We discussed others we wanted to tell about Save'Em. For one thing, Nina had a lot of contacts at Los Angeles Animal Services, since in addition to working here she also volunteered several evenings a week at East Valley Animal Shelter. .

That meant she'd been able to inform me now and then about their wonderful activities to save endangered pets, like a recent puppy mill rescue. In turn, Animal Services cooperated with private shelters like HotRescues to allow us to take in animals in danger of being euthanized by them because of lack of space.

"Did you talk to Matt yet?" Nina asked from where she was still typing on the computer keyboard, a smile in her eyes as she looked up at me.

"No," I said, "but I will." Matt had several important teams reporting to him: SmART, which was the Small Animal Rescue Team, D.A.R.T., the Department Air Rescue Team for saving larger animals like horses, and Emergency Preparedness Services. He'd be interested in Save'Em. He often told me about animals that needed to be rescued at Animal Services so I could pick them up or find another shelter that would, and now he'd have another resource, too.

Before letting Nina get any busier with the tasks I'd assigned, I asked about the visitors to HotRescues that day while I was gone. "Any potential adopters?"

"A few. I had Bev take them around after they filled out the initial paperwork." Bev, a delightful senior citizen, was one of our longtime volunteers. "You'll need to check with her about whether any were serious—and whether they looked like you'd approve them."

For now, I went down the nearby hallway to my office, Zoey following close behind.

I like my perfect-sized den at HotRescues. It's all business on one side, with a not-so-antique L-shaped desk that I had refinished when I helped to start the shelter. On the other is a conversation area with a designer-like sofa that has brown, leathery upholstery, fluffy beige pillows, and curved wood legs. In between is a handy wooden bookshelf that also pretends to be a file cabinet. I have a window view of part of the shelter area, although I often keep the shades drawn.

I called Matt first. We decided to meet for dinner that night. That way, I could give him details about Save'Em—

ones he could use to encourage Animal Services to let us know about special-needs pets that Bella could save.

Next I called Dante DeFrancisco. With his vast network of HotPets stores, he had resources beyond my comprehension. In addition to his funding HotRescues and HotWildlife, a nearby wildlife sanctuary, he sometimes donated money to other worthwhile pet assistance organizations.

Now that could include Save'Em.

"Everything working out all right with the new and remodeled facilities?" he asked.

"It's all great," I assured him, leaning my elbows on the desk near my clunky, aging computer. We discussed particulars for a few minutes, and then I told him the reason for my call.

"Save Them All Sanctuary," he said in a musing tone as I watched Zoey circle the woven area rug under the desk, preparing to lie down. "The founder is Bella Frankovick, right?"

"Yes, do you know her?"

"She's a shrewd enough lady. Came to talk to me about donating food. Until she's well established and I'm impressed with her facility, I'm not giving her anything for free but I've cut the price substantially. I like the idea, and I like her. But she's new at this and I had some misgivings, so we'll see."

"Well, I liked what I saw so far. But I'll keep you informed about anything else I learn about Save'Em."

"Good." He said good-bye and hung up.

Dante had set an irritating little fly of unease buzzing around my head. Was Save'Em all it appeared on the outside?

I was still going to try to send as many special-needs pets in its direction as I could.

But I would also have to make sure that my first impressions of Bella Frankovick and her shelter were indeed correct.

Chapter 3

Matt and I took a detour before eating that night.

We went to Save'Em.

That little fly kept buzzing around in my mind after my conversation with Dante. Yes, I'm impulsive at times. Compulsive, too.

I'd called Bella first and asked if it was okay for me to bring another friend to see the sanctuary. She was truly gracious, saying I could bring as many friends as I wanted, whenever I wanted.

That didn't sound like someone with anything to hide.

Plus, I wanted an official Animal Services opinion about the shelter. Well, sort of official. Matt wasn't assigned to review private shelters, so his opinion would be just that.

He picked me up at HotRescues. I left Zoey again. Nina had gone for the day, but our security director, Brooke

Pernall, would be there with her dog, Cheyenne, so Zoey would have company.

Matt had changed out of his official Animal Services uniform. He wore a black plaid sport shirt tucked into black jeans, an informal, sexy look. I supposed he would look sexy in anything, at least to me.

Matt was a tall, muscular guy with short black hair. His features were craggy, and I always enjoyed how he regarded me appreciatively with his toasty brown eyes.

"This is your second trip there today?" he asked as I slid into the passenger seat of his Animal Services vehicle.

I nodded. "Just want your opinion. I don't want to influence it, but—well, I was favorably impressed."

The Save'Em parking lot was less crowded than it had been earlier that day. We walked through the gate and were met inside by Bella, who had already told me that she lived in a small cottage at the rear of the property. She greeted us as warmly as she had greeted Carlie and me that morning.

"I'm surprised to see you again this soon, Lauren," she said in her charming British accent. She looked as lovely as she had earlier in the day. I was sure Matt noticed.

"I've just been talking about Save'Em so much that Matt wanted to see it himself." And then, to be fair, I mentioned, "He's an officer with Animal Services."

Bella's perfectly made-up blue eyes widened. "Did you see something wrong, Lauren?" Her voice choked. "If so, I wish you'd told me. I'd have done anything to correct it. Anything at all."

"It's nothing like that," I assured her.

The tour was nearly the same as earlier, and Matt seemed impressed, too.

"I still love it," I told Bella. "I'm letting other private shelters know you're available to take in special-needs animals. Plus—well, I've talked to Dante DeFrancisco. He said you'd already spoken with him. I've put in a good word for Save'Em." I didn't mention that we'd left things somewhat iffy. I'd be sure to tell him, though, that my opinion hadn't changed after a second look.

I would mention that I had brought Matt here for a quasi-official appraisal. That way, I wouldn't appear even a little wishy-washy—which I wasn't.

"Thank you," Bella said. She gave me a hug, and Matt and I left.

We stopped for dinner at a Mexican restaurant on our way back to HotRescues. Over a taco salad, I asked Matt for his first thoughts on Save'Em. They were as favorable as mine.

I didn't need to feel vindicated. I usually only cared about my own opinion. But it didn't hurt to have the backup of Carlie from before, and now Matt. Especially when I had to report about it to Dante.

But enough of that. Matt and I had something else important to discuss.

"The HotPets Rescue marathon?" Matt said. "Good. I want to talk to you about that. I'm getting a lot of Animal Services folks to run, but any donations they get will be designated for city shelters."

"Are you running?"

"Of course. You?"

I looked down at my body. I'm in fairly good shape for

a forty-something lady and I exercise when I can—by walking dogs and hefting large bags of pet food. I'd wanted to participate in the upcoming marathon since Dante first mentioned it. He liked to hold events to benefit, and call attention to, pet rescues. We had even gotten Matt to authorize a demonstration by the Small Animal Rescue Team at HotRescues a few weeks ago.

I'd get as many sponsors as I could now for the marathon—ones whose donations would be for HotRescues. And now I'd add Save'Em.

But I had to get into better shape.

Not that I intended to win. But I'd have to finish that race if I started it. If I make a commitment, I produce.

"Yes," I said firmly. "I'm running."

"So when are we training?"

It was late Thursday evening. The weekend was fast approaching.

"Sunday," I said. "Why don't you come to my house with Rex? We'll take both dogs out and run."

"It's a date," he said.

For the next couple of days, Zoey and I got to HotRescues late, a rare occurrence. But as soon as I woke in the morning, she and I took a run around the gated community of Porter Ranch, where we live. That way, I'd be prepared when Matt and his dog, Rex, a black Lab mix, joined us.

Matt and Rex joined Zoey and me late on Sunday. We ran together through my residential neighborhood. I waved as we passed neighbors and their dogs, as I had during Zoey's and my earlier outings. Their formerly amazed expressions—if I hadn't imagined them—had been replaced by friendly encouragement.

Dinner tasted good that night, after I'd showered and sent Matt into my kids' bathroom to shower, too.

And later—well, I somehow got my energy back. Enough of it, at least, to spend a very pleasant night with Matt.

More than a week passed after my first marathon practice with Matt. On most days, I took at least a short run with Zoey, who clearly loved it. My stamina definitely continued to improve. I intended to be in great condition by the time of the actual marathon, a few weeks away.

It was early Monday morning. I had just awakened and let Zoey into the fenced yard for her first evacuation of the day.

I often watch morning news shows on TV as I get ready to head to HotRescues. It's usually just background noise. Today, though, the local news got my attention. I heard the announcer ask, "What is your opinion of Save Them All Sanctuary, Dr. Drammon?"

I rushed over to the aging TV perched on a dresser in my bedroom—not nearly as nice as the one in the living room that had been chosen by my son, Kevin.

I had already showered and put on my blue HotRescues staff shirt, but hadn't yet pulled on my slacks. I'd run a comb through my hair and begun putting on the light makeup I generally wore. Now I perched my butt on the edge of my mattress as I watched.

The man who sat in a chair to the left of the screen was a usual anchor for the show. The man in the chair facing him did not look familiar. He was lean, with a hairline that had started to drift back on his head. What hair was left was dark, peppered with gray. He wore narrow, black-rimmed glasses and looked sincere as he responded to the question. "I've been a veterinarian for more than fifteen years. I'm all for saving as many animals as possible. That's what I do. But quality of life is so important. And I worry about the dogs and cats that are kept at Save Them All."

"Why is that?" asked the anchor.

"Because its professed purpose is to take in senior animals that are not otherwise adoptable. Those with disabilities, too. In theory, it's a wonderful idea. But if the animals are elderly, how long should they be allowed to grow older? Suffer? Same goes for the handicapped. A few can, perhaps, be helped. But once again, prolonging their lives can lead to suffering."

"Then you think that a shelter like Save Them All Sanctuary is a bad idea?"

"Unfortunately, yes. Private shelters generally take in mostly younger animals, those that are healthy, because those pets are far more likely to find loving homes. Just keeping animals in poor condition alive, well . . ." He trailed off, removing his glasses and rubbing his eyes with his thumb and forefinger, almost as if wiping away tears.

He appeared so sincere. So caring.

I wanted to confront him immediately, ask why on earth he had become a veterinarian if he believed so strongly in euthanizing just because.

The announcer got that, too. "So at your veterinary clinic, if a pet is old or has problems, you believe it's best to put them down."

Drammon nodded. "For their own sakes. So they don't suffer."

I had a hard time listening after that. The interview fortunately didn't last much longer.

I grabbed my BlackBerry from its nightstand charger and pressed the button to recall Bella Frankovick's number. Did she know about this?

I got her voice mail and left a message to call as soon as she could. No details, though. I'd wait till I spoke with her to see if she knew about this Dr. Drammon and the interview.

She and I had met for coffee a few days back. Talked about our philosophies on saving pets, which were similar. We'd even called each other a couple times to touch base. And, surprisingly, we'd begun sending each other text messages now and then, as if we were half our ages. I got a kick out of it.

That was why I texted her next, telling her to call me.

I needed to finish getting dressed. Quickly. Before I decided to punch out some defenseless furniture in aggravation.

When Zoey and I took our customary morning walk-through HotRescues that morning, I remained irritated enough to be abrupt at first with Nina and other staff members and volunteers, though my ugly mood wasn't their fault.

Most understood. Our handyman, Pete Engersol, cleaning a kennel, just grinned as I snapped a criticism at him. He was used to dealing, now and then, with my bad moods if animal welfare was at stake.

I ran into Dr. Mona Harvey, our part-time shrink who counseled people interested in adopting our residents. She bent to pat Zoey until her tweed skirt nearly touched the ground, then stood and looked into my face through narrow glasses. "Do you want to talk about it?" she asked, obviously seeing my irritability without my having to say a word.

"No, thanks. I think Nina said someone interested in one of our cats will be coming by later today. Will you be able to meet with them?"

"I've got it scheduled," she said. "And you're changing the subject."

"Yes, I am. See you later."

Bev, our older volunteer who could practically run the place, also virtually ignored me as Pete had. Some younger volunteers like Ricki just skirted around Zoey and me. A college-age African American, Ricki had just started school to become a veterinary technician but still managed to visit HotRescues when not in class.

Then there was Mamie Spelling. The short senior citizen with curly, red-dyed hair had been playing with two terrier mixes in our fenced park area when I ran into her.

Mamie had been my mentor years ago when I first became interested in pet rescues. Recently, she had turned into an animal hoarder. And a murder suspect. She was aging and confused, the only reasons I'd sort of forgiven her. After her hoarded animals had all been saved, and the real murderer had been caught, I'd encouraged her to move into a senior facility near HotRescues and volunteer here, where I could keep an eye on her.

She'd given me a teary look as I'd walked past before,

but now she approached and gave me a hug over the waist-high fence. "Tell me why you're upset, Lauren, dear," she said.

Feeling guilty for being in such an obviously foul mood, I complied.

After I finished my story, she nodded her agreement with my judgment of the TV vet. "Anyone who criticizes heartfelt pet rescues is a jerk."

I laughed. But this interaction with Mamie finally got through to me. I was letting that miserable interview, with someone I didn't know and who clearly *was* a jerk, bother me too much.

I took Zoey to my office. She sat, watching me as I settled behind my desk, her head cocked. "Time to deal with this in a better way," I told her. She seemed almost to nod, then curled into a ball on the rug at my feet.

I called Carlie. She always had good perspective on everything.

Yes, she was aware of the interview. She had friends at the station where the interview was conducted who kept her informed about animal-related stories. That was where her guy friend Liam worked.

She didn't know Dr. Victor Drammon, but after watching a replay of the interview she'd looked him up on the Internet. He had a clinic near Beverly Hills. She'd seen nothing especially critical either in his online ratings or from the veterinary review boards.

"I'll counter what he said when I do my show," she assured me. "Although, Lauren, he actually has a point. You don't rescue the kinds of animals Save'Em does."

"Not usually," I admitted. "And I feel so awful that I can't always save the especially needy pets like them."

"Of course. But you know the drill: HotRescues' function as a private no-kill shelter is to save and rehome as many pets as possible. If you took in the old and infirm, you'd fill up and wouldn't be able to save as many healthy, young pets in their eleventh hour because the public shelters that house them need more room. Have you talked to Bella yet?"

"I left her messages. And I'm going to one of those public shelters this morning."

That was one reason I was overreacting—maybe. Nina had worked out a visit for us at the East Valley Animal Shelter, where she'd volunteered for HotRescues to take in some animals that morning—dogs and cats that otherwise might not survive until tomorrow if we didn't bring them here.

I couldn't save them all. And I definitely didn't want to hear things like that damned uncaring vet had said about how it might be better to assume that the special-needs pets I couldn't rehome were suffering and deserved to die. It happened much too often, and it just shouldn't be.

HotRescues is a no-kill shelter. The definition of that term varies, but my favorite interpretation is a place where animals are euthanized only when they're sick and possibly suffering, with no hope of recovery. We don't kill for behavior issues, and we certainly don't kill just because an animal is old or disabled. But having someplace wonderful to take special-needs animals with only slim chances of getting new, loving homes was a big relief to me.

I mentally thanked Bella Frankovick for creating Save'Em

as I rounded up my crew to go save as many animals as we could that day.

I went to Save'Em late that afternoon. I wasn't alone this time, either.

My companion wasn't Matt or Carlie or any other person. It was an adorable, senior-citizen dachshund I'd seen at the East Valley shelter that day whom I doubted I could place in a loving home. But I also couldn't leave him behind knowing he wouldn't have lasted more than another day at the public shelter.

I'd finally gotten a text message back from Bella. She had seen that interview. Wanted to talk but not just then.

I'd texted her back requesting the okay to bring my new, old friend to Save'Em. Yes, she'd said, Durwood the dachshund was welcome.

So here we were. I'd kept Durwood in a crate in the backseat, for his safety. Now, I took the small wiener dog out. He was primarily black with some brown spots, as well as a lot of gray around his muzzle.

Mostly, he was sweet, very happy to be in my arms, nosing at me and giving doggy kisses.

How could anyone have left him at a high-kill shelter? The story was that he'd been an owner relinquishment, someone's pet who had been given up simply because they didn't want him anymore.

He was a dog I'd love to have kept at HotRescues. But he was thirteen years old, slow in his gait. He was unlikely to be adoptable, despite my wishes. I'd have kept him at my shelter if there hadn't been a better place for him, of course.

I'd have done my best to find someone to at least foster him—and preferably adopt him.

But I knew that at Save'Em he'd have a better chance at finding a new, wonderful home with a loving family—or he would be kept there and well cared for, for the rest of his life. Maybe he'd become Ignatz's new best friend.

I snapped a leash onto Durwood's collar and he walked with me from the parking lot to the front gate. Slowly. And when we got there, he sat down, panting.

Poor guy hadn't much energy. But he had been checked out by a vet while at the East Valley Animal Shelter and had a clean bill of health—except for age. Unfortunately, that wasn't curable.

The person who let me in the front door was Peggy, the volunteer in a red shirt who had greeted Carlie and me the first time I'd come. "Hi, Lauren. Is this Durwood?" She knelt and held out her hands, and the dog wiggled up to her, tail wagging hard enough almost to knock him off balance. Peggy hugged him, then stood. "Bella told me to show you inside. She has someone with her but will say hi when she can."

She brought us into the main building, *tsk*ing a bit when poor Durwood struggled to keep up. I lifted him into my arms. "No need for you to do anything that's too hard for you, boy," I told him.

"Hi, Lauren," said Kip Schaley when we got into the entry. "Bella told me you were bringing us a new resident." Save'Em's spectacled accountant patted Durwood, too. Once again he held a bunch of files and appeared distracted. "I'm waiting for a call in my office, but I'll look in on him later."

A staff member wearing a black shirt came into the tile-covered entryway to greet us. She appeared to be in her twenties, a bit plump, with an attractive face highlighted by curly, silver-blond hair. "Hi," she said. "I'm Neddie. Come along to my office and we'll get the paperwork started to take in this sweet fellow."

Peggy gave Durwood a last pat before heading through the archway into the main facility. Neddie's office was to the right, the opposite side from Bella's. I followed her and sat on a stiff folding chair, keeping Durwood on my lap.

Their procedure was similar to that of HotRescues—filling out forms about where the dog had come from, providing any background information we had, and handing over copies of vet reports, all of which would be entered into the computer.

"He'll need to be checked out by our vet, too," Neddie said. "We have a new one—I think Bella said you recommended her clinic? She's that woman whose show I watch on the Longevity Vision Channel, Dr. Carlie Stellan."

I smiled. "She's a wonderful vet."

"Unlike our last one," Neddie muttered. "That damned Dr. Drammon." She looked up at me with angry gold-tinged eyes. "He's a traitor."

"I heard his interview." My expression undoubtedly mirrored hers.

"We're not supposed to talk about it. Would you like to see where we'll keep Durwood after his quarantine period?"

"Sure."

This time, it was Neddie who stooped and lifted Durwood, who wagged and licked and acted like a wonderful, loving dog.

Good thing that the paperwork that came with him from the East Valley center hadn't identified his former owner. Otherwise I might have given him a piece of my critical, angry mind.

When we exited Neddie's office back into the entry area, Bella was there with a man. He wore a dark suit and an even darker scowl.

Bella, as always, was lovely in her black Save'Em shirt with a light suit jacket over it and matching slender pants. Her makeup was perfect, but her eyes looked sunken and her expression pale.

"I don't want another tour of this damned stupid place," the man, taller than she, shouted down at her. "It would only make me even angrier about how you're wasting my money."

"It's my money, Miles," she retorted coolly. "Even though you're stopping me from collecting some of it. I earned every penny of our community property. You should have paid me more to put up with you."

So this was her ex-husband, the Beverly Hills plastic surgeon. His eyes were inky brown and as cold as a winter night in the San Bernardino Mountains. His high cheekbones underscored those small eyes, and his narrow chin had a wattle of flab hanging down that quivered like gelatin on a moving train.

He looked as if he could have used some of his own surgical skills on himself.

"You were nothing but a barely successful screenwriting hack before," he continued, hands clenched into fists at his sides. "At least if you'd kept doing that, it would only be you I'd have been forced to support now, not this ridiculous façade, too. If you had to pretend to love and save animals, why not purebreds that someone might actually spend money to buy from you, not pathetic things at the ends of their lives? And why you have to house them in luxury like this—"

"It's not luxury. It's a warm, loving environment and they deserve it. A lot more than you ever did. You're the pathetic thing, not my animals."

"Well you'd better warn that damned lawyer of yours to get ready for the next round of our fight. You'll never see another cent of rental income from my real estate. And I'm going to get the rest of my money back, too, you'll see."

"Over my dead body," Bella spat. "Rather, your dead body." Her grin was malicious.

I saw those fists of Miles Frankovick rise as if he planned to use them on Bella. I quickly grabbed my Black-Berry from my large purse and aimed it at him. "This thing takes great pictures. That'll make a wonderful one to send to the cops. And it'll look great plastered all over the Internet." My turn to grin.

He pivoted toward me, and I wondered if he would instead punch me. But he just aimed another furious glare first toward me, then at Bella. "This is far from over," he spat, then walked briskly toward the door.

In moments, he was gone.

Chapter 4

Bella was visibly shaken as she thanked me, then insisted on meeting Durwood. Neddie was still there, saying nothing, but she looked scared as she accompanied us back to the quarantine area.

"He's so sweet," Bella said, stepping into the kennel, lifting Durwood and giving him a hug. "We'll take good care of him, you'll see." Her voice quavered.

"I know you will."

I needed to get back to HotRescues, but I hated to leave Bella alone. Well, she wouldn't exactly be alone, but I wanted to provide whatever support I could.

"Let me call my assistant," I said. "If Nina can hang around for a while, let's go out for dinner. We can chat about good times and great pets."

"I'd love that."

Fortunately, this was one of the evenings Nina wasn't volunteering at the East Valley Animal Shelter. Plus, she told me our security director Brooke had already shown up with Cheyenne and was taking her initial walkthrough of HotRescues for the night.

Before we left, Bella invited me to meet her own dog, Sammy. "He's out in the rear yard helping to get our more frightened new residents acclimated to being around other dogs as well as people. Come on. I'll introduce you."

Sammy was a Belgian Malinois, which resembles a German shepherd. They're particularly smart dogs, also frequently used in law enforcement. As we reached him, he was lying down on a grassy area while a nervous-looking greyhound sat beside him, apparently ready to bolt if he hadn't been on a leash.

"Everything okay?" Bella asked the staff member observing the encounter who held the other end of the lead.

"Absolutely. Sammy's got Godric all calmed down."

"Excellent! Come on, Sammy. Time for dinner."

That apparently made Sammy happy. He followed us to the small cottage at the far end of the Save'Em property, which was framed in light blue with white trim. The inside was cottage-like, too, with entry straight into the living room. Bella showed me around. A doorway at the far side led to the hall to the kitchen and two bedrooms.

"Cute place," I told Bella.

I didn't understand why her laugh was so wry until she said, "Definitely. But a far cry from the Beverly Hills mansion I moved out of."

I had to ask. "Which do you like better?"

"Silly question. I'm free here. No fights every day, and I can pick my companions. Right, Sammy?"

After she fed Sammy and exchanged her Save'Em shirt for an attractive peach blouse, we headed for the place we'd agreed on for dinner, a chain steakhouse not far from Save'Em. I drove. I didn't have to ask Bella what was on her mind. The forced smile on her lovely face told me that she, like me, was rehashing that awful conversation with her ex. She responded to my questions, but otherwise didn't say much.

Inside the restaurant, though, she opened up after we ordered our food and hit the salad bar. Unfortunately, we couldn't get wine in the family joint, but that didn't matter—not when I started a topic of conversation that obviously appealed to her.

"Tell me how you decided to open Save'Em," I asked as soon as we sat down at our booth once more.

The false, brave smile on her face segued to a real one. "As soon as I'd made the decision to leave Miles at last, I considered what I wanted to do with the rest of my life. He hates animals, so we didn't have any pets for the horrible ten years we were married. I missed them. I also knew what it felt like to live in hell and need a change, a sanctuary."

"I'm so sorry." I thought of my own horrible second marriage and how my decision to go into pet rescue had been similar, but she needed to talk, not listen to my tale of redemption.

A server brought our meals—both burgers. As I cut mine in half, Bella continued, "The idea came to me while watching some TV shows when Miles wasn't around. A couple of them were Carlie's, about animal rescue and pet health. I finally dumped Miles more than a year ago. I was smart about it, carefully moving my half of our community property out of our bank and stock accounts first. We're still arguing about that, of course. He claims I had no right to it. A judge granted our divorce but left property division open. We're continually fighting about money and our interests in the rental properties we own, too. But that's not what you wanted to hear. I looked for the right place, bought it in my own name with a down payment from the money—*my* money, which I had rightfully taken from our accounts—then remodeled it as soon as the divorce was final. That was why I only started taking in special-needs pets a few months ago."

"What a wonderful story," I told her as she bit into her burger. "The creation of Save'Em, I mean—not the rest. When Carlie interviews you on her show, you'll have to tell it to the world."

"Of course." She grinned. "I want everyone to know and feel happy about what I did—and donate as much money as possible, since what I have won't last forever." She seemed to wilt for a moment as her mind again circled her ex. "It may not last long at all if I have to continue to use it to fight Miles off legally. And if he wins our property battle—"

"Don't even think about that," I told her. "You're entitled to what you got and undoubtedly more."

"You're a dear, Lauren." Her pretty blue eyes brightened as she regarded me.

"Of course I am." I smiled. "Now, let's just enjoy our dinner and not even think about our ugly exes."

"You have one, too?"

I still hadn't intended to mention mine. The thought had just slipped out.

"Yes." I gave her the short version.

"We've got a lot in common, then, Lauren," Bella said when I finished, her voice soft and emotional. "I think we're going to be good friends."

"Me, too. Now let's stop all the gushy stuff and eat."

When we were done eating, I drove Bella back to Save'Em and parked at the rear, close to the little house where she'd left Sammy.

"Want to come in and check on Durwood?" she asked.

"I'd love it."

She unlocked the gate to the wooden fence surrounding the rear of the place and let us both in, then locked it again behind us. The property was lit similarly to HotRescues, with energy-saving halogen lights at safe intervals to illuminate the yard around the cottage, the park area, and the backs of the animal shelter buildings.

"Just a sec. I'll get Sammy." Bella went through a similar procedure to unlock the house while I approached the rear of the main building. In a minute, she came back outside with Sammy at her side, unleashed but looking attached to her. "Let's go see Durwood."

"Are you the only person here at night?"

"Usually. Some staff members stay till nine most of the

time, and others come in at around six in the morning, so I'm not alone much. And if you're worried about my being alone in an emergency, they're all on call."

"Still . . ."

We were inside the building by then. It, too, was lit by dim lights. "This way," Bella said. Sammy stayed beside her.

Most dogs we passed didn't look up from their comfortable-looking beds on the tile flooring. An occasional muzzle lifted; eyes opened halfway, then closed as the dog went back to sleep. None even barked at Sammy, which showed they were familiar with him.

That demonstrated to me that the dogs had no major fears about where they were. A wonderful testimonial to Save'Em.

We were soon at the isolation ward. Bella told Sammy, "Sit. Stay." Of course he obeyed. I liked that dog. My obedient Zoey and he would get along well.

Bella and I went inside. Durwood was in an enclosure. Unlike the others, he didn't stay asleep but stood immediately as we neared him. He didn't bark but made a quizzical snuffling sound, like, "Did you come to take me out of here?"

"I know it's too soon to tell," I said to Bella, "but do you think there's any chance of his getting adopted? If not, maybe I should take him back and see if I can get anyone interested."

"We'll see. You can always retrieve him if you want. But even if he doesn't find a new home, he'll be loved here. In fact, once he's out of isolation, I want to introduce him

to another dachshund who's one of our favorites here—
Ignatz. I think you met him the first day you were here."

"Of course. He's adorable."

"He's also in need of a pack member. I've got Durwood
in mind to fill that role, assuming they get along."

"That's what I'd hoped!" I said. "And if anyone comes
along who's interested in adopting one—"

"I'll make it a condition that both are adopted together."

I gave Bella a quick hug of approval. "Thank you so
much! I won't worry about Durwood, at least for now."

"Come visit him anytime. In fact, visit him—and me—
often."

We continued walking around the main building. When
we looked in on the cats, a couple were on the prowl within
their special habitat, but most were asleep, too.

I was finally ready to leave. I still had to go to HotRescues to pick up Zoey on my way home. In fact, if I'd been
away for a while I almost always visited my shelter before
I could settle down for the night. Micromanaging? I'd been
accused of that by my nasty ex and, at the time, had felt
hurt. Now I happily admitted to it as one of my special
talents.

Bella and Sammy walked out the back gate with me
toward my car. It wasn't alone in the parking lot. Apparently Bella noticed the other vehicle, a black Mercedes
sedan, at the same time as me. She dashed toward it,
Sammy at her heels. "What the hell are you doing here,
Miles?"

The driver's window rolled down. "Just keeping an eye
on my unwanted investment," he said. "The property is

okay. I'm deciding what the best use for it is, after I get you evicted."

"I own this property! It's mine. You can't have it."

"You own it only as long as you make payments to the bank. When I get my money back, you'll lose it."

I had approached behind Bella. Sammy stood at her side looking highly uneasy, obviously aware of his mistress's rage.

"You have no business here now," I said over Bella's shoulder. "You probably never will. It's time for you to go."

"Oh, yes, you're that woman who runs HotRescues. For the moment. Did you know that Dante DeFrancisco is a friend of mine?"

I wondered how he knew who I was. No matter. The guy was obviously a liar. "I'll ask him, but even if you know him I doubt that you're friends. He's an animal lover. You, apparently, are a creep who likes to make trouble." I pulled my BlackBerry out of my pocket, where I'd just shoved it. "But I've got some friends in the LAPD. Let's see if the cops are up to an arrest for trespassing this evening."

"Don't bother." Miles's window rolled back up, but not before he called out, "Like our former governor used to say in the movies, 'I'll be back.'"

"The hell of it is," Bella said as he peeled out of the driveway, "he undoubtedly will be back."

"This isn't his first time harassing you at night?"

She shook her head.

I lifted my phone again. "Then I will call the cops. You should at least report this. While we're waiting, I'll tell you all about EverySecurity, the company we use at HotRescues. It's not the best—we've had problems with them in the past—but they've improved. They work for Dante and cover most of his HotPets stores. Because they screwed up a while ago, I also have a former private investigator as our security director who supervises them, and she or her staff are around all the time at night. I'd suggest you do the same."

"I'll think about it." Bella's tone seemed to say that she would drop the whole idea as soon as I left. "But I'll be fine. As I said, this isn't the first time. I'm sure he just wants to rattle me so I'll give in. But that's not going to happen."

I tried to stay a little longer, but I did need to leave. Once again, Bella promised she would be fine.

I only hoped she was right.

Chapter 5

Bella was okay the next time I talked to her, the following morning.

I was at my breakfast table still in my robe, a cup of coffee in one hand and my BlackBerry in the other. Zoey sat beside me on the floor, hoping for a handout of cereal. "How about a biscuit instead?" I asked her and she wagged her tail as I complied.

No, Miles hadn't come back, Bella responded to my first, concerned question. She had kept an eye out for him while holding her cell phone until she had gone to bed. She had made sure that Sammy was loose in the house and ready to play watchdog, if necessary. He was good at that.

"But I would love a break, Lauren," she finished. "Once I've got my staff here and busy, would you mind if I visited

HotRescues? I'd enjoy seeing your facility and how you run it."

"Mind? I'd be delighted!"

I quickly dressed in grubby clothes. "Ready, Zoey?" I asked at our front door, not that there was any question about her eagerness to go on our morning's practice run. When we finished our course, I went inside and fed my sweet dog, who showed little indication of being out of breath. As Zoey ate, I showered, dressed, and put on a little makeup. Then we headed for HotRescues.

Bev was behind the leopard-print welcome desk. "Nina's in the back checking things out," our senior volunteer said. "You'll like these phone messages." She handed me some papers on which she had written notes in her neat handwriting. A young couple and a family who had each been here before were coming back to fill out our final adoption form. If all went well, both might even be able to take their new pets home with them today.

"I already met them and liked them," I told Bev. "Did you schedule their times?"

She had. The couple would arrive around ten that morning and the family about three-thirty, after the kids' school let out.

I walked around the corner and down the short hallway to my office and left the messages there. "Do you want to come?" I asked Zoey, inviting her, as always, on our initial walk around the shelter facilities for the day. The happy look in her expressive amber eyes gave me the answer I expected. "Let's go."

To my delight, when we exited my office Bella was in

the reception area chatting with Bev. She wore jeans and a denim work shirt with the Save'Em logo over her T-shirt.

She looked at me, then downward. "This must be Zoey. What a sweetheart!" She knelt and hugged my dog. If I hadn't already liked Bella, I would now.

"I've heard of Save Them All Sanctuary." Bev came around the desk to join us. "You're the person who started it? Lauren said you might be visiting today." Bev was short and thin, with a hint of a stoop that suggested possible osteoporosis. She wore a yellow HotRescues volunteer knit shirt. She was here often enough to be a staff member. I'd even offered once to hire her, but she had laughed and said she didn't want to feel obligated to be here—though she was certainly around a lot.

"Yes, I founded Save'Em," Bella admitted with a shy-looking smile.

"Then I want to shake your hand." Bev did so, her grin wide and delighted.

"I didn't think you'd come this early," I told Bella as I started her tour of HotRescues.

"I needed to get away for a little while," she said. "But I'll be fully refreshed when I go back."

With Zoey at my side, I took her out the door at the building's rear and into the shelter. Our presence immediately excited a lot of the pups and most started barking—something I did not encourage.

The area looked far different than it had a few months ago, before Dante bought the property next door and expanded our facilities. He'd also had this area remodeled. The cement walkway was still lined with kennels for medium and larger dogs, but much more attractive ones with wood and glass in addition to the standard chain-link fencing. Similar ones around the corner at the rear weren't as large and housed small and toy dogs.

The kennels on the new property were much like the ones here had previously been—but newer and updated, made with better materials. Each was still mostly outdoors, with an indoor area at the rear where dogs could veg out or avoid bad weather.

"Hi, Abel," I crooned to the black Lab mix in the first kennel on the left. He had been brought here a few months ago as an owner relinquishment and remained unadopted. We weren't sure of his age, but he had a lot of gray around his muzzle.

"Looks like one of our guys," Bella observed.

"He hasn't been here long, and I'm hoping to find him a new home—but if that doesn't work out, I might be in touch about him." Unless I could find him a loving fosterer. One way or another, he'd remain well cared for.

He behaved well, not barking or jumping like some of the other dogs who'd gotten excited just to see us. Bella and I went inside his enclosure and fussed over him. Zoey waited outside for us, sitting tolerantly.

Soon it was time to move on. I introduced Bella to other dogs, most of whom were fairly new since we were fortunate enough to find homes quickly for a lot of our residents. I took her into the building on the right, at the center of this row of kennels, to show her the new kitchen and the upstairs had been converted into an apartment for the security person who slept here overnight. "Hint, hint," I told her. "You should have someone like that."

"I do," she said dryly. "Only, it's me."

I shook my head and led Zoey and her back down the stairway. I gave her a tour of the rest of this kennel area, pointed out our storage building at the rear, which held our laundry facilities, then around the back pathway onto the new property. I showed her the newest kennels and the large building that now contained upstairs offices for Dr. Mona and our part-time dog trainer, Gavin Mamo. Downstairs was a second kitchen and areas to house small animals like rabbits and guinea pigs, although we didn't have any right now. One part was designed to hold puppies and some of our tiniest dogs. Plus, this was where our groom room was—the area where our new on-staff groomer Margo worked.

As we walked around, I introduced Bella to our staff and volunteers. Quite a few were around that day, caring for and socializing our residents. We passed Nina as she hurried back toward the greeting area, and she seemed delighted to meet Bella.

I also pointed out to Bella our new cat house as well as the latest quarantine building on the new property. We kept all animals there for at least a couple of weeks when they first arrived at HotRescues, as well as any ill creatures who needed to get well before going back into the general population.

"It's wonderful!" Bella kept exclaiming, which I thought was sweet. Of course it *was* wonderful. I had helped in the original design, as well as the current one. It all worked well.

But Save'Em was wonderful, too.

Our tour ended when Nina came to get me. "Our first prospective adopters of the day are here," she said.

I hurried toward the welcome area with Bella and Zoey, greeted the people who waited for me, and told them I'd be right with them. Then I walked Bella to her car. "I'm just so happy that I got a chance to see HotRescues," she said as she slipped inside. "Of course you know I'm jealous."

"Why?" I blurted. "Save'Em is state-of-the art, too. It's fantastic."

"But more of your residents are likely to find great forever homes," she reminded me. "I'll make my residents' lives as happy as possible even if they stay with us, but still—"

Her cell phone rang, and she pulled it out of her pocket—and frowned. "Damn him," she whispered. I immediately knew who it was.

"You don't have to answer," I said. "Let it go into your voice mail."

"He'll only call again. And again." But she did as I suggested.

"And remember that you can't talk on your cell while driving," I told her.

"Yes, Mom." She laughed despite the strained expression on her pretty face. "See you soon, I hope."

"Definitely."

But if I'd known at the time the circumstances under which I'd next see Bella, I might not have spoken so quickly.

That afternoon, I checked my e-mail while grabbing a quick sandwich that Nina had brought in for me—trying not to give Zoey pieces despite her adorable begging stare.

A message from Carlie was there, and I opened it first. She had attached a link to a promo she had filmed for her upcoming TV show that would feature Save'Em. I immediately clicked on it.

Her clip was fantastic! It made clear that, on her show, Carlie would counter the nonsense from Dr. Drammon's interview about how older or disabled pets shouldn't be allowed to live, that all of them should be assumed to be suffering. Since segments of that interview were still being aired on TV, this promotion was even more necessary.

"As with everything else," Carlie said to the camera, "every situation should be judged individually—and my opinion about Save Them All Sanctuary, and how it treats its special-needs residents, is all good. Tune in to my upcoming show, 'Hug'Em at Save'Em.'"

I called her, and she answered right away. "What a great way of contradicting that nasty S.O.B who'd have closed Save'Em's doors and killed all its residents," I said. "When will this spot air? Everyone who loves animals and doesn't want to see them die will watch your show."

"I always like to jump in and use any advance publicity," Carlie said. "I decided to take advantage of Drammon's ridiculous interview by shoving it back into his face even before people can watch my show. This spot should start airing soon—and frequently, at least on the Longevity Vision Channel and some of its affiliates."

"Well, hugs to *Pet Fitness* and to you, too." I smiled as I hung up.

Later, I smiled again. The other set of eager adopters visited HotRescues—two African American parents with their son, age ten, and daughter, age fifteen. They were interested in a year-old standard Schnauzer mix.

I was always careful when a family with young kids wanted a puppy. I sometimes didn't approve the placement. Too much attention might be required by both—and they might even hurt one another. But both these kids, and the dog, were old enough to constitute a potential good fit.

We sat outside in the park area with the Schnauzer, whom we called Gervis. Of course they would be able to change the name if the adoption worked. I hadn't yet visited their home, although they had brought pictures. It appeared to be large and well decorated, with a substantial backyard.

One of the photos of the yard showed a doghouse, which waved a proverbial red flag at me.

I checked their application again. "So you did have a dog before?" I asked the mother. "Another medium-sized one?"

"That's right," she said. "We lost poor Roselle a few months ago. Old age."

"Did Roselle sleep outside?"

The teenage daughter was the one to answer, her tone accusatory, which I didn't like. "I know why you asked that. It's because of your rules. You won't let anyone take a dog if it'll be outside a lot by itself."

"That's one reason, yes." I regarded her calmly, and her belligerent expression softened.

"We'll keep Gervis inside always, I promise, except when he needs to go potty. Or when we're walking him. Or when he just wants to play there. That's the way things were with Roselle, honest." She sounded almost ready to cry.

I aimed my gaze first at her, and then at the rest of her family. All except her brother, who was on the ground roughhousing gently—yes, an oxymoron—with Gervis. The pup was clearly loving it. "That sounds good," I said noncommittally.

The mother nodded. "It's true. Your application says we'd need to allow you to come for visits. You can check our home out first if you'd like, or come anytime." She aimed a gentle smile at her widely grinning son. "I think Darian has already adopted Gervis. With your okay, of course."

"The indoor-outdoor question was nearly my final concern." My turn to smile. "One more, though. Where will Gervis sleep?"

"My room," Darian said immediately.

"Or mine," his older sister contradicted. "We'll let him choose."

"I will want to visit now and then, at least at first." I directed this to the parents. "But although I want to go over a few more things with you, I think Gervis has found a new home."

I was beaming for the rest of the afternoon. When I received a call from Matt asking to join me for dinner, I felt as if I were walking on air.

Two potential adoptions that worked out in one day. Sure, I've even had three now and then. But as few as one felt wonderful when I believed I'd helped another pet find love forever. Two made me euphoric.

Even Nina commented on how happy I looked as I watched the family leave together, including Gervis. "Pretty proud of yourself, aren't you?"

"Yes," I said simply.

She rose from behind the welcome counter and gave me a hug. "You should be."

I walked around HotRescues after entering what I needed to about the adoptions into our computer system. Zoey came along. The staff and volunteers I ran into apparently found my smile contagious—much better than when I'd walked around in a snit.

"Another one adopted?" Bev walked up with Dodi on a leash. Dodi, a sheltie mix, had been at HotRescues for a few months now. She was a sweetie, but the right people hadn't come to look at her yet. Bev was taking her for a final walk of the day on the street outside.

I nodded at the question, and Bev slapped me on the back with as much energy as someone half her age. "You go, girl!"

I laughed.

Our final walk through HotRescues took half an hour. It was past visiting hours—at least for potential adopters—when I returned to my office. Matt was there, though. Nina had let him in before leaving to volunteer at a city shelter that evening.

"Hi," he said to Zoey first as he stooped to pet her. I knew there was a reason I liked this Animal Services officer. Then he rose and looked down into my eyes with his sparkling brown ones. I stretched up to meet his kiss.

"Have you been running?" I asked. His body had always seemed toned, but, though I might be imagining it, he felt even more muscular now—and we'd only seen each other a few days ago.

"Sure have. You?"

I nodded.

We decided on a restaurant for dinner that wasn't far from my home so I could drop Zoey off first. He had left Rex at his place, so it would just be us this evening.

Dinner was good. Conversation was better, at least until we squabbled amiably over the check. I thought I'd won the right to treat until my BlackBerry rang. I checked it. Bella.

It was fairly late by then, and I was curious so I answered.

"I think you were right, Lauren." She sounded breathless.

"About what?"

"Needing better security. Someone's here, I think. I hear noises, and Sammy keeps pacing and barking."

"Have you called the police?" I knew my alarm sounded in my voice. Matt, who had handed his credit card to our server, looked at me in concern.

"Well, no. I might be imagining—"

"Assume you're not. Better to be safe than—"

"Sorry. Yes, I know. But with the bad publicity Save'Em already had after Vic Drammon was interviewed on TV, I'll take my chances. I shouldn't have called you. I was hoping you'd come, but that was stupid. Just in case there is someone here, you'd be in danger, too. I'll talk to you tomorrow. Sorry." She ended the call.

I couldn't believe how frustrated I felt—and how absurd I thought her attitude. I explained the situation to Matt.

"Let's go there and find out," he said, making me want to hug him all over again.

L.A. Animal Services officers were sometimes permitted to carry weapons, in case they had to put down a suffering animal. I knew Matt locked a gun in his car, and he had driven us here.

He drove us to Save'Em. I called Bella and told her we were coming. Despite her protestations, she sounded relieved.

I showed Matt where to turn so he could park in the back near Bella's house.

"Well, hell," I said as he pulled into the parking lot. A car was already there. A familiar car.

Miles.

I told Matt why I recognized it, including the confrontation I'd had with Bella's ex yesterday.

"No wonder she heard things. The jerk is stalking her, trying to scare her while he fights her for the money she's entitled to. I'm ready to scare him right back. Could I hold your gun?"

Matt's laugh was grim. "Let me," he said.

I didn't really anticipate we'd find Miles just sitting there, though. If Bella and Sammy had heard noises, it was likely that he'd sneaked onto the grounds to scare her—or worse. Even so, I slowly approached the car to rule out his presence, leaving Matt to extract his weapon.

The lights in the parking lot were dim, but as I got near the car I saw a figure in the driver's seat. "He's here," I called to Matt, and I stepped up my pace.

When I got to the door, I reached out, ready to pound on

the window since the creep didn't even look in my direction. He was staring straight ahead, through the windshield, toward the nearest part of the shadowed wooden fence.

Only . . . he wasn't moving at all. A chill crept through me. Instead of pounding on the window, I rapped gently.

He still didn't move.

Trembling, I shifted so I could see him better in the faint illumination—and saw exactly what I'd been afraid of. A dead man.

A knife was sticking out of Miles's chest, and there was blood all around.

Chapter 6

I called 911 right away as Matt nodded his agreement. He used a handkerchief to open the car door and reached in to touch Miles's throat. Judging by the grim set of Matt's mouth, I knew he didn't feel a pulse.

I called Bella next and told her to come out to the parking lot because there was something she needed to see. I didn't explain why.

Matt's scowling opinion was a lot iffier about that.

"I need to see her reaction. I am sure she didn't do this. She couldn't have," I told him. We both moved away from Miles's car. I knew Matt was watching the shadows. Listening. So was I, wishing I shared a dog's keen sense of hearing.

The murderer was out there somewhere. Were we in any

danger? I didn't think so, but I'd still feel relieved when the authorities got there.

"If Bella acts the way I hope she does," I continued, "then I'll feel confident she didn't kill Miles. She did hear an intruder, after all."

"You should wait till the cops take charge. Let them judge her reaction. If she did kill him—and I'm not saying she did—she could have been lying when she talked to you. Making things up about hearing someone. Or, maybe she did hear someone: Miles. But considering where we found him, this doesn't look like self-defense."

He wasn't wrong. But I figured that as long as we didn't touch anything—except for his necessary and limited contact with the car door—we weren't interfering with the investigation.

Bella came out her front door, Sammy in front of her. The dog reached us first and I grabbed his collar before he could dash over to the car. Matt hadn't completely shut the door. I didn't want the curious dog to start sniffing and perhaps contaminate the scene even more.

I watched him put his nose into the air, though, and wriggle his erect Malinois ears. What did he sense— anything helpful? Or was he simply acknowledging the presence of death in a canine way?

"I'm so glad you're here," Bella said as she reached us. She was dressed more casually than I'd ever seen her— frayed jeans and a tight, faded T-shirt. Her makeup was far from perfect, assuming she even had any on. She looked toward the car. "I'm not surprised to see that, damn it, though I didn't know he was here. He parked at an angle so

I couldn't see the car from inside, but my first thought was that my intruder had to be Miles. That's why I didn't call the cops. But maybe I should have."

"Bella, I think you need to look more closely at the car. But please be careful. And remember I'm right here with you." I began having second thoughts about my plan immediately. Matt was right. If she was a killer, she'd already lied enough times that her reaction now could be meaningless. And if she wasn't, she was about to receive a terrible shock without any warning from her so-called new friend.

She looked at me quizzically. "Did he leave something on the seat that he intended to gift me with—a stink bomb? Something else I'd hate? Where is he now?" She shook her head and started walking briskly toward the car. I rushed to catch up with her, thinking I should stop her before she reached it, but I was slowed down by holding Sammy back and she was moving too fast. "Honestly, I just wish the jerk would accept how things are and agree to divide our finances fairly. I don't care whether he likes what I'm doing or not. Save'Em is what I intend to do with my life from now on."

She was right by the car now. I took hold of her arm, stopping her.

"There is something I should tell you . . ." I began.

"Listen, he was just playing games with me before, trying to scare me by making all those noises. I hate what he's doing. I could just kill—"

"Don't say it," I warned her.

"But—"

63

That was when, leaning toward the car window, she screamed.

The sirens now audible in the distance formed an eerie chorus behind Bella's sobs. A least I'd grabbed the hysterical woman before she could touch the car door.

I should have waited for the cops. Bella's reaction had definitely convinced me of her innocence, and it might have helped to convince them, too. But surely the hard evidence would do that anyway. Someone's fingerprints were likely to be on the knife. On the car—besides Matt's. Other evidence, too, that I wouldn't even consider looking for.

A police car lunged into the parking lot, and Matt, who'd been watching us intently, hurried over to meet it.

In a short while, I was separated from Bella to await the Robbery Homicide Division detectives and the investigators from the Scientific Investigation Division. I now knew the drill. Not that I wanted to. But this was, amazingly, the third murder to affect me within the last few months.

Interestingly, one of the members of the LAPD who arrived in the second wave of cops was Detective Stefan Garciana. He had been in charge of the investigation when I was suspected of murdering someone I'd despised, right on the HotRescues property. He had been hard on me, but he had also given me a bit of insight into how his mind worked while he conducted investigations. I used some of his techniques when I helped to find the culprit in another murder where my former mentor, Mamie, had been accused.

"Ah, Ms. Vancouver," he said, approaching me. "We meet again. And at another animal shelter, I understand." He glanced around, as if assessing our surroundings. Only part of the Save'Em shelter was visible from this rear parking lot, but I had no doubt that he would get to see the rest of it soon.

"Yes," I confirmed. "This is Save Them All Sanctuary."

"Are you affiliated with this place, too?"

"No, but I'm friends with its administrator. Plus, I really like its approach to caring for pets with special needs."

"So it's a better place for animals than HotRescues?"

"Of course not. It's different, but—" I glared into his amused dark eyes, then shut up. He was just trying to goad me. He had been good at that before. But I'd learned how not to react—most of the time. I hadn't seen him for a few months, though, so I had to reboot the lessons I'd learned.

Garciana wasn't a bad-looking guy, with his dusky Hispanic features, but because of his job and his attitude I found him as attractive as a coyote stalking a cat. He was thin, with wavy dark hair and expressive eyebrows. He wore the same kind of black suit I had seen him in before.

As I watched, his amusement disappeared. He was obviously ready to get to work.

Bella sat on a lawn chair outside her house with Sammy's comforting head on her lap, looking pale and frightened as a uniformed cop questioned her. Matt was closer to the car, from which paramedics had removed Miles's body, then covered it to await investigators.

That meant I had Garciana all to myself to question. Even though I was sure he figured he would have me all to himself to interrogate.

He would soon learn better.

"Why don't you tell me your version of what happened here." He regarded me with a gaze suggesting he anticipated that, whatever I said, it would be filled with lies, or at least butt-saving exaggerations.

"Here's the short form." I proceeded to tell him about Bella's frightened call, my arrival with Matt, and our discovery of Miles's body.

"Okay, how about a longer form? I think there must be some helpful details that you're leaving out."

I grinned, crossed my arms, and leaned against the rear of the building. "I'll tell you what I know, and what I think. But I haven't yet figured out who the least likely suspect is. I'll want to stay in touch with you as you conduct your investigation. We should be able to help each other that way." I just wanted to hassle him right back. I had no interest in getting involved any more than I already was.

His gaze became half stony, half amused. Maybe it was the way his eyebrows turned into a waving caterpillar of multiple expressions. "I think I'd better call our Personnel Division folks. I didn't know you were now a detective with the LAPD."

"Wouldn't want to be," I told him. "I've had more than enough contact with murder cases to know I never want to be near any again. But I've also seen that some members of your department like to take the easy way out—choose the most obvious suspect and ignore other possibilities." I cocked my head as I regarded him. "You, of course, told me that you like to focus on the least likely suspect, too."

But no matter what he had professed to be his method, I had seemed the most likely killer to him in the case where he'd investigated and I'd been closely involved. He had latched on to me and had only let go when I'd helped to turn his sights onto the real culprit.

He hadn't been involved in the last case I'd had to look into, for my old mentor's sake. His counterpart in that case, Detective Joy Greshlam, had been even harder, in some ways, to convince of the truth, but I'd been able to help there as well—with a little assistance from my security manager Brooke's guy friend Antonio, who was a detective with the LAPD's Gang and Narcotics Division.

"I gather from this silliness that you want to direct me away from whoever you believe to be the most likely suspect. You again?"

I shook my head. "No. From what I've already told you, I'm sure you've glommed onto the person who's the most obvious possibility."

He nodded. "I assume you're talking about the vic's ex-wife."

"Right. But like I told you, she called me really frightened about the noises she heard. Apparently either the victim or the murderer, or both, were sneaking around the grounds of Save'Em. And when she saw Miles's body, she really freaked out."

"So she's either very innocent or very smart. Tell you what, Ms. Vancouver. I'm not about to let you interfere in another police investigation. But tell me what you know about the situation and what you suspect. You've been helpful before and I have grown to respect your opinion, so I'll make a special note of what you say that could lead to showing that Ms. Frankovick is innocent, and will keep that at the forefront of my mind during the investigation. If you're wrong, I won't be able to help her, or you. If you're right, then I'll already be sifting through other leads with the assumption that the ex-wife isn't the killer. That's the best I can do."

I stared at him for a long moment under the dim parking lot lights. I'd been so focused on him that I'd lost track of how many people were arriving, the sounds of a multitude of voices—as well as a chorus of loud barks in the buildings around us.

Those who were barking were the main reason I wanted Bella to be innocent. It wasn't just our new friendship. If she had to fight an arrest for murder, who would be in charge here at the shelter? Who would help the poor creatures whose causes she had taken up and now championed?

No, I couldn't really count on Detective Garciana to keep me informed. I would, however, keep him informed about everything I learned that would help to clear Bella.

Not that I'd be searching much this time, but I would certainly keep my ears open.

"That sounds fair enough," I said, stretching the truth like the smallest rubber band. "As long as you not only keep an open mind, but give Bella the benefit of any doubts you have—and I'm sure you'll have a lot if you continue to investigate—I know you'll find who the real killer is."

But as I walked away from him, toward Matt, who was talking with another man in a suit, I had to steel myself against how my mind already pondered Miles Frankovick's life, friends, and acquaintances. It might take more than Detective Garciana's open mind to figure out who had hated Miles even more than Bella—and who had killed him.

But it wouldn't be me.

Chapter 7

The media were coming. That was a given, in a situation like this. I glanced around the parking lot, which still bustled as if it was a set for one of the popular TV crime shows. Of course I'd heard that fictional shows depicting crime scene investigations were just that: fiction. They supposedly took a lot of liberties in the interest of enhancing the drama.

Even so, the reality seemed pretty dramatic to me.

In any event, I didn't know whether the news vultures stuck GPS trackers on all police cars or just eavesdropped on supposedly secure communications between cops, or how they did it. All I knew was that in the prior situations in which I'd been involved, they had almost immediately shoved their microphones and intrusive questions into my face and the face of everyone else around.

I hadn't seen any media sorts yet, but I was still in the

parking lot that was now secured by the authorities. Even if some had arrived, they were probably being kept away, at least for now. Which meant they were likely to pounce on anyone who emerged from the Save'Em facility. I didn't want to talk to any of them, or even be accosted with a microphone.

Maybe it was a good thing that I couldn't leave yet anyway. Matt was still being questioned, and he had driven us here.

There was one TV personality I should contact now, though. Carlie wasn't a media sort in the problematic tradition of reporters and paparazzi. Even so, a murder connected with a very special pet sanctuary like Save'Em would be of interest to her—especially since she had met Bella and already intended to film a show here soon.

Consequently, I slipped onto the walkway between the rear of the main building, where the special-needs animals were housed, and the separate cat building. The crime scene investigators were buzzing around doing their job, but that area remained fairly empty and no one stopped me from heading in that direction. The light was even dimmer than in the parking lot, and as long as I stayed nearer to the cat building than the main one the constant barks remained in the background rather than being so loud they interrupted my thoughts.

I pulled my BlackBerry from my large purse and called Carlie. Only then did I take a quick look at what time it was: about two in the morning. I expected the call to go straight to voice mail, but instead I heard a groggy, "What's wrong, Lauren?"

She'd obviously seen my name on her screen since I'd

called her smartphone with mine. "I'm at Save'Em," I said. "Miles Frankovick has been murdered."

"Did Bella do it?" Carlie's voice was stronger, and I pictured her sitting up in bed, now wide awake. She had heard Bella's threat over the phone when we first met her, too, so I wasn't surprised at her question.

"No," I said firmly, because I was pretty much convinced of her innocence. I quickly related to Carlie the call I'd gotten from Bella and what had happened since then. My voice grew raspy as I described finding Miles in his car and seeing the knife in his chest.

"I'll be there in about half an hour," she said.

"That doesn't leave you much time to get dressed," I said. She lived not too far from her veterinary clinic in Northridge.

"I'll just throw on some clothes. It's not like I'll be going in front of a camera."

I wasn't sure why I felt a little relieved as we hung up. I was a mature adult who was comfortable being in charge not only of herself but dozens of dogs and cats needing homes, plus the staff and volunteers who helped to care for them. The prior situations I'd been involved in where people had been murdered in my vicinity also gave me experience in dealing with this kind of situation.

But I was as uneasy as if I was a suspect.

Maybe people who dealt with murders all the time never got used to them. I intended not to find out any more than I already had.

This time, the cops would surely find the perpetrator, and soon. The LAPD had a good crime-solving record. My assisting by directing them to the right suspect twice was probably a fluke. Well, based on intelligent analysis, but still . . .

As I returned to the parking lot area, I considered what to do for the next half hour till Carlie arrived. If anything was different from the way it had been before I made my call, I couldn't tell—except that Miles's body had been removed by the coroner's office. Matt was still near Miles's parked car, talking to some guys in suits, including Detective Garciana. They were all probably trading information. Matt was, after all, an officer of the law, but the laws he was in charge of enforcing involved animals more than people.

I didn't see Bella but figured she was inside her house being interrogated about her deteriorated relationship with Miles, and whether she had killed him.

I hoped she, too, watched cop shows—enough to know not to answer incriminating questions without a lawyer present.

For now, I decided to let the cops who were near the entry to the back part of the property know that a vet would soon be arriving to make sure that any animal here that needed attention would be cared for. Carlie could do that, of course, if necessary—even if that wasn't her real reason for coming.

Then, I would interrupt the official conclave among Matt, Garciana, and the others. As I drew near, I saw Matt scowl in my direction. Apparently he didn't want me to butt in.

I pondered a few seconds, then decided to trust him. Since he wasn't part of LAPD, he wasn't likely to be included in anything too confidential. Whatever they let him in on should, therefore, be something he could impart to me. I could then let Bella's lawyer know.

For the moment, I had nothing to do. I hated to feel as if I was extraneous, with no way to help.

Time for me to go visit some special-needs pets.

I had to show my HotRescues ID to a couple of uniformed cops, and explain that Detective Garciana knew me and I was there to look in on the animals. After a quick phone call or two, presumably to Garciana, I had no trouble going into the rear part of the main building, into the area where pets with disabilities were housed. I'd check on them first, then head for the other end of the building to look in on the senior dogs.

About a week had passed since my first visit. Unlike with HotRescues, where we tried hard not to keep residents any longer than it took to find them wonderful new homes, these were almost the same animals that had been around when I was last here. A couple seemed unfamiliar and had possibly been added since then, but I recognized the three-legged pup I had seen before, as well as the deaf one, the blind cat and the one with spinal curvature.

I especially recalled the Basset hound mix who had captured my attention and sympathy most during my earlier visit, the dog who had no use of his back legs. I checked the slip at his entry gate to confirm that I remembered his name correctly: Nifty. Most of the other dogs were barking as I entered, and on seeing me they aimed their irritated comments at me. Not Nifty. He just sat and watched me with interest, as if I was the one inside an enclosure waiting for attention and he had to decide whether I was worthy of his giving me any.

Ignoring the others' barks, I opened Nifty's front gate and slid inside. I noted the shelf of cloth and paper towels and plastic bags above him and the fact he had soiled the area behind him. I did a quick cleaning job and noted that he had moved away soon enough not to dirty himself.

"You're such a good dog, Nifty." I sat down on the clean tile to give him a hug. He gave me a lick on the cheek. I again considered what would happen to him and the others now. If Bella was even arrested, let alone convicted, for Miles's death, were there other people who could step in and take charge of Save'Em?

What if that horrible vet who had been interviewed on TV—Drammon—got his way, and all the senior and disabled pets here were destroyed simply because whoever took over here assumed they were suffering?

I felt wetness on my cheeks that wasn't solely due to the kisses Nifty was deigning to give me. I hugged him closer.

"You'll be fine, boy," I said. "I promise."

I felt a lot better about having given that promise after I finished walking through the main building and checking on the other inhabitants. When I went back outside, Carlie was there.

If she did what she'd said and featured Save'Em on her show, she could put out a plea for donations. I'd also approach Dante for help. I would suggest that at least some of the participants in the HotPets marathon that I was going to run with Matt designate Save'Em as the charity where their sponsored donations would go.

But I really hoped that Bella remained in charge. She had been the one to dream of, then implement, the Save Them All Sanctuary model.

Carlie must have been there for a while since she was surrounded—not by paparazzi, who had not yet infiltrated the parking area, but by cops.

She couldn't be a suspect. I wouldn't be interfering with an investigation by joining her—so I did.

So did Detective Garciana. Matt remained near the car where Miles's body was found, still talking to other guys in suits.

"So you're just here because you're a veterinarian?" Garciana was asking. Carlie and he were at one edge of the parking lot, close to Bella's house. He was scowling, as if he wasn't happy about the interruption caused by her presence.

"That's mostly right," she said.

Despite the fact she had done as promised on the phone and hurried here, apparently taking enough time only to put on a Longevity Vision Channel T-shirt, jeans and sneakers, and no makeup, she looked pretty good.

"I'm also concerned about the ongoing condition of this pet sanctuary," she continued. "With a homicide here, it could be subject to negative publicity. And since what I heard was that the victim is the ex-husband of Save'Em's founder Bella Frankovick, it's a logical conclusion to think that Bella may be considered a suspect. If so, her attention may be diverted from Save'Em while the investigation is going on."

"It may be really diverted if she's arrested," I added.

"You're that veterinarian who's on TV," one of the three uniformed cops who remained near Garciana said to Carlie. She looked about as young as my college-age daughter, and her brown eyes were open in a wide stare that looked admiring. Her nametag read Wilfred. "I like your *Pet Fitness* show. I watch it all the time. I heard on the last one that you plan to do a feature on this place. Right?"

Carlie nodded. "That's my intention."

"Wait a minute," Garciana said. "You're on TV? I told my officers to make sure that all media people were kept out of this crime scene."

"I'm not a reporter," Carlie said. "My show is about animal health."

"And you're going to contradict everything that other vet said in his TV interview about what a bad idea this kind of pet sanctuary is, aren't you?" asked Officer Wilfred.

"What are you talking about?" Garciana growled.

The young officer told him about seeing the interview of Dr. Victor Drammon on television, and how he'd said that Save'Em's policy of keeping older and infirm pets alive was abusive.

"Dr. Stellan's show about this place hasn't aired yet," she concluded, "but when she mentioned it she hinted about how wonderful a place like this is, and how good it is for special-needs pets."

"That's something the victim and his ex-wife were heard arguing about." I was surprised both that Garciana knew about that already and that he mentioned it in front of Carlie and me. But I recognized the look of speculation on his dark-featured face that changed immediately to an innocently sincere expression—the way he looked when interrogating someone he thought could be a suspect. I'd learned that the hard way.

But Carlie, a suspect? No way.

"You didn't know Miles, though, did you, Carlie?" I quickly interjected.

"No, and I'd only recently met Bella." Her worried glance at me suggested she understood why I'd asked.

"I'd like to take you into the main building, Carlie." I nodded in its direction. "There are a couple of dogs I think you should examine." Not really, but I hoped that would put her visit back into perspective.

"Sure." She stole a glance toward Garciana. He didn't object.

"It's okay if you both go there," he said. "I've already put the word out that Ms. Vancouver can look in on the animals and make sure they're all right as long as she stays out of the way. But I'd like some contact information from you." He nodded toward Carlie. "We may want to interview you."

"And I may want to interview you, Detective," she said. "On my show. If there's anything about your investigation that might endanger the operation of this sanctuary, I'd like my viewers to know about it."

Don't push your luck, I wanted to shout to Carlie. Apparently Garciana, despite his speculative look, was willing to let Carlie go about her business without subjecting her to an interrogation—for now. But if he thought she was somehow going to interfere with his investigation—or if he thought there was any teensy but real possibility of her being a suspect—antagonizing him by suggesting she wanted to interview him on-camera might only make things worse for her.

"That might be interesting for both of us, Dr. Stellan." Garciana eyed the card she'd pulled from her purse and handed to him.

From the corner of my eye, I saw that Matt had left the group of investigators he had been talking to and was approaching us. He wasn't looking at me, though.

Instead, his gaze was aimed beyond where Carlie, Garciana, and I stood, toward the house.

I turned to see what he was so focused on.

Bella Frankovick had just come through the door. Another uniformed detective emerged behind her.

She moved slowly. An exhausted, ragged expression made her usually lovely face sag.

And she was crying.

Chapter 8

Bella apparently wanted to talk to me then as much as she wanted to be confronted by the media. Or maybe she simply couldn't talk. Her smile was brave as she came over to where we stood, but her face and demeanor made it clear how unhappy and scared she was. She didn't meet my gaze.

Since the door had been left open, Sammy had followed her out, and the alert Malinois sat obediently at Bella's feet, ears moving as he obviously listened to what was going on around him.

"Has anyone checked on the animals?" Bella asked, making it clear that, despite the hell she must be going through, her priorities were not affected.

"I walked through the main building a little while ago and everyone looked fine," I said. "I haven't checked on the cats, though."

"I'll do that now," Carlie said. "And I'll take another look at the dogs and special-needs animals as well."

"I'll come along. We'll probably leave after that." I looked at Bella quizzically, ready to change my mind if she needed us to stay.

She gave a quick nod. "I need to take care of a few things," she said. "But I'll be here tomorrow." That said a lot. Apparently she didn't believe she was in danger of imminent arrest. A good thing. Maybe she wasn't at the top of the suspect list.

Even so, I wondered if she had called her lawyer. She at least had someone on call for matters relating to her divorce. If whoever that was didn't do criminal work, Bella still might be able to get a referral. If not, I knew someone I could recommend.

"I'll talk to you then," I told her. I'd ask, when we spoke, what her attorney situation was.

I hoped she wouldn't need one, but suspected she already did.

I called Brooke Pernall from the car as Matt drove me home from Save'Em. Since our security director was on duty that night at HotRescues, she wasn't soundly asleep. I told her what happened, asked her to get whatever insight she could the next day from her boyfriend since Antonio was a detective with the LAPD Gang and Narcotics Division, and requested that she hang around until Nina arrived and was in charge for the morning. I wouldn't arrive as early as I usually did.

I thought about inviting Matt to stay with me for the rest

of the night. Even told him I'd considered it—then decided against it. I didn't want him to leave Rex alone, especially after he had already been by himself for so long. Although I did want to hear everything Matt had learned that day and told him so.

"Nothing important," he said, and as he drove, he gave me a brief rundown that convinced me he was right; he hadn't learned anything helpful.

He not only understood but agreed with my suggested plans for the night. He'd planned on just dropping me off, too. That was one of the things I liked about him. A lot. Not only did he work with animals, but to him pets were as important as people.

"As long as you're okay after all that happened tonight," he said. When I assured him I could deal with it, he added, "Okay, but one evening soon we'll grab dinner together again when things aren't so exciting. Spend more time together."

"I'd like that," I told him, and enjoyed a long kiss good night at my front door.

I allowed myself to sleep in the next day, but just a little. For one thing, Zoey hadn't changed her schedule and she wanted a morning walk. Maybe she just wanted to assert some alpha control over me since I'd come home so late.

We didn't do any training for the marathon, though. I was eager to get to HotRescues. I was also too tired for a workout that would only buy me more exhaustion.

I turned on a local morning news show as I got ready to go. I wasn't surprised to see a segment about Miles Frankovick's murder.

One of the people interviewed was another plastic surgeon from his office, a woman named Dr. Serena Santoval.

She was crying so much that it was difficult to understand most of what she was saying. The gist of it was that Miles had been a fine colleague, an excellent doctor, and an all-around wonderful man.

I didn't believe a word of it, but I had no doubt that Dr. Santoval did.

Which made me wonder about the true relationship between Miles and her. She seemed pretty upset for a coworker.

Not my problem, of course. But if I dropped a hint into Antonio's ear for him to pass along to Detective Garciana, maybe the investigation would focus on the grieving doctor instead of Bella. Who knew? Perhaps this woman had had a motive to get rid of her colleague.

"They want to adopt Abel!" Nina sounded as excited as her words made me feel.

Zoey and I had just arrived at HotRescues. We had no sooner entered through the door into the welcome room when Nina leaped up from behind the counter and hurried over to us.

"One of the volunteers has taken them back to look at him again," Nina continued. She thrust some papers in her hands at me. "They were here a couple of days ago and filled out the preliminary application. You liked them then, remember? The Oakes? Here's their additional paperwork. If it all goes well, they'd love to take him home with them today."

Abel was an über-sweet black Lab mix who had been with us for a while. His gray muzzle suggested he was middle aged, and his adoring personality had made me especially eager to find him a new, loving home.

Maybe this was Abel's day.

I went into my office to leave my purse, then Zoey and I entered the shelter area for our first walk-through of the day.

We ran into the Oakeses, unsurprisingly, at the first kennel on the left. They were inside, sitting on the cement, playing with Abel. They looked up and smiled as I came over.

The volunteer who had been showing them around was Mamie Spelling. She was grinning widely.

"How is Abel today?" I asked.

"Absolutely wonderful!" said Mrs. Oakes, a large woman about my age in a long-sleeved T-shirt and jeans. Her husband, even stouter than she, nodded. Their application had indicated that they had just become empty nesters, with their youngest daughter now off at school, and they could devote a lot of time to a dog, especially since the woman worked at home selling things over the Internet.

An excellent situation.

They'd even brought photos of a very nice single-family home with a large, fenced yard. I'd go visit it, of course, but in this instance didn't feel compelled to check it out before the adoption.

"I'll be finished with my walk-through in about five minutes," I told them. "If you'd like to meet me back in my office, we can finish up Abel's adoption—assuming that's what you want."

"Yes!" they said at once, then laughed at each other. I joined them, and so did Mamie.

I'd give Abel some final hugs of my own later. For the moment, I let him revel in the company of his about-to-be family.

. . .

Mamie walked with Zoey and me along the rest of the first row of kennels. She wore loose jeans beneath her yellow knit HotRescues volunteer shirt. "I'm so delighted for Abel," she said.

I agreed, of course, then asked, "So how are things with you, Mamie?"

She looked up at me, her wrinkle-shrouded eyes smiling. "Couldn't be better, thanks to you. I love where I'm living now." It was an assisted living facility, which Dante helped to pay for, not far from here. "And the fact that Herman can be with me is so wonderful." Herman was her dog—the one canine she had really designated as her own when all the animals she was hoarding were taken into protective custody by Animal Services. They'd all been saved and, to my knowledge, each of the private shelters who'd eventually taken them in had found them good homes. Mamie had eventually been allowed to reclaim Herman, though. "Thank you again, Lauren." She reached up and gave me a hug.

She turned to go back to where we had left the Oakeses, and Zoey and I continued through the shelter. We had a few empty kennels, which happened more now that our facility was larger. I'd have to check first with Nina because of her volunteering at a high-kill city shelter to see if we could rescue even more dogs and cats soon. If she wasn't aware of any pets in immediate danger, I'd talk to Matt. As an officer of Animal Services, he had his fingers on the pulse of the whole organization and could determine which care centers were in need of someone to take in pets that otherwise would be put down to make room.

Linda O. Johnston

In a short while, Zoey and I had looked in on all the dogs and cats. We'd run into Angie Shayde, our part-time vet tech, who had been checking out our residents to make sure they all looked well—and was also examining a few recent arrivals in the quarantine area.

When we returned to the welcome area, the Oakeses were waiting. I showed them back into my office and told Nina to have our groomer, Margo, give Abel a quick bath.

That was another advantage of having a larger shelter. We now had a groom room and didn't have to take our animals out to the nearest HotPets location for clips and baths—a necessity for keeping them looking their best for potential adopters.

The adoption paperwork and advice took about an hour. I never rushed through the process. Plus, I had a whole spiel about expectations that I bombarded them with— gently, of course. I wanted each adoption to work both for the adopters and their new family members.

Soon, it was a done deal. The Oakeses seemed thrilled. Abel obviously knew something important was afoot, since the usually mellow dog pranced and rubbed up against his new mom and dad as soon as he came back from his bath.

We walked out to the welcome area. I handed the leash—a gift from HotPets, of course, along with a collar and some initial food—to the Oakeses, then bent to hug Abel a final time at HotRescues. I would visit him at home at least once, though.

My congratulations were echoed by some staff members and volunteers who'd come into the area to say good-bye.

They were echoed as well by Bella Frankovick, who had just entered through the door.

I was surprised to see her but smiled a greeting. She knelt to give Abel a hug, too, as though she knew him. She'd seen him once, of course, during her prior visit, but her affection had to be more out of happiness for the event than for the specific dog.

When the Oakes family, including Abel, left, I turned to Bella. "How are you doing?" I chose to ask that instead of the myriad of other questions that whirlpooled in my mind.

"Not bad." The strain on her face belied her words, though. "I came to invite you out for coffee."

"Sounds good. Just give me a minute."

I spent a little longer than that in my office, putting some notes about Abel's adoption into the computer system so I wouldn't forget them and handling the minimal donation we required from adopters. Then I told Nina, at the computer in the welcome area, that she was in charge, asked Zoey to stay with her, and Bella and I left.

I drove us to the nearest of the chain coffee shops. There, Bella ordered something so full of whipped cream and sugar-laden ingredients that I figured fully loaded coffee was her comfort beverage of choice.

I just ordered some brewed coffee, although I added some additional pizzazz via a sugar-free flavored sweetener.

We sat at a small, round table in the corner, and I was surprised that we got something as secluded in the crowded room. More people were outside, though, so maybe an inside seat wasn't at as much of a premium.

"How are things at Save'Em?" I asked. That was a good, neutral way to inquire about why she really had come to see me.

"Hectic today." Her British voice sounded dejected, almost fearful. "I needed to get away for a short while." Her blue eyes looked straight into my green ones. "I left one of my best employees in charge, naturally."

"Naturally." I didn't doubt it. Whatever else was going on in Bella's life, I knew she would try to keep it from harming the animals in her charge.

"I would prefer not to talk about any of this," she went on, and I knew that, despite her preference, she was going to spill her guts. I just hoped that didn't include confessing to a murder.

Not that I thought her guilty.

"But that police interrogation last night was frightful. I despised Miles but I didn't kill him, Lauren." Her gaze remained on my face, as if she hoped to see inside to my brain to determine my opinion.

"I don't see how you could have," I said neutrally. "You called me all panicked about hearing an intruder, and then Matt and I found Miles's body. The coroner will have to figure out time of death and all that, but I don't believe the timing could have worked for you to have stabbed him and returned to your house." Actually, I was fibbing a bit. She could have stabbed him and then called—but the coroner's report might prove, or disprove, that. And so far I hadn't heard the origin of the knife.

"I know a former spouse is a perfect suspect in a murder, at least when the couple remained in touch—which, unfortunately we did. And we were arguing. People knew about that, even you."

I nodded.

"The detective who questioned me was not overbearing,

but he was insistent. I know enough from television shows that they don't tell you that you have the right to remain silent and have an attorney present until they arrest you, but I believe I was cautious in the little I said."

"Very good." That alleviated some of my concerns about her interrogation, at least.

"This morning, the detectives waited until some of my staff and volunteers arrived and questioned them, too. Poor Kip was especially rattled. My accountant, Kip Schaley?"

Her expression suggested that she was questioning if I recalled him, and I gave a nod that I did.

"He didn't like Miles. He is extremely sweet to me, and I think he believes he will take Miles's place in my life. For the moment, I don't even want to think about another relationship. People—men—seem to enjoy turning on me."

Men plural? I wondered what she meant but didn't want to interrupt her to ask.

"I don't think Kip would have killed to help me, but he is the only person I can think of—besides me—who might have had a motive to kill Miles."

"What about someone Miles worked with?" I asked. "Another plastic surgeon in his practice?" I thought of the woman doctor who had been crying on television.

"You see? You look beyond the obvious. You know the right questions to ask. First, though, I would like for you to refer me to the attorney who helped when you were accused of murder—if you liked his, or her, work, that is?"

First? What was second?

"I did," I told her. I'd give her the contact information for Esther Ickes when we returned to HotRescues. "I take it that your divorce attorney doesn't do criminal work."

She nodded.

"And, also. . . ." Her hesitation told me that I was about to hear whatever was second, and that I wouldn't necessarily like it. "Lauren, I know you stood in my shoes in the past when you were considered a murder suspect. Plus, I have heard that you helped someone else who was wrongly accused of murder, found who the real killer actually was."

"Well, yes, but—"

"Please, Lauren. As long as you don't believe I killed Miles—you don't, do you?"

I shook my head, my mouth open to refute what I knew she was about to ask.

"Then, please. Help me learn who really murdered him. For the sake of all of the poor creatures now at Save'Em and all of those to come. Let me stay there and run the place and save as many elderly and infirm animals as I can, and not go to jail for something I didn't do. Please, Lauren. Help me."

Chapter 9

I took a sip of coffee as I pondered how to respond. The noise in the shop seemed to grow louder, a Greek chorus of voices underscoring the battle going on in my mind, or maybe I was just more conscious of it.

Bella and I weren't yet the closest of pals.

But we had started to cultivate a real friendship. We definitely had a lot of interests in common.

Bella wouldn't be able to focus on rescuing special-needs animals if she was busy fighting to stay out of prison.

But I'd already told myself not to get involved.

"You realize, of course, that I'm not a detective." I stared right at her. "My success in those instances you mentioned could just have been flukes." Or maybe not. I had developed plans, done research, conducted my own investigations that didn't only rely on where the police were looking.

"I know you can't guarantee anything. That's not what I'm asking. But, Lauren, I'm so afraid. Weren't you scared when you thought the police were sure you were a murderer?"

I took another sip of coffee. It was growing cooler. Or maybe my blood was thinning as I considered how I had felt back then.

Scared? I didn't like to admit to being frightened, even to myself. But I had definitely been uneasy. Worried. Really anxious. And . . . Yes, I had been scared.

"It doesn't matter how I felt but yes," I told Bella. "I can understand what you're going through. And from what I saw, the police, although fairly competent, like it when they think they've zeroed in on the most likely suspect. Although . . ."

"Although what?" Bella leaned closer, as if I was about to tell her something really important.

In a way, I was.

"One of the detectives who came to Save'Em to work on the investigation was the head detective when I was a suspect. We talked quite a bit then. He admitted to me that he also liked to identify the least likely suspects, just in case. Then he would eliminate them if he could."

"He sounds smart. And fair."

"Anyhow, that's what I considered when I got involved with helping in the last investigation. I'll do it now, too, if I decide to help you."

Bella's smile was uneven yet sure. "You've already decided, haven't you?"

My laugh sounded rueful, even to me. Even as I'd told

myself to stay out of it, I'd already been considering who could have killed Miles.

I am not an indecisive person. Which told me: Yes, I had already determined I'd help Bella.

"Maybe," I told her, not quite ready to commit to her, even though I'd made a commitment to myself. "But if I say yes, you'll have to help me, too." I removed the strap of my purse, which I'd slung over my chair, then reached into the bag and extracted a small notebook and pen. "Let's talk about who you consider the most—and least—likely suspects."

Bella didn't hang around after I drove us back to HotRescues, but said, as we exited my car, "Thank you so much, Lauren. I can't tell you how much I appreciate this."

I had agreed. And I never second-guess myself.

I therefore had to ponder how I would go about clearing her and come up with an investigative strategy.

Zoey immediately greeted me as I entered the welcome area. "Hi, girl," I said as I bent to pet her and get a doggy kiss.

Bev was behind our desk. That was a good thing. Nina knew me well enough to read from my demeanor that something was up. Bev just gave me a rundown about a family who had come in, filled out our paperwork, and visited our available pets.

"They seemed most interested in cats," she said. "Maybe two. I told them you would look over their application and call to find out when they could come back to talk to you about adopting."

"Sounds good," I said.

I took my usual walk around the facility with Zoey, greeting staff, volunteers, and, most important, our residents.

But my mind wasn't entirely on what I was doing.

Returning to my office, I brought up, on my aging but stalwart computer, the files I had put together for both of the cases I had already worked on. I had maintained a separate computer page for each suspect, then kept rearranging them in the order I thought was correct, from the most likely to least. I pulled the notebook out of my purse and started files on the people Bella and I had discussed. There weren't many, but she promised to come up with more.

I had to put Bella herself on my list. Then there was Kip Schaley, the Save'Em accountant who had a crush on her. She hadn't liked considering him a suspect, since if he'd killed Miles he had undoubtedly done it for her.

Bella had given me a rundown of some of the people who worked with Miles in his cosmetic surgery office. One was the woman, Dr. Serena Santoval, who had cried for him on TV. There were a couple of other doctors, too, plus his assistant.

I couldn't tell from this who was most, or least, likely to have killed him.

But as I copied the names into the files I had created, I realized what my next step had to be.

As ridiculous as it felt, I was going to look into having my face lifted.

I spent some time that afternoon visiting homes of people who had recently adopted pets from HotRescues. As I'd anticipated, they all seemed to be good fits. Always a relief, of course—even though I wouldn't permit an adoption that I thought might not work. Of course a few didn't and pets were returned to us. That was a requirement in our contract—that we get the animals back if any issues arose. Fortunately, that seldom occurred.

That evening, I called both of my kids. Not that I was about to tell them what I was getting involved in for Bella.

But I wanted to hear their voices. Catch up with them. They had each just started a new year at their respective schools, and I missed them—both had stayed around their campuses for most of the summer for jobs and more classes.

Maybe that was why I missed them so much.

I sat on the sofa in my living room, settling myself on its blue upholstered seat and leaning back against one of its many fluffy pillows. Across from me was the huge big-screen TV that my son Kevin had chosen, but I didn't turn it on.

I called my daughter, Tracy, first. Twenty years old, she had just started her junior year at Stanford.

"Hi, Mom," she said, answering at once. "Everything okay?"

"Sure," I said, hugging Zoey, who had joined me on the couch. "Why do you ask?"

"Because you don't usually call on a Thursday evening."

No, I didn't. I called my kids anytime I felt like it, but had gotten into a habit of usually making it Sunday, Wednesday, and Friday, unless there was something special to discuss.

"Consider this a special occasion," I told Tracy.

We didn't talk long. I chose not to mention anything at

all about visiting Save'Em and what a great rescue facility it was, in case she Googled it and learned what else had gone on there.

My conversation with my son was similar. Kevin was eighteen and had just begun his sophomore year at Claremont McKenna College in the town of Claremont, just east of L.A., which was much closer than Stanford. Even so, he didn't come home often on weekends. It was better that way for him. He was mature, a good student, and didn't need to take care of his old mama. Even though he called me more often than Tracy did.

"I'll be coming home this weekend," Kevin said as we ended the conversation. "A couple of guys from high school have something going on so they'll be back in town, and I want to see them."

"Sounds good," I said, my heart swelling. It would be wonderful to see him. Even though I doubted he'd spend much time here with his friends around.

Feeling all wound up, I thought about calling my parents in Phoenix, or my brother, Alex, who also lived there with his family, then decided against it. All that family contact might make me feel as if I was worried, second-guessing myself about my decision to help Bella.

And, like I said, I never did that.

I got to HotRescues early the next morning—in plenty of time to see our security director, Brooke, before she and her dog Cheyenne left for the day.

I had called ahead to make sure she was awake. "Come

up to the apartment as soon as you get here, Lauren," she'd told me. "I'll have coffee ready."

That sounded good to me, so as soon as I'd arrived and done a quick jaunt around the facility with Zoey, I went into the center building of the original shelter and walked up the stairs to the new apartment that was now there.

It wasn't the most glamorous residence, but it served its purpose: a nicely furnished apartment-away-from-home for whatever security person was there each night at HotRescues so they could have a place to crash when not patrolling. It was larger than a studio apartment, with a bedroom, living room, and tiny but sufficiently equipped kitchen. The bathroom had only a shower stall, no tub. There were no laundry facilities, but when towels and bed sheets needed to be washed, the regular HotRescues washing machine was available.

It worked. And Brooke seemed pleased enough with it that she spent more nights here herself than bringing in her independent contractors who helped out.

"How are you?" I asked when she opened the apartment door to let Zoey and me in.

I always asked that, no matter how fit and rested she looked—as she did that morning. She wore her traditional black T-shirt that read SECURITY STAFF over matching black jeans. Her brown hair, highlighted and gleaming, framed a face that had once been pale and gaunt but now looked healthy and attractive.

The first connection Brooke had had with HotRescues was when she had attempted to relinquish her sweet golden retriever Cheyenne so we could find the dog a new home.

Brooke had been let go from her job as a private investigator and was about to lose her house. And her life. She had a heart condition, no insurance, and no way to pay for medical treatment to save herself.

She hadn't wanted her dear pup to suffer as she did.

That turned out to be one of the infinite number of times I was grateful that our benefactor, Dante, cared about both animals and people. He had donated enough for Brooke to get medical treatment and save her house. Then, when she was well enough, he'd authorized our hiring her as the security director of HotRescues, a smart move since EverySecurity, the pricey independent security company he liked to use for his HotPets chain, had badly flubbed its job here and we needed someone to ensure that didn't happen again.

Brooke did a superb job with that and more around here.

Now Cheyenne and Zoey sniffed each other, then walked into the kitchen together to jointly beg for treats. I smelled the coffee Brooke had promised to brew.

"So what's on your mind?" Brooke asked as we settled down at the compact kitchen table. "Is it about the Miles Frankovick murder?"

I nodded, then sighed. "Bella asked me to get involved and help figure out who killed him, and the way she did it I couldn't say no."

Her grin was much too amused. "I know you better than that, Lauren. You never agree to anything you don't want to do. Besides, you were already involved. You know, though, don't you, that private investigators need licenses?"

I sat up straighter, practically banging my coffee mug on the table. "I'm not a P.I. And I certainly don't want to become one."

"Are you insulting P.I.s?"

"Do you still have your license?" I countered.

"If I say yes, does that mean you're insulting me?"

I laughed. This was turning into a ridiculous conversation, and I was sure that Brooke had started it to help lighten my mood.

She had succeeded.

"Since you're a P.I., I definitely think highly of the breed," I said. "But you wouldn't want me as your competition, if you ever go back to actively being one."

Her turn to laugh. "You're right about that." Her mouth segued into a grim line. "Can I talk you out of it?"

I shook my head.

"I figured. I don't like it, Lauren. You— All right. You already asked me to get whatever insight I could from Antonio. So far he hasn't been very helpful. I may be able to fix that, though." Her raised eyebrows suggested that she would find a way to get what she asked for by seduction, and I grinned.

But then I grew more serious, too. "When I asked you that, I was at the crime scene, and I was curious. I really hadn't planned to get involved. But now . . ."

"You were already involved," she countered. "How do you plan to go about your investigation?"

"The same as before. Lots of interviews and questions and notes."

She nodded. "So what do you plan to do next?" I told her, and she shook her head as she uttered a laugh as wry as a frustrated dog trainer. "Good thing no one at those doctors' offices know you, Lauren. For one thing, you look damned good for a forty-something woman."

I opened my mouth to protest. She'd spoken in a tone that suggested she referred to a senior citizen, someone twice my age. She was only about ten years younger than me, so it wasn't like she was a teen who looked at anyone over twenty-five as antique.

"For another thing," she continued, "anyone who knows you would be certain you won't do anything beyond maybe dressing up a little more for some occasion and adding a bit of makeup to change your looks. Nothing invasive like surgery. You're too smart, and pretty, for that."

I shut my mouth again. She had me pegged. Except for the pretty part. I'm not horrible looking, but I'm fairly average.

"That should be one interesting doctor's appointment," she finished. "Wish I could at least go along, but that might add to any suspicion. Just be sure to let me know how it goes. And Lauren?" I looked at her. "I still don't like it."

Chapter 10

It turned out that the doctors in Miles's office were not taking appointments for the next day, which was Friday. In fact, when I called that afternoon from my office at HotRescues, the receptionist sounded weepy when she told me that, at the best of times, appointments were usually not available for a week or more. Now, due to a death in their professional family, this was the worst of times.

That gave me an even better idea of the snobbery undoubtedly at work there along with the plastic surgeons' knives. People who actually wanted to have wrinkles cosmetically altered or lips collagened into frozen pouts would probably believe that, if they had to wait for an appointment, those who could do it best were in high demand.

Maybe they genuinely were—although that made me

shake my head, with its unaltered features, in incomprehension.

As I talked on the phone, I eyed my computer screen, viewing the list of files I had created for Bella's situation. How could I start filling in blanks if I had to wait for eons to talk to people in the office where Miles had worked?

"I do have a cancellation on Monday, though," the receptionist said after a pause. "For Dr. Santoval. I think she'll be seeing patients again then, although . . ." Her voice tapered off.

"I heard on the news about what happened to Dr. Frankovick." I lowered my voice with sympathy. "Such a terrible situation. I'm sure you're all in mourning." She was unlikely to be the object of my planned inquiry, but getting anyone to talk could lead to something helpful.

"Yes, we are." Her response was a combination of hoarseness and sob, and I perversely felt tears rush to my eyes. I knew what it was like to mourn someone. Despite Miles Frankovick's attitude toward saving pets and his treatment of Bella, he'd undoubtedly left behind some oblivious people who cared that he was gone. Like his staff. His coworkers—and maybe particularly Dr. Santoval, if her performance on the news wasn't just an act.

"But life must go on, I guess," the receptionist continued bravely. "It'll be hard around here, but we were told that the best way to deal with what happened to Dr. Frankovick is to continue on as well as we can, in his memory. So—well, we did happen to have a cancellation. If you could come in at ten in the morning on Monday . . . ?"

"Yes," I said, and gave her my name and cell phone number. I didn't have to reveal that I was the director of a no-kill animal shelter like Dr. Frankovick's ex-wife. But even if they learned who I was, I could still genuinely want to have cosmetic surgery done to improve my looks.

My horrified rejection of the whole idea would not show up on any Web site if they Googled me.

The weekend went fast. Maybe it was because time always seemed to pass quickly these days when my kids were around. I managed to see Kevin now and then between his get-togethers with friends. As always, I remarked—internally and nostalgically—about how much he resembled his dad. Kerry had been tall and slim, with deep red-brown hair and a ready laugh. That also described my sweet, smart son.

I was glad I got to cook a meal at home for him on Sunday night. That way, I spent a couple of extra hours with him.

Kevin was aware that I was training for a marathon, even got to see Matt and me run with our dogs a little before he'd taken off to join his friends on Sunday morning. He was fine with my inviting Matt to join us for dinner that night. He'd met Matt before and seemed to enjoy talking to him about his work with Animal Services.

I supposed that if I decided to intensify my relationship with Matt, Kevin wouldn't mind. Tracy might not, either. But although Matt and I now had a "friends with benefits" sort of thing going on—and maybe more—I didn't want to rush things.

Neither did Matt, fortunately. He was astute enough to realize I wasn't ready for anything too serious. Not yet, at least.

Matt had been married before, too—back when he had been a Navy SEAL. He had divorced around the time he'd left the military and become a K-9 officer in the police force of a small California town. Soon after was when he had moved to L.A. to join Animal Services. He had only recently revealed his former marriage to me, and we had been seeing each other for months. No kids, though, and he seemed to regret it. Maybe that was why he was so kind to animals.

Too soon, Kevin had to jump into his car and head back to his college campus, east of our home. Matt and Rex were still there when Kevin left. Enjoying their company made my son's departure easier.

They stayed the night, too, and my activities with Matt helped even more with the transition.

When I need medical attention, I don't head for Beverly Hills. There are other good doctors who staff reputable hospitals much closer to where I live. Dante funds generous benefits to the staff, including me, at HotRescues, so my medical insurance might cover the extra costs of going there. But why bother?

The office where Miles Frankovick's medical practice had been was in the eighth-floor penthouse of a building on Wilshire Boulevard. I pulled my Venza into a metered spot along the street and hoped that I had overpaid for the time I would spend there. I didn't want a Beverly Hills parking ticket.

The building was, inevitably, ritzy for a place housing many medical offices, with lots of glass and gold trim decorating the marble façade. The elevator unfolded proudly to reveal the entry to the office I sought. The carved oak door was labeled ornately with BEVERLY HILLS' PREEMINENT COSMETIC SURGERY FACILITY. To one side, a display case as elegant as a piece of antique furniture framed a list of half a dozen names that included Miles and also Dr. Serena Santoval.

The waiting room looked as if it belonged in a European castle. Its gleaming slate floor was covered with plush braided area rugs and had several conversation areas with richly upholstered chairs and European-looking tables laden with magazines. Several people sat there leafing through the publications. I glanced around to determine whether I thought any needed plastic surgery.

They didn't.

Neither did the two receptionists behind the desk that led into the medical areas. The women themselves were either hired for their model-like beauty, or they'd partaken of some of the services here as part of their compensation. Or both.

"Hello," I said. "I'm Lauren Vancouver. I have an appointment at ten."

"Which doctor?" asked the gorgeous brunette with cheekbones as sculpted as any famous starlet's beneath her perfect complexion. Her lips were poufy enough to suggest that she had, indeed, received collagen injections.

"Dr. Santoval, I believe." I leaned over the desk conspiratorially. "I've heard good things about her, but, well . . ." I pretended to hesitate. "I heard even better things about Dr. Frankovick."

The receptionist's hazel eyes widened and grew damp.

Despite looking like a resident promotion for the doctors, she was, apparently, human. Maybe she was the weepy person I'd spoken with on the phone. Was that part of the image, too?

"He was a good man," she said. "His patients swore by him." She straightened her shoulders beneath her white medical top. "But Dr. Santoval is quite good, too. The only thing is, we've had to switch your appointment to Dr. Renteen. He is excellent as well. All of our doctors are. But he was the one who worked most closely with Dr. Frankovick. I'm sure you'll like him."

She was well programmed. Did I want to talk to Dr. Renteen? Sure, whoever he was. But would I like him? Probably not. And what had happened to Dr. Santoval?

I only had to wait for about five minutes before I was shown from the waiting room into the examination area. This part of the office was almost as showy as the reception room, with artwork along the wall that I was sure included limited-edition prints by names even I would recognize, and more carved wooden doors for the individual rooms.

The chamber I was nearly bowed into was more like an office than an exam room—again, pretty snazzy. The man sitting behind the desk had a thick head of ebony, wavy hair and a smile that revealed gleaming white teeth. His shoulders didn't appear especially broad beneath his white lab jacket, but maybe that was because it was difficult to modify shoulders by unnatural means. "Hello, I'm Dr. Abe Renteen." He held out his hand.

"Lauren Vancouver," I said, shaking it.

He proceeded to ask gently prodding questions about the kind of cosmetic work I sought. I'd already rehearsed what I hoped was a credible intro. It nevertheless sounded like garbage to my own disbelieving ears as I recited it to him—something about feeling as if I was aging too quickly because of the extra skin under my chin and the lines near my eyes.

I watched his gaze move from one location on my face to the other. In a way, I hoped he would just reassure me that I looked fine, but that wasn't, of course, his job—or the way he would scoop in the barrels of money he undoubtedly received from anyone who actually followed through and had him rework their appearance.

When I was done, he rose and motioned for me to stand, too. His critical examination of my face made me shrivel defensively inside, but I hid it. Hell, I know I look just fine for someone my age.

"I'd heard such wonderful things about Dr. Miles Frankovick," I said, tossing that out even before I had intended to so I could draw Renteen's fault-finding to a screeching halt. "I'd been hoping to consult with him . . . but of course I heard what happened."

"Yes," said Dr. Renteen. I'd initially assessed him as maybe five years younger than me or more, even with whatever work he'd had done, but his frown aged him to way beyond my own mid-forties. "It was so sad." Interestingly, his tone didn't sound especially regretful.

My mind raced to decide how to follow up. "Maybe it was just as well I didn't see him, though. You know, I heard on some of those awful TV gossip shows that he and his wife had just divorced and were still involved in some ugliness. I watch those shows all the time, and for a while their situation was right there in every program, very nasty. There was even some talk that they split because he was involved with a professional colleague."

I was reaching a bit with that one, to see if I'd get any reaction.

None came, though, so I continued, "All that discussion of cosmetic surgery gave me the idea of coming here and getting a consultation with Dr. Frankovick, but I delayed. I'd figured it was hard for a doctor to really concentrate on doing things well when he's preoccupied, and for a cosmetic surgeon to possibly mess up . . ." I let my words trail off—and as I watched Dr. Renteen's face, I believed that I had somehow hit a nerve.

"He would have done a good job." That came out through gritted teeth. Ah, a reaction at last. "He was a professional. But all of those paparazzi, those terrible shows—his personal life was just that. Personal. It should never have been allowed to reflect on this office, even when he was alive. And it did. Too much. It—" Dr. Renteen paused. A look of dismay washed over his face, as if he only just realized he was venting to a patient. His eyes closed for an instant, and when he opened them he smiled with no emotion. "But of course it didn't really reflect on us. Or even on him. He was a fine doctor. Those reporters are just trash-talkers. Now, though we'll miss Dr. Frankovick, we'll continue in his fine tradition. Now, let me tell you what I would suggest for you. I'll then have it written up into a report, which will also contain our estimated charges. You can choose the entire package or whatever parts of it you would like."

Not a single knife scratch, I wanted to hurl back into his face.

This seemed as easy as if I'd written the Hollywood script, the way Bella used to do. Dr. Renteen had just given me a good motivation for him to have killed his medical colleague: resentment over bad publicity that could have hurt their whole practice if it didn't stop. He surely didn't talk to all his patients like this.

Then again, not all of his patients would necessarily mention watching Miles Frankovick's ugly divorce being dissected in the media.

I dragged my feet, almost literally, when Dr. Renteen showed me out of his office. I'd have liked to have gotten all the other doctors' opinions of Miles Frankovick and his divorce and how the publicity might have hurt their medical practice.

I thought about requesting consultations with his colleagues so I could select the one I liked best, but doubted that would go over well.

There was definitely one I wanted to talk to, though: Dr. Serena Santoval.

A couple of other people dressed in white jackets like Dr. Renteen, who were probably doctors, walked down the hall as I asked him a few more questions about timing and recuperation and whatever else I could think of.

Several others in more colorful lab coats darted about like tropical fish, probably nurses or aides to the drably clad physicians.

The woman I recognized from TV finally appeared, coming out of one of the other examination rooms.

"I'll look forward to your written suggestions," I told Dr. Renteen. "Thanks." And then I hurried toward Dr. Santoval.

She stopped to talk to one of the colorfully garbed nurses who had a handful of files. I glanced back and no longer saw Dr. Renteen—a good thing. I dawdled a bit, and when Dr. Santoval started away from the nurse I caught up with her.

"Hi. I just talked to Dr. Renteen about having some cosmetic surgery done, but I was wondering if a lady physician would be even more empathetic with a female patient. Could I possibly consult with you?"

"I'm afraid I don't have time just now, and Dr. Renteen is quite a good doctor." I hadn't paid much attention to Serena Santoval's appearance when I had seen her on TV. Now I noticed that, although she was attractive, I didn't see any indication that she'd had cosmetic surgery herself. Divots parenthesized her mouth, and a few small lines radiated from the corners of her pale blue eyes. Maybe both were caused by recent exhaustion and grief instead of age, though.

I drew a little closer and began to speak as if sharing a confidence. "I really had hoped to see Dr. Frankovick . . . but of course that's not possible. I saw you on the news being interviewed about his death. I'm really sorry. I could tell you must have been close. Not that it's my business, but were you . . . I mean, were you more than professional colleagues? With your obvious grief—well, some of those shows implied that he was involved with a coworker. Was that you?"

Yes, I sounded like some kind of blithering, mindless groupie, but who cared? I was hoping to shock a useful response from her.

She hadn't been looking at me when I began speaking. Now she gazed right into my eyes. Hers looked as horrified as if I'd stripped off my clothes. "I—I hadn't heard any of that. And if anyone identified me . . . it was nothing like that. It was . . ." She pulled her wrist up in a gesture that suggested she was searching her wristwatch for an excuse to leave. "Oh, it's time for me to meet with a patient. Dr. Renteen will do a fine job with you. You'll see."

But what I saw was that my made-up, pseudo-news story about Dr. Miles Frankovick being involved with one of the other doctors here had most likely not been so made up after all.

And it gave at least a couple of those doctors a possible motive to have killed him.

Chapter 11

"You're here early," I said to Brooke.

It was four thirty in the afternoon, and she had just knocked on my office door.

I had returned to HotRescues after my pseudo-medical appointment and took a longer walk than usual through the grounds with Zoey. After spending so much time with people I neither liked nor trusted, I needed a good dose of animal time.

When I felt better, I worked on inputting data into my computer for most of the rest of the day. Nearly all that data involved our residents, and I smiled constantly when I added things about our most recent adoptions. This was stuff Nina usually dealt with so a lot of surface information was there, but I always liked to add things about my personal evaluation of the adopters. Maybe it was a bit much, but I liked to justify to myself—and to our staff who might also read this stuff online—why I thought the people would be good to our former inhabitants.

Then I made myself work on the computer pages in the files I'd begun about possible suspects in Miles's murder. I was able to add a page and a motive for Dr. Abe Renteen, as well as my impressions of Dr. Serena Santoval.

So far, though, I didn't have enough to point to either of them, or anyone else, to clear Bella.

I hadn't realized so much time had passed until Brooke came in. Zoey went to the door to greet her and Cheyenne, who, as always, was with her.

"I'm here to talk about your acting as a P.I.," Brooke informed me, her tone wry.

"Do you want to handle it?" Not that I'd let her take this on by herself even if she said yes.

"No, but I may have some information you can use. Rather, Antonio may." My door opened wider, and Detective Antonio Bautrel of the LAPD followed them inside.

As usual these days, Brooke looked amazingly healthy, all the more so, it seemed, when she was with her significant other. There was a glow in her pale amber eyes and a smile on her full—unenhanced—lips as she preceded the detective into the room.

Antonio was clad as I'd almost always seen him, in the businesslike, I'm-in-charge suit of a detective. Today's was a light brown, contrasting well with his short black hair. He was just a little taller than Brooke, but he filled out his suit well enough to boast of all the cop training he did. Nor was he gorgeous, but his slightly large nose and jutting brow adorned his face quite nicely. I could see why Brooke was attracted to him.

They both took seats in my conversation area, so I went around my desk to join them.

"This must be good," I said, "for you both to be here."

A look of triumph on Brooke's face suggested that what they were about to impart could be more than good. "We may be saving you a lot of time," she said. "There's no sense in doing a lot of useless digging in a case that's pretty well solved."

"Meaning?" That couldn't be good for Bella—not if she was the one the cops had set their narrow, unimaginative vision on.

"You can't attribute anything to me, Lauren, or I could get into a lot of trouble," Antonio said, "but I'm going to let you in on what's currently going on in the investigation. There's a lot of evidence against your friend Bella Frankovick."

"That doesn't mean she's guilty." I waved my hand as dismissively as if he had accused Cheyenne.

Antonio's look was sympathetic. "It doesn't mean she's not, either. We have motive, means, and opportunity— you've heard of them?" At my brusque nod, he continued, "Motive is that he was trying to take back all the money she had removed from their joint accounts before their divorce and to keep her away from the real property he claimed should only have been his, despite it being in both names. Their divorce was final, but the judge said they could work out their settlement afterward—and they hadn't. Money is always a good motive. Means was the knife. It wasn't anything special, a carving knife made by a well-known manufacturer, one that could have been picked up at any chain kitchen store. No fingerprints were found on it, nor were any besides Miles's and Matt's on the car, but she probably wore gloves. And opportunity was—"

I interrupted. "She didn't have opportunity unless the timing is being ignored. She called me when she panicked about an intruder. She was still inside the house when Matt and I arrived. Miles was dead by then, in his car in the parking lot."

"Or her plea to you could have been contrived," Brooke said. "You already know that."

"But I don't buy it. I heard how frightened she sounded on the phone. No one else did."

Antonio held up the palms of his well-worn hands. "Okay, it's not foolproof. In fact, I'll admit that the detectives on the case don't yet believe they've collected all the evidence that will allow for an arrest and conviction. But they're confident they'll get it."

"Well, they shouldn't be." I had folded my arms as belligerently as if I held myself back from thrashing him. "I'm not hearing anything new from you. The cops are sure it's Bella. They already thought so. The only thing you're convincing me of is that I'd better hurry even more to determine who killed Miles. It's the only way I can protect Bella from a false arrest."

"Lauren—" Brooke's tone and expression suggested she was about to try to talk some sense into me—from her perspective.

From mine, I already knew how sensible I was.

"If I'm acting like a P.I.," I said, "so be it. You can help me, Brooke. Or not. But I'm going forward with this."

. . .

No hard feelings, at least. I invited Matt to join the three of us for dinner that evening. We all met up at a British pub not far from HotRescues. The place was charming—dimly lit, a television tuned to a soccer game, the aroma of baking shepherd's pie, and a menu filled with other delights such as bangers and mash, fish and chips, and Cornish pasty.

Good venue. Great company. I like Brooke and her guy. And I'd come to care about Matt. A lot.

But it turned out to be as bad an idea as if they were there to steal from me. Which they were, in a way—my excellent plan. My confidence.

My fun, peaceful evening.

Three against one. Matt might not have bought into the current official version of what the investigation had yielded, but he clearly wasn't happy that I remained involved.

I had met him not long before the first situation in which I'd been forced to determine the identity of a murderer or be arrested myself. He understood, I'd thought, that when I'd gotten involved in this kind of situation, it wasn't exactly by choice.

"You didn't make a fuss either time before when I started looking for the killer, even last time when I wasn't a suspect," I accused all three of them. "Why start giving me a hard time now?"

I'd just met Brooke around the time of the first situation and hadn't even known of Antonio's existence at the time, but was glad for his help with my next case. They'd been helpful and even a bit sympathetic, without telling me to butt out.

"Both of the last times you could have gotten hurt," Matt said, leaning toward me from his chair beside mine at the square wooden table. "Badly." He took a hard swig of Newcastle ale from a filled glass. "It made sense for you to try to do something to protect yourself. I get it. And even, maybe, to help your longtime friend. But you don't know Bella well, and you can't guarantee her innocence. Back off now, and stay safe. Enough is enough."

He had come right from work, wearing a khaki-color Animal Services knit shirt that emphasized his muscular build. Under other circumstances, I'd have thought about how sexy the guy was, and how nice it was that we were seeing each other. But not now.

I made myself take a long, pensive drink, too, before responding. What he said was correct. I liked it a lot that he cared. But that wasn't the point. Responding emotionally wouldn't help, though.

"I came out of both just fine," I said, proud of how calm I sounded. "And I found out the truth. Besides, what you said confirms that everyone seems to be zeroing in on Bella as the killer. If it is her, she has no reason to hurt me." I looked at them. "Or do you agree it could be someone else?"

No answer. Not till Brooke said, "If you won't be reasonable about getting out of this, then at least promise you'll be careful. Call on any of us anytime if you need help or backup."

"Or for a reminder of why this kind of amateur investigation isn't a good idea," Antonio said. So what if I had thought him a nontraditionally good-looking man? At the moment, he didn't look, or act, at all attractive to me.

"But, honestly, Lauren," Brooke said. "You should stay out of it this time. You don't even know how dangerous it could be."

I glowered at them all as the men nodded their agreement. They could be right. I knew that.

But all of them except Antonio knew that once I'd made up my mind, I wouldn't change it. Period. Possible danger or not.

We fortunately got off the topic of me and onto the thing the three of us had in common: pet rescue. Antonio wasn't as engaged as the rest of us, but he, too, loved animals, so talking about some that Matt had heard were in danger of being euthanized within the next couple of days was a topic we all could jump into with sincerity. I assured him I'd have room for a bunch at HotRescues and that I would also post a request on the Southern California Rescuers Web site for other facilities that could take some in.

By the end of the meal, and another round of ale, they were all more mellow. I was, too. No more demands about what I should or shouldn't do.

Even so, I rode back to HotRescues almost silently with Brooke and Antonio without inviting Matt to join me that night.

Though I hadn't had any intention to heed what those browbeaters had said to me at dinner, my own priorities limited the amount time I had that week to dig into helping Bella.

Good thing I heard that a memorial service for Miles was going to be held that Saturday. Even if I had no opportunity to do much investigating or digging before then, I'd attend.

First, though, I focused on some adoptions of particular sweetness to me at HotRescues. One was Babydoll, a loving shepherd mix with an unusual coat that suggested she wore a skirt. She had been a resident of ours for quite a while, but despite the plethora of attention she received from all of us, including our wonderful volunteers, she needed a forever home of her own. And now, she had finally found one.

Then there were Fitzwalter, a cat we had taken in when released to us after a hoarding situation, and Alta, a kitty who had been a recent owner relinquishment and obviously needed a home to lord over. Both were chosen by families who appeared to be good fits.

Of even more intensity were the visits to a couple of city shelters where some wonderful cats and dogs were in immediate danger. I hustled there with some of my staff, including Pete and Nina, to grab up as many as possible. Some colleagues who also posted on the SoCal Rescuers Web site were there, too, and we divvied up the animals graciously—and with exuberance. We were all in this together, saving as many pets as we could.

Then there was a very special day. On Thursday, I went to visit Save'Em. I was there because Carlie was coming. She was starting to film her "Hug'Em At Save'Em" episode of *Pet Fitness* here, which would be fun.

Even more important was that she was about to initiate some extraordinary veterinary help for a special-needs pet.

She was bringing a wheelchair for Nifty, the Basset hound mix with a dysfunctional hind end.

We met in the parking lot outside the front of Save'Em—fortunately not the same area where I had found Miles Frankovick's body. I didn't want to think about that today, though it was hard not to.

Carlie arrived with a van from the Longevity Vision Channel containing a small film crew. But I was most excited to see what she would extract from the vehicle.

Someone else removed the apparatus from the van, though. Carlie introduced Paul, a guy she'd filmed a few months ago who co-owned ProsthaPetics, a company that sold animal assistive devices and prosthetics.

"That's it?" I looked over the contraption that I knew to be a doggy wheelchair. Basically, it looked like a *U* of small pipes, with the free end containing a halter and the base attached to two wheels.

"That's it," she confirmed.

A different volunteer opened the door for us that day. Her nametag identified her as Daya. Like Peggy, she wore a red shirt, but she appeared to be mid-twenties instead of a teen. She bared large, irregular teeth in a smile as she let us in. "Bella told me you were coming. This is so cool. Can I be on the show?" This, of course, was directed to Carlie.

"Let's see how things work out." I loved Carlie's tactfulness.

Bella emerged from her office as we gathered in the entryway, clad in her usual Save'Em work shirt over jeans. I was happy to see my friend, but I told her right off that I had nothing new to report. She looked relaxed and delighted about what was to come, and I suspected that she had enhanced her usual makeup in anticipation of being part of the filming.

Carlie introduced her staff and Paul, and Bella smiled and shook a lot of hands. Then, leaving Daya in charge of the greeting zone, Bella showed us through the archway into the open, two-story kennel area. A lot of volunteers were in enclosures, socializing some of the older dogs. Some of the canines nevertheless barked at us as we went through to the rear of the structure, where the special-needs animals were housed.

They, too, had quite a few visitors playing with them. No Kip, though, or Peggy. I remained pleased about how active Save'Em was in recruiting people to help with the animals. HotRescues had as many as we needed, too, of course, so I didn't need either to give or take any lessons.

Carlie knew the location of Nifty's kennel. The sweet dog maneuvered himself from lying down into a sitting position as Bella and Carlie entered.

"How about some better mobility, sweetheart?" Carlie picked him up as easily as if he were a toy dog instead of a forty-pound-or-so Basset and carried him out of the enclosure.

There, she did a quick veterinary checkup as cameras rolled. Bella was filmed, too, as she answered some of Carlie's questions about Nifty's general health and ability to get around, including how he managed to evacuate.

"He's surprisingly agile about getting out of the way," Bella said. I felt certain that one or more of the three cameras was recording her smile, as proud as if she was a mama discussing her child.

"Okay," Carlie finally said. "The moment of truth. I

think Nifty is ready to begin his new life. Let's give your wheelchair a try, Nifty." She motioned to Paul, and together, with the cameras rolling, they fastened the halter around Nifty so the wheels were at his back end and his limp, unusable legs were comfortably hooked up to the rear. Then they both moved away to give the cameras a better view of the obviously confused pup. Poor Nifty kept turning around and trying to nip at the things now attached to him.

Carlie brought some treats out of her bag. With Paul's help, they lured Nifty forward slowly as he used his front legs. The movement sent him ahead faster than he probably expected and he stopped.

After a few minutes of this, the treats were placed farther in front of him. Amazingly, marvelously soon, he was moving steadily and gracefully with his new wheelchair attached.

"This is so wonderful!" Bella's enthusiasm was undoubtedly captured for posterity—and the *Pet Fitness* show. It was genuine. Mine, too, but I expressed it off camera. Carlie understood that I didn't want to be an official part of this, no matter how delighted I was to watch.

"I'll give you further instructions, along with a handout you can share with your staff," Carlie said. "It'll include advice on how to encourage him to go to the bathroom with the wheelchair attached. We'll be back to check on Nifty's progress in a few weeks."

The filming was over. We were all so excited for Nifty. Some of Bella's official staff had been watching from around where I stood, and Bella told them how to handle this—encourage Nifty individually and not confuse him any more than he already was.

She showed us back to Save'Em's huge, well-equipped kitchen, downstairs and toward the center of the main building, where we all toasted over coffee and soft drinks. Kip joined us there. The accountant had apparently been lashed to his office computer and had just broken free.

"Thank you so much, Carlie," Bella said as we got ready to leave. "You, too, Paul, for bringing Nifty's wheelchair. Maybe we could work out prosthetics or other equipment for some more animals?" She looked hopefully toward Carlie, who nodded.

"As long as I can film it for *Pet Fitness*, I'll be glad to help. We'll work out who pays whom and all that another time. This one is definitely on me."

Bella's grin widened even more.

She continued to smile as she showed the entire group of us out of the main building toward the front door. Then she stopped, clutching the door, paling noticeably as her mouth gaped open.

I moved around the crowd and looked outside.

Detective Stefan Garciana stood there. "Hello, Lauren," he said. "I didn't expect to see you here. I have some more questions for Ms. Frankovick."

Chapter 12

Bella looked shocked. But I had gone through something similar before, so I wasn't as surprised.

I moved closer and said into her ear, "Remember cop shows. Don't say anything without your lawyer present. You did contact Esther Ickes, didn't you?"

She nodded grimly. "I've met with her, too."

"Good. Then call her right away."

Esther was the attorney specializing in criminal law to whom I'd referred Bella. Esther was a wonderful, crafty senior citizen as well as being an outstanding lawyer. She had helped me when I'd been accused of murder. I'd been referred to her in the first place by Dante's lady friend Kendra Ballantyne, a pet-sitter who seemed always to be attempting to solve murders for her friends.

I grimaced at the thought. So, unfortunately, was I these days.

I smiled, though, as Carlie edged in front of us in the doorway, motioning to have her camera staff join her and film the scowling detective.

"Hi," she said pertly. "You may remember me. I'm Dr. Carlie Stellan, a veterinarian, and I've just been filming an episode of my *Pet Fitness* show here for the Longevity Vision Channel. I gather you're not here to do anything to benefit the animals." Garciana opened his mouth as if to reply, but Carlie didn't give him time. "You know, having the authorities storm the door this way might be a great contrast to the good things we've already gotten today. Could make for great TV. Thanks for coming." She turned back to her staff. "Fellows, be sure to get this officer's contact information in case we decide to be in touch." She strutted out.

Bella and I had been shunted over toward one side. "I'd stay and help if I thought it would do any good," I told her. "But even though I'm not big on paparazzi-type stuff, I think having Carlie's guys filming here might be useful to you. Like I said, though, call Esther right away."

Her smartphone was up to her mouth as I followed Carlie outside.

Unlike with real paparazzi, the filming Carlie had done wouldn't wind up flashing on pseudo-news shows on TV, or even on the Internet.

That's what I assumed, but I called her as soon as I got

back to my office at HotRescues to make sure that wasn't really her plan.

"I thought you knew me better than that, Lauren." She actually sounded hurt, and I repented having asked.

As usual, Zoey was on the floor near my feet. I bent to gently pat her behind her perked-up ears as I said, "I do. But—well, in a way it might be to Bella's advantage, gain her some sympathy, if it looks to the world like she's being hounded by the cops."

A moment of silence. Then Carlie said, "You know, maybe I should side with Matt, Brooke, and Antonio on this. You're getting too involved again, Lauren."

My turn to chomp on my tongue for a beat. I should never have mentioned my irritating dinner conversation the other night to Carlie. "Maybe so. I'll think the situation through a little more. Meanwhile, keep me informed about when your episode on Save'Em will air. At least I haven't seen any more of those ads for a while from that vet who wanted Bella to close her doors for the animals' supposed sake. The one your promo spots countered."

"Maybe he had some humanity in him after all," Carlie said. "Even if he didn't care about saving special-needs animals, he might have decided to shut up about the whole situation after Miles was killed."

"Or maybe he figured that the situation would result in Bella's arrest and the end of Save'Em anyhow," I finished.

What I hadn't mentioned to Carlie, or anyone else with qualms about my helping Bella, was my plan to attend Miles's memorial service.

It was scheduled for Saturday, at a church in Beverly Hills. There'd been no word about when his actual funeral might be, since apparently his body remained in the hands of the coroner. But someone who cared about him—his fellow plastic surgeons, maybe?—had put together a service anyway. That made the news, even if Carlie's filming of Detective Garciana at Bella's didn't.

Maybe the oddest thing about my going was that I planned to accompany Bella. Yes, she, too, had decided to attend.

"I might have come to despise him," she'd told me over the phone that Thursday evening. That was the same conversation in which she related that, thanks to the intervention of her attorney Esther, the visit to Save'Em by Detective Garciana that afternoon had been a nonevent. "But we were married for ten years. A handful of those years were enjoyable, and even though things turned bad quick, I never wished him dead . . . at least not till we started arguing about our division of assets. I wonder if the fight will just end now, with him gone."

I didn't mention how that could factor into the cops' unimaginative assessment of motive. "I assume he has heirs—family members or whoever," I said. "I hope you get along with some, at least, or you may continue the same kind of financial fight."

Once again I was stroking the soft, warm fur behind Zoey's ears—this time as she sat beside me on our living room couch at home. The rest of the afternoon at HotRescues had gone by fast, especially considering that a class from a nearby grade school had come for a visit to see what an exemplary no-kill shelter for homeless animals looked like. I'd greeted Brooke on her arrival for the night but hadn't meandered into the Bella situation with her again—maybe by tacit agreement.

On getting home, I didn't change out of my HotRescues clothes but now vegged out in front of the muted TV, sipping a cup of herbal tea.

"I never got along well with his brothers," Bella said with a sigh, "so I guess it's not over. Depending on how he's changed his will, of course."

"Of course," I agreed. Too bad I didn't know its contents.

Maybe Miles had been killed out of someone's greed—and that someone wasn't Bella.

The All-Embracing Church of Beverly Hills wasn't a venue I'd heard of before. I'd looked up its Web site to extract the address to program into the GPS my kids had recently bought me. It was a multidenominational house of worship, and its photo on the site made it look like a house of high incomes.

In person, on Saturday, it appeared even more impressive, tall and solemn and forbidding, its façade done up in white-trimmed terra cotta tile around the windows and on the roof. Many towers stood at attention around the central building. The large crucifix rising from the one to the right of the front entrance appeared surprisingly plain to be a symbol of the otherwise uninviting church.

Bella had picked me up at home since I was more along her route than she was mine. Like fraternal twins, we both wore black dresses. My shirtwaist was more conservative than her above-the-knee, sleeveless one. So was my plain silver-link necklace, compared with the diamond-encrusted one she wore.

I figured I'd see the two cosmetic surgeons from Miles's office whose services I had pretended to be interested in. I didn't particularly want to explain anything to them, so I disguised myself a little. I slathered on more makeup than was my norm. I also pulled my hair severely from my face, clipping it beneath a black, small-brimmed hat that I assumed was a current style since I found it in my daughter Tracy's room.

Bella parked her upscale Lexis in the church's parking lot. It looked at home among the other luxury vehicles.

As she exited her car, she smoothed her dress and her face, taking a deep calming breath. I was looking forward to this as much as I would a dental exam, but it was even more of an ordeal for her.

"You okay?" I asked.

"Sure. Although I'll bet your detective friend from the LAPD will be here, too—to watch me, not necessarily to look for anyone else who might have wanted Miles dead."

That's why I was there, but I decided not to vocalize it. Bella probably assumed it was at least part of my reason, but I'd just offered to join her for moral support.

A lot of people walked from the parking lot, up the steps and through the wide doors that opened into the church.

A woman dressed in a white robe adorned with a long red stole stood near the door greeting people. I assumed she was the clergyperson. We nodded in greeting, then passed by without Bella introducing herself. Me, neither. Bella seemed to want to sit near the rear of the sanctuary, but I urged her forward toward the middle.

By then, people had recognized her. Several said hello, and Bella greeted them back gravely, with no appearance of discomfort. Others stared and whispered. I trained my gaze on a few of them until they looked away. They probably wondered who the heck the antagonistic broad was, but who cared?

A few rows on the right, near the front of the sanctuary, I saw what must have been the area chosen for Miles's colleagues and office staff. I recognized the two doctors I'd talked with and a few other staff members. They all talked among themselves, ignoring everyone else.

"Bella." A hushed male voice sounded from behind us.

Bella went as rigid as one of the outside towers before she pivoted toward whoever had spoken. I turned, too, and recognized the veterinarian from the TV interviews criticizing Save Them All Pet Sanctuary. Bella looked away without responding.

The clergywoman must have slipped by us somehow. She was at the front of the room, on the dais. "Everyone please take your seats," she said into the microphone.

The service was brief and poignant. If the little I'd seen of Miles hadn't convinced me that he was an animal hater, as well as a jerk of an ex-husband, I might have felt very moved by it.

Two medical practice colleagues rose to eulogize him at

the front of the room, standing behind a dais in the middle of an arch of flowers. One was Dr. Serena Santoval. I felt pretty certain that I'd gotten it right and she had been Miles's lover, judging by how weepy and personal she was. I didn't know whether that relationship might have precipitated Bella's divorce from him, but it could have. Either way, despite her sobs, I couldn't eliminate this good doctor from my suspect list.

The other I hadn't met before. I gathered from what he said that Dr. Pass Pearson was the newest doctor to be added to the practice. He was therefore perhaps the least likely to have cared enough about Miles either positively or negatively to have killed him.

Eventually, the service was over. I had chosen the aisle seat so I kept Bella from rushing from the sanctuary, instead letting most of the seats in front of us empty and the occupants file out.

We'd heard there would be a reception downstairs in the church. I wasn't hungry, but I did want to talk to as many people as I could—and eavesdrop on the rest.

Bella curbed her reluctance to head to the stairway when I whispered that there'd be a lot of potential suspects down there.

"Then that *is* why you're here." She sounded somewhat pleased that she had assumed the truth.

I nodded and entered the crowd navigating the stairs. Bella would follow, I was sure.

"Bella!" The voice came from behind us. Kip Schaley was there, in a gray suit and athletic shoes.

"I didn't know you were coming," she said.

He edged close, his back toward me, as if he was trying to take my place. Interesting. I'd already wondered if he had a crush on her.

"I wanted to be here for you." He smiled down at her uncertainly.

"Thank you. Let's go downstairs."

So now I followed them. If I hadn't had a purpose here, I'd have felt like a third wheel.

At the bottom, I entered the reception room and watched as the two moved forward. As they reached a table occupied by coffee urns, Bella started pouring herself a cup.

Kip turned toward me, peering through his glasses. In a low voice he said, "Bella said she asked you to help find out what really happened to Miles. It's nice of you, but unnecessary. I'll help her."

"That's nice of you," I replied, "but if you find anything useful please let me know. I've already promised to do what I can, and I don't break promises."

"But—" At my glare, the poutiness of his look disappeared, replaced by a pleasant nod. "With both of us checking," he finished, "we're bound to figure it out."

"Sure," I said.

As he got in line for coffee, I edged between some people and moved toward Bella. Her eyes remained on the crowd still trickling down the stairway. "I'm glad Kip is here," she said. "I'd have invited him if I hadn't thought it inappropriate to look like I brought a date . . ." Her words trailed off, and I glanced at her, trying to figure out her apparent non sequitur.

That was when I saw the veterinarian from the critical

TV interviews wending his way from the stairway and through the droves of people toward us.

Interesting. I'd wondered about him when we saw him before, but he had moved away when the service began and I had no idea where he'd been seated.

I wondered about him even more now, and why Bella was reacting so strongly.

Again, she stood straight, glaring at him. His appearance was softer, or maybe that was because he regarded her through small, thick-lensed glasses.

"Hello, Bella," he said.

"Vic." She said his name, then turned her head to look beyond him.

"It's good to see you." He wasn't bad to look at in person. His receding hairline only emphasized a narrow, handsome face, and he looked quite at home in his dark suit. But I saw beyond his looks to the cold, heartless man beneath.

Bella's gaze returned to him as if it was hard for her, too, to look only at the surface. "That's a strange thing for you to say."

I felt as if I was in the middle of a dramatic performance after entering a theater for the first time after intermission. They obviously had a history, but I didn't know what it was and I didn't think I'd get much opportunity to dig into it until these two played out whatever was going on here.

"Hello, Dr. Drammon." I remembered his name from TV. I didn't hold out my hand since I despised the guy, but I introduced myself. "I'm Lauren Vancouver. I run Hot-Rescues, a no-kill pet shelter, and unlike you, I very much applaud what Bella is doing with Save Them All Sanctuary."

"I do, too, only—"

"Only you think that saving older or special-needs animals is a form of torturing them. Good-bye, Vic." Her firm chin high, Bella moved away. Kip joined her, and I followed them without saying anything else to the despicable vet.

I'd want to hear more about their history later. I was very curious.

When we walked away, I noticed that some of the men in suits included Detective Stefan Garciana. He was deep in conversation with the woman who had officiated over the service. I tried to keep my back toward him, but Bella noticed and gasped.

"Ignore him." I continued moving. Kip hurried to keep up with us.

They stayed with me, at least until I veered toward the table with coffee urns. I needed a drink, and caffeine would have to do. When I turned back, Bella and Kip faced three people: two men and a woman. They all looked angry, and Bella, holding Kip's arm, was clearly uncomfortable.

I joined them again.

"These are Miles's brothers." Bella introduced them, as well as her former sister-in-law—Edson, Brewster, and Eleanor Frankovick.

"You have some nerve showing up here." Eleanor's hiss made her resemble a snake even more than her thin body, narrow face, and uplifted hairdo. I assumed she was married to Brewster, since she grabbed his arm.

"I just wanted to pay my respects." Bella's quiet response

swathed her in dignity, which was clearly lacking in the people she faced.

"You should have done that before," Brewster said, "instead of killing him." He looked more like his deceased brother than the one beside him, with his dark brown eyes and turkey wattle beneath his chin. Edson's eyes were lighter and even more spiteful, his features gaunt.

"Don't grace that with a response," I interjected, glaring at them and motioning for Bella to move on. Kip, grasping Bella's hand, led her through the crowd while I stood my ground. Bella's former relatives turned away first, and I felt a small, absurd sense of victory.

When I pivoted, I saw that Bella and Kip had wound up near the gathering of doctors and staff from Miles's medical office. Had Bella intended to stop there? I doubted it, but the crush of eating and mourners didn't appear to let her move away easily.

The medical personnel stood in the middle of the room near a table filled with veggies and dip, a nice, healthful snack area that would undoubtedly make a good impression on anyone considering getting work done by them. As he said hello, Bella nodded at Dr. Abe Renteen and kept walking, with Kip trailing behind, but a young lady with long legs revealed by a short skirt approached them. I thought I recognized her as one of the office personnel in brightly colored lab jackets—a nurse, perhaps.

"Hello, Mrs.—I mean, Bella."

Interesting catch. I assumed the office staff had been instructed to address doctors' spouses formally, but no one, least of all Bella, considered her Mrs. Frankovick any longer.

"Hello, Keara." Bella seemed to hesitate, then she said, "I'm glad to see you're still with the office. You are, aren't you? You were such a good assistant to Miles. Have they assigned you to someone else?"

Keara's large blue eyes moistened and she nodded. "But I—we—miss him. He . . . well, when you two split he seemed so lost at first." Really? That didn't sound like the situation as I understood it. "I wanted to—"

Whatever it was she wanted was obliterated as Serena Santoval planted herself in the way.

"How does it feel?" the emotional doctor asked. "You were already rid of him, Bella. You didn't have to kill him."

I saw Bella's eyes widen in shock, but she stood her ground. "I didn't. I had no reason to. I was through with him, and he was through with me. But you, on the other hand—"

"Are you accusing me?" the woman hissed.

"Only as much as you're accusing me," Bella said.

"You belong with those damned filthy animals Miles said you were throwing his money away on."

They looked ready to attack one another. Interesting, but it wouldn't get me the information I sought.

I noticed Detective Garciana watching—not good for Bella.

"I don't think we'll solve Miles's murder here." I arranged myself so my shoulder was between them. "Let's assume, for now, that neither of you did it, shall we?"

"But—" Serena the harpy began.

"I said *assume*. If you have any ideas who else could be a suspect since you worked so closely with Miles, it wouldn't hurt to share."

"Are you a cop?" Serena demanded.

"Of course not."

"But you are . . . you're bogus, aren't you?" That was Abe Renteen. He stared at me with narrowed amber eyes, as though considering me again for a face-lift.

"What do you mean by bogus?" I countered his question with my own.

"You were at our offices this week asking about having some cosmetic surgery performed, weren't you?"

I hadn't thought my disguise to be flawless, but it clearly hadn't worked at all, at least not with him.

"Was I?" I stared coldly, as if he had insulted me.

"Ms. . . . Vancouver, isn't it? In case you weren't aware of it, people in my profession learn quickly to study details of faces they're considering enhancing. That nose of yours, the wrinkles I could help with—"

I winced. Yes, I had a wrinkle here and there but they weren't really so bad.

"Why were you really there?" he demanded. "I can guess, seeing you here with Bella. Are you trying to figure out who to point the blame at in Miles's death besides her?"

I was about as inclined to answer him as I was eager to choke on the carrot I'd picked up. "I assume you're not going to admit it right here," I told him. "But anyone else on your staff who you suspect? Or—"

To my surprise, he laughed. "All of us are innocent, of course. We believe that dear Bella, there, must be guilty because she and Miles hadn't stopped arguing about money. That's the thing—if you're trying to solve a murder, follow the money. It's kind of you to attempt to protect Bella, even if it's futile. In the unlikely event that it's not her, there is another place you can look where money is at issue. It's been kept relatively quiet, but if you Google the names Al and Clara Traymore, you might just get another couple of names for your little suspect list. Real or not, Al thinks he has a motive. So go bother them and stay out of our clinic."

Chapter 13

"Did Detective Garciana try to talk to you?" I was watching Bella's stony expression as she began driving us away from the church. Since Kip had come on his own, he left at the same time we did but drove himself.

Bella's perfectly manicured hands clenched the steering wheel. I'd noticed them before and been surprised that the polish on her nails wasn't chipped, since I knew she was a hands-on shelter administrator.

Maybe she had redone her nails just to look perfect and unfazed at the memorial ceremony.

In any event, she didn't appear to be mourning her ex. Not that I figured she would. But I wasn't able to read her emotions.

I did read, though, that she was filled with them. Anger? Hurt? Fear?

She darted a glance toward me. Her blue eyes flashed with what appeared to be rage. But as she caught my inquisitive yet sympathetic gaze, she seemed to melt.

"No." Her voice sounded much calmer than I'd anticipated. "I caught him looking at me from across the room at the reception, as if he wanted to unnerve me. He succeeded, but I kept as stiff an upper lip as I could."

That sounded very British, and I smiled.

I waited till she stopped the car at the next traffic light. "Okay, then. Let's forget about him for now. I want to go over a few thoughts with you, learn what you know about the people there and who had motives to kill your ex."

"Fine," she said, not surprisingly since she had requested my help to do just that.

But I wanted to catch her a little off guard. "First, though, tell me all about Dr. Victor Drammon."

Mistake. Though the light had changed and she had started moving ahead with the flow of traffic, she slammed on the brakes. Fortunately, no one had been tailgating us, so we merely stopped just beyond the intersection.

She slowly pressed on the gas again. Without looking at me, she asked, "Why do you want to know about him? He's not who you're looking for."

"You don't consider him a suspect in Miles's murder? Okay—maybe. But I saw that there was something between you, even though you didn't talk to him much. He obviously wanted to talk to you, and you shunned him. I already know that he was the first vet you considered for Save'Em before he started saying nasty things about the shelter on TV. So tell me about him."

"And if I tell you that isn't your business?"

She might be right. There appeared to be something personal between them, and I didn't need to know about it. Except that he could be a factor in hurting innocent animals despite being a veterinarian, and I couldn't rule him out completely as a suspect in Miles's murder.

"It is my business because you asked me to look at every angle to help find out who killed Miles," I contradicted her. "And my life revolves around saving pets' lives, and that vet might be intentionally killing them—or at least discouraging people from trying to allow them to live out their lives as long as reasonably possible."

Her shoulders drooped beneath her black designer dress. "That's exactly the problem." Her voice was so low that I had to strain to hear it over the outside ambient noise of rushing air and traffic. "I'd thought—well, all right. Here it is." She pursed her lips as if considering what to say, then continued. "Vic and his ex-wife were good friends of Miles's and mine for years. In fact, Vic's veterinary clinic is just outside Beverly Hills, not far from Miles's offices. We all got together for dinner now and then, that kind of thing. He divorced first but remained friends with Miles and me. And when things really started getting terrible with Miles . . ."

Though she let her voice trail off, I guessed what she was thinking. "He was there for you. Tried to help you through it."

"Exactly." We were stopped at a traffic light near a turn onto a freeway on-ramp, and she looked at me. Her lovely features looked both pained and sheepish. "We never talked about the future, of course, but when I finally made the decision and left Miles, I thought Vic would still be there for me. The one thing we had talked about was how to help special-needs pets, and I had assumed that, when I started Save Them All Sanctuary, he would be our veterinarian for the long haul. I don't know why he changed his mind about helping the old and infirm. And when he made his opinion so public . . . well, it really hurt."

"I see."

"He sided with Miles about Save'Em. Became his good friend again instead of mine. But that's behind me. I don't want to talk to him ever again, and I can't wait till Carlie's episode on how wonderful things are at Save'Em airs. That will show him. Now, let's discuss some of the others. I don't know who might have killed Miles, but we can brainstorm a bit."

"Fine." I had another question for her first, though. "Do you know the Traymores, the people Dr. Renteen mentioned?"

We were now cruising along the 405 Freeway, headed north. Her brow wrinkled slightly, as though she was thinking. "No, I'm afraid not. But let me know if you find anything out about them, will you?"

I agreed.

For the rest of the ride, we did a kind of debriefing, where we discussed the people Miles had worked with, and the likelihood of the guilt of each one of them in his death.

"I kind of like his assistant Keara for it," I said, not necessarily believing it but wondering how Bella felt about the young lady who'd obviously had a crush on her boss.

Bella didn't immediately dismiss the idea, which interested me. "Maybe," she said pensively. "She comes across as such a sweet young thing, doesn't she? But before Miles and I split, there were times that she just seemed to drip honey all over me yet somehow be critical all the same. I neither liked nor trusted her. But as a killer . . . well, don't cross her off the list just yet."

"I won't."

One by one we dissected the others, too. I likened Dr. Serena Santoval to a conniving witch. So far, she was my favorite suspect. Keara or not, I believed that Serena had considered herself Miles's next main squeeze once Bella was no longer his wife. Had he agreed? If not, would rejecting her have made her angry enough to kill him?

But Dr. Abe Renteen was a close second. He'd been outspoken about despising the negative publicity Miles's divorce fight had engendered for their medical practice. Had he thought that getting rid of Miles would somehow improve their reputation?

There were a couple of other doctors we examined, too—including the newest guy in the practice, that Dr. Pass Pearson. Bella hadn't known him before she separated from Miles, so she had no idea if there'd been any animosity between them.

Then there was Kip Schaley. He was so enamored of Bella that he might have wanted to help her by getting rid of her argumentative ex. That might be why he didn't want me to try to find the killer. I didn't mention him to Bella, though. I felt that, even though she'd recognized he might have done something rash to help her, she'd have defended him now.

We had already turned west on the 118 Freeway and were getting close to the exit she would take to get me back to HotRescues. "One last thing," I said. "And this could be the most telling information of all. We touched on it before.

Who might inherit from Miles on his death, now that you were divorced—those relatives at the service today?"

"Quite possibly," Bella said, her tone once again pensive. She made a turn onto the Hayvenhurst exit. "Miles's parents are from New England and still live there, too infirm to travel, unlike his brothers. Some or all of them are definitely his most likely heirs—but of course I don't know whether he drew up a will that left money to them or to someone else. I may be able to find out who inherited from him when I talk to my divorce lawyer. He'll need to figure out who it is and whether they're going to argue the same way about our marital money and property as Miles did."

"Good thing to know," I agreed.

Yes, I was curious about the Traymores and why Dr. Abe Renteen had tried to sic me on them as the possible murderers.

But, no, I didn't try looking them up that late afternoon. Our trainer, Gavin Mamo, was at HotRescues for a special session with a few of our dogs who needed a refresher on how to act at least somewhat obediently—and therefore become more adoptable.

We always had Gavin do a private session or two with our newest canine residents when they first came out of quarantine. He also worked with our staff and the volunteers who helped to socialize dogs, to at least attempt to reinforce that training.

Since it was Saturday, a lot of our help was around, and I'd put out an edict that as many as possible were to be there to participate in Gavin's session.

He had set things up in the center court in the new part of HotRescues, between rows of kennels. Mostly medium and larger dogs were housed in that area, and each had been taken out of their enclosure and tethered on a sturdy leash. Volunteers and staff members had been directed to hold the leashes so no dog could get more than a couple of feet away.

So many of our volunteers were present that I had to smile. Even our most senior, Bev and Mamie, were participating. The dogs they'd been assigned to were not among the most rambunctious, but the training refresher would do them as much good as the younger folks like Ricki, the future veterinary tech; Sally, who volunteered at HotRescues only on weekends; and Margie Tarbet, who was there with her son Davie, a teen who'd needed some training to lasso in his keen interest in pet rescue.

Participating staff members included Pete and Nina. And me, of course. Dr. Mona wasn't there, but she didn't usually work directly with the animals. And although our new groomer, Margo, was around, she didn't get involved with training, either.

I had put Zoey in the office, but she knew all this stuff and did it well. I didn't need for her to get better trained. But other dogs around here definitely needed it.

I had Dodi on a leash—an adorable sheltie mix who had been at HotRescues longer than almost any other resident. I needed to make sure she was trained well enough to find a new home, although I doubted her behavior was a factor in no one having yet chosen her. Sometimes, people and pets just have to jell, and the right combo hadn't yet worked out for poor Dodi.

"Okay, now, everyone listen up," called Gavin. He was a large guy and liked to flaunt his Hawaiian extraction by wearing colorful muumuu shirts. Today's was bright green with magenta flowers. "We'll just go through the basics today. First, we'll walk in a circle, and I want you to give the command 'heel.' You'll make sure your dog obeys by how closely you hold the leash and how often you reward them with a treat. Then we'll go through 'sit,' 'down,' and 'stay.' Everyone ready?"

For the next ten minutes, that was exactly what we did. Dodi obeyed perfectly. Most other dogs did, too, although we had a few who tried to assert their canine pack alphaness over the people holding them. Even they became highly obedient, though, in exchange for treats.

When we were finished, I bent down and hugged Dodi. "You need your forever home soon, girl," I said. She panted her agreement.

I congratulated my staff and volunteers, then shook hands with Gavin. "Thanks," I told him. "On behalf of all of us, most especially our residents."

His toothy grin split his round face as he embraced me in a hug. "Why so formal, boss lady? You know what to tell me."

Actually, I did. "Gavin, you rock!"

The pups were back in their kennels, most exhausted enough to nestle right down on the wonderful bedding from HotPets. The human gang had dispersed, almost all leaving HotRescues for the night.

I was still here, though. Zoey, too. My sweet pup hadn't

complained about being locked in the office by herself for nearly an hour, so I'd taken her for a walk outside our grounds in the pleasant commercial neighborhood. She now lay by my feet as I worked on the computer.

My door was partly open and I was startled when someone knocked on it. I looked up. Brooke stood there, Cheyenne at her side. Zoey rose, and the two dogs exchanged nose sniffs.

"Hey, I ran into Nina as she was leaving," Brooke said. "She told me about the good training session Gavin led. Wish I'd been here."

"You'd have had to arrive for work early," I reminded her. "I'll give you notice next time, but you don't have to attend. You've already got Cheyenne trained as a security champion."

"I know." She walked farther into the room, skirting the dogs. She looked ready to patrol our grounds in her black security staff shirt and jeans. She looked as great as she usually did lately. A good job, adequate income, and happy love life apparently all agreed with her.

I decided to shelve my annoyance with her that reappeared in my mind from our last get-together.

She settled into a chair across from my desk and swung one leg nonchalantly over the other, revealing her short-topped boots. "So, did you find anything interesting online just now about Miles Frankovick's murder?"

I glared. "What makes you think I was looking into it now?"

"The expression on your face. Plus, I know you, Lauren. When you get something on your mind, you obsess about it. Yes, you let things interrupt—especially things relating to HotRescues—but now, alone in your office, you looked so absorbed. I know that's what you're up to. Besides, there was something on the news today about a memorial service for Miles, and I'll bet you were there. Right?"

"Could be." I ignored her self-satisfied grin. But I had a thought. She had a good mind for solving puzzles, especially those relating to crimes. Did I dare try to utilize it? "If I did happen to be doing some checking," I said, as nonchalantly as if I was discussing whether I'd been cleaning out cat litter, "are you going to give me a hard time about it?"

"Would it do any good?"

I shook my head.

"I figured. So . . . did you find anything interesting?"

"Maybe," I said. "Care to brainstorm?"

She laughed. "So tell me who your latest suspect is and why."

Chapter 14

I brainstormed a lot with Brooke before I'd left for home last night. Had even gotten her to call Antonio on my behalf.

That was why I'd left Zoey at HotRescues this Sunday morning and headed for the L.A. Sheriff's patrol station in West Hollywood.

I had learned online that Al Traymore, the guy Dr. Abe Renteen had suggested as the ideal suspect in Miles's killing, was a deputy sheriff. Despite being one of the three-against-me department the other night, Antonio had been nice enough to schedule me for a meeting with Deputy Traymore.

Not that they were colleagues, exactly. The Los Angeles Police Department was in charge of everything within the city of L.A., whereas the Sheriff's Department took care of all the rest of Los Angeles County, including some small towns like West Hollywood that were carved out of the main city's boundaries. Confusing.

I parked outside the West Hollywood station on San Vicente and went inside. I asked the uniforms behind the desk for Deputy Traymore, and he soon emerged.

"Ms. Vancouver?"

I nodded, smiled, and held out my hand. The cover Antonio had provided me with, according to Brooke, was that I was interested in moving to an apartment I'd found in West Hollywood and wanted to talk to someone about the crime rate in the area. I didn't know why this deputy would know what to tell me, or how Antonio had actually finessed this conversation. But what I knew about Brooke's guy friend and his intelligence suggested that he was smarter than the proverbial fox—a good trait for a detective with a major urban police department.

Not that he was perfect—he had taken the side of his fellow detectives and judged Bella guilty enough to want me to back off looking into the murder. But he was man enough to rise above his prejudices and help me anyway.

I assumed he had looked into what this deputy's assignment was and found a way to get me in under the pretext of needing the kind of help he gave. But I'd done some online research and discovered why Deputy Traymore had a grudge against Dr. Miles Frankovick. I intended to pursue that today.

"Thanks for agreeing to see me, Deputy," I said. He led me to a seating area in the entry and waved for me to sit down. Not exactly the most private location, but I didn't intend to shout my questions anyway.

I began by asking generally about the crime rate in West Hollywood—a nice mix of residential and commercial areas.

Deputy Traymore wore the beige uniform of a sheriff's deputy, with its yellow-trimmed green patch on the shoulder. He had a thick jaw that suggested belligerence, and wavy salt-and-pepper hair. He began spouting statistics from a printout he had brought with him. The number of annual robberies was significantly more here than the national average, and violent crime was a little higher, but most other kinds of crimes were around the same as that average.

I tried to focus on what he was saying so I could respond, but finally blurted, "You know, I'm thinking of getting a face-lift when I settle into my apartment. Do you think that's safe?"

He stopped talking and stared as if he was trying to bore his way into my skull with his furious silver-gray eyes.

Which only made me feel as if I'd asked the right thing. I was now taking control of this discussion and hoped to get some answers to the real questions I'd come with.

"Are you a damned reporter?" he growled. I could see his thick fists clench and was glad we remained in public.

"No, I'm not. But I'm someone who is very interested in the cosmetic surgery that your wife received and what went wrong."

"Then you're an investigator from the offices of the

lawyers representing those damned plastic surgery hacks. Well, you can tell your bosses and their clients that I'm not dropping my lawsuit. I'm going to get every cent they've ever made and will make in the next hundred years and make sure they pay it all. I deserve it. Do you know how much it costs to keep my wife in the hospital, thanks to that jerk Frankovick? She's having reconstructive surgery done. And her state of mind . . . well, she's under psychiatric care, too."

"I can only guess the cost," I responded calmly. "What hospital is in? Doesn't insurance help?" I assumed he had health insurance through his position in county government.

"None of your business which hospital she's in. I tell you and you'll probably go bother her."

I'd hoped to do just that, if possible. Talking to the woman would give me a better sense of her mental condition—and whether she, like her clearly angry husband, made a realistic murder suspect.

To do that, I had to learn where she was. I wasn't the kind of official investigator Deputy Traymore had assumed I was, but I doubted he would believe any other reason I tried to give him for wanting to see her—even though my mind scrambled for one.

"I'm not an investigator, but a concerned citizen," I said. "I admit that I'm not interested in plastic surgery for myself. But a friend of mine had a bad experience with that same plastic surgery outfit, so I'm looking into ways she can get back at them." Not a bad improvisation. But until I saw where this led, I wouldn't congratulate myself.

"I'll bet your friend's experience wasn't as bad as this." Traymore's tone was soft but furious. He reached into his pocket and pulled out a wallet.

He flipped through several photographs that depicted a woman's face, which looked a thousand times worse than I'd imagined possible. All the features seemed swollen or puckered and out of alignment. I felt terrible for the woman.

I also could see the motive for either her or her husband to kill the doctor who did it to her.

"Was it this bad?" he insisted when I remained quiet, shoving the photos closer to my eyes.

"Not quite," I responded softly.

He yanked back the pictures, shoved his wallet into his pocket. "I'd love to mangle that damned Dr. Frankovick the way he did to my wife. Instead, and in answer to your other question, yes, I have insurance. But I have a deductible and some limits on coverage. There are also expenses it doesn't cover, like pain and suffering . . . and all the other stuff in the papers my lawyer has filed against that quack and his office."

"But . . . are you aware that Dr. Miles Frankovick has passed away?" I used the euphemism about Miles's murder purposely, to see the deputy's reaction.

His guffaw seemed to come from way down in his craw. " 'Passed away'? You mean, someone with guts and brains did exactly what I wanted to. What I might have done if I wasn't an officer of the law. Some people get away with it. I know enough to probably have not gotten caught. But I have too much to lose by getting revenge that way. Like, all the money those damned, maiming scalpel-wielders who're still around are going to ultimately pay me. I want a lot more than they're insured for, and I plan to get it."

The conversation with the angry Deputy Traymore gave me a lot to think about for the rest of the day after I returned to HotRescues. I'd brought Zoey, of course, and we said hi to everyone here—including our sweet, affection-craving residents. I indulged a bunch of them, slipping into their kennels to give them hugs and attention.

Then we returned to my office. Instead of working, I was musing—not a good thing.

Was Al Traymore crouching behind his profession of being an officer of the law while aiming knives at enemies, or was he truly innocent?

I'd have loved to run my questions by his wife. Maybe I'd still find a way to do that. Find *her*. But the deputy's angry words had confirmed what I'd learned on the Internet. Clara Traymore was currently a patient at an exclusive hospital in Brentwood. Presumably, she was having more surgery to correct what had gone wrong with her face-lift.

This particular hospital was also known for its psychiatric wing. Detective Traymore had mentioned that she was under psychiatric care.

Had she been driven totally crazy by the sight of her own disfigured face in the mirror?

Where had she been on the night Miles was murdered?

"Come on, girl," I said to Zoey. I didn't want to spend the entire afternoon puzzling over the Traymores or even about Bella's problems. It was a lovely October day, and I was at my wonderful pet shelter. Weekends tended to bring in a lot of people interested in adopting pets.

Zoey and I would walk around the grounds for a while and be ready to greet them.

The next day was Monday. Not a bad time to go shopping in an exclusive pet boutique in Beverly Hills.

No, that's not really my style. As much as I love animals, I hate to admit I think they're cute dressed up, especially in outfits that resemble what their owners are wearing. But I prefer keeping them au naturel.

If I ever changed my mind, perhaps dressing up my charges at HotRescues to attract possible new family members, I'd undoubtedly turn to a HotPets store and get a discount.

But in my research into the Traymores, I had learned that Clara was part-owner of BHark Shop, a high-end pet store on Rodeo Drive. I could browse—and maybe ask a few questions about the absent proprietor.

I arrived around one in the afternoon. I glanced in the front window and saw a lot of really cute accessories for dogs and cats, including jeweled collars and bowls. In most places, I'd have assumed the bling was all false—but this was Beverly Hills. Maybe some were the real thing.

I walked inside, immediately surrounded by displays of luxury pet things on tables and hanging from racks. The store was long, narrow, and well stocked. An aroma like sweet dog biscuits filled the air. Colorful leashes hung alongside collars, and mannequin dogs and cats on counters were adorned with some of the items that were for sale.

I found myself smiling at all this human-alluring ostentation—and even wondering which things Zoey would like best.

I was greeted right away by an elegantly dressed African American woman in a caramel-colored sheath dress. She looked as posh as if she were an associate at a local women's boutique and emitted a scent I recognized from visiting—but not buying from—high-end human boutiques. "Hi, and welcome to BHark. How can I help you?"

"Oh, I'd just like to look around," I said. The last thing I usually felt was self-consciousness about what I was wearing, but I now wished I had put on something a little dressier than a short-sleeved cream sweater over beige slacks. At least I wasn't wearing jeans or any low-cost cologne. Nor did I have on anything with the HotRescues logo, but under the circumstances I hadn't wanted anyone to associate me with any kind of pet shelter. No one was likely to assume any connection between Miles's wife and me, but why take any chances?

"Are you interested in items for dogs or cats?" she inquired smoothly. "Or do you have another kind of pet?"

I noticed that she wore a nametag, which read Mercedes. This, then, as I'd learned from my Internet research, was Clara's partner. I saw one other person behind a counter at the back of the store, a peon, I assumed, who rang up sales.

"I have a dog, and I'd like to get her a new collar and leash set," I improvised. "But . . . well, I was referred to this shop by a friend. She says everyone here is great, but she told me I should specifically ask to be helped by Clara Traymore. She's one of the co-owners, isn't she?"

Mercedes nodded. She had a narrow, taut-skinned face

that looked all the more elongated as her smile faded. "Yes, she's my partner, but she's not here today."

"Oh, I could come back tomorrow." I pasted a clueless smile on my face, even as I surmised what was going through her mind. Should she divulge anything at all to this random customer?

"I'm terribly sorry, but Clara is . . . well, she is unwell, and I'm not sure when she'll be back."

"Oh, my." I stepped back carefully to avoid knocking into a table stacked with luxurious doggy sweaters. "My friend will be so upset to hear that. What's wrong with her?"

"She'll be fine soon." Mercedes's tone sounded as firm as her unwrinkled skin—and I wondered if she, too, had availed herself of Miles's clinic's cosmetic surgery, perhaps more successfully.

"Is it something contagious? My friend will want to visit her, if possible."

"Who is this friend?" Mercedes interjected. "Perhaps I know her, too."

I pondered how to handle this. "Oh, she didn't want to mention her name." I raised my hand to my mouth and giggled a little. It almost hurt to do that. It's not me, and I don't like playing roles. I much prefer being candid and direct. Plus, I had backed myself into a corner, which I hated. "Okay," I said after lowering my hand. "Here's the truth." Well, it wouldn't be exactly the truth, but she didn't need to know that. "I'm actually a neighbor of the Traymores. A friend. I heard some nasty rumors about Clara being hospitalized after some botched plastic surgery, and Al won't talk about it. I'd really like to visit her, but I don't know where she is. Can you help?"

Her narrow shoulders seemed to relax, and she closed her highly made-up eyes. "If you value your friendship with her, I'd suggest you not visit. Please, come here." Some other customers had entered the store, and Mercedes gestured toward the woman behind the counter to go help them. She preceded me into a side aisle. "I went to see Clara right after she had her surgery and—well, it was terrible. Her lips were so swollen she couldn't talk. Her skin was nice and firm in some places but under her chin . . . well, she looked even worse than before. And her eyes looked so wide that I doubted she could close them. She was a wreck, physically and emotionally. I believe . . . well, I think she's under a psychiatrist's care now, as well as another cosmetic surgeon."

"I see," I said thoughtfully. "Poor thing. But maybe she's better now. Do you know when she had the surgery in the first place?"

"Around two weeks ago. She hasn't been back here since."

Interesting. "I'll bet you miss her around here."

"Absolutely. She's so—well, she's so take-charge when she's around. I can't wait until she's back."

"Was she hospitalized immediately after that terrible procedure? I haven't seen her in our neighborhood."

"She's only been in the hospital for about a week now. From what I gathered, she just hid in her house before that."

Which meant Clara was potentially out and about at the time of Miles Frankovick's murder.

I didn't stay much longer. But I did buy a package of

fresh, gourmet dog biscuits. Zoey would have first dibs, but I'd let others at HotRescues taste them, too.

I'd accomplished some of what I'd wanted to here. But instead of being able to eliminate Clara Traymore as a murder suspect, she was now near the top of my list.

Chapter 15

There was one other place I wanted to stop before leaving the Beverly Hills area. Not Miles Frankovick's former plastic surgery office. I might want more information from the doctors and staff there eventually, but I didn't have any questions that needed immediate responses—unless one of them was ready to admit to killing Miles. Not likely.

Instead, I headed my car toward the veterinary clinic where Dr. Victor Drammon worked. Yes, he was a vet, and they had to deal with animal life and death all the time. Maybe his opinions were well reasoned, based on his experience. But I nevertheless despised the one-sided, kill-them-all position he had taken.

I was also curious about his relationship with Bella. The way she had acted and spoken about him had made me think she'd anticipated something really special between them after she rid herself of Miles—the usual way, I mean. By divorce.

Not only had Vic Drammon nixed that, but he had done it in an ugly, public fashion that all but slapped Bella's lovely face about the way she was caring for special-needs animals.

He had known Miles, too. But just because I couldn't stand the position Drammon had taken didn't mean he was a killer. Of people, anyway. To the contrary, Bella had described the way the friendship between Miles and Drammon had evolved once the two couples, who'd once been friends, had both divorced. If what she'd said was true, Drammon was an unlikely murder suspect.

But now that I had taken on looking into who killed Miles Frankovick, I intended to talk to everyone I learned had known him, even a little, no matter how unlikely it was they were his killer. Maybe they'd give me insight into others who were more probable.

I pulled into the nearly full parking lot of the Santa Beverly Animal Hospital off wide and traffic-laden Santa Monica Boulevard. The building looked fairly large, with a white façade and red-tiled roof—standard pseudo-Spanish style that was popular in Southern California. The outside looked a bit dingy, though. It could have used a coat of paint, and I noticed as I drew nearer that the wood trim around the windows was also more gray than white, and it looked pitted.

Apparently the veterinary hospital had been around for a long time and had probably cared for a lot of patients over the years. What was important wasn't appearances. It was how the animals were treated.

I recognized how unlikely it was that I'd be impressed by anything concerning Dr. Victor Drammon. And my real reason for being here? To assess, in person, the care of patients by this anti–special-needs pets veterinarian.

A guy with a Great Dane on a leash held it tightly as a woman with a Basset hound mix walked out of the front door. Another woman just entering was clutching a large case, which I assumed held a cat.

There I was, without an animal. How would I get to talk to the vet? I'd have to wing it. A challenge, sure, but I was good at making up things that got me the results I wanted.

I followed the others into a waiting area unsurprisingly filled with humans and pets. At the counter, a nearly filled sign-in sheet sat on a clipboard with most of the names crossed off.

I pondered at warp speed. Should I use a false identity or my real one? False. I quickly jotted down the name Lauren Earles—which had been real once, before I divorced Charles the jerk. I checked the box labeled new patient, then wrote in the reason for visit, "Need second opinion from Dr. Drammon about how to handle senior dog." He was a self-styled expert in that, after all. I knew what his answer would be. Kill the poor, nonexistent creature.

I sat down on a bench with cracked yellow cushions, between the lady with the cat—a ginger kitty that peered out of the crate with a tolerant gaze—and a young man holding a pit bull puppy on his lap. "This is my first time here," I told the lady. "Is this a good veterinary clinic?"

"I've been coming here for years and think the doctors are great," she said.

Then how old is your cat, and have you taken it to see Dr. Drammon? But I didn't voice that aloud.

I looked around. A sign on the wall near the counter listed the vets in the practice. Drammon was at the top, and there were a half-dozen other names below his. I wondered how many had as much seniority as he did in veterinary medicine, and whether any of his colleagues followed his beliefs about getting rid of aging or infirm animals.

In a short while, a young lady in a medical smock called my name. I almost didn't want to respond to "Earles" because it brought back such terrible memories. But I'd assumed it temporarily, and for good cause. I'd drop it again as fast as a torch lights gasoline the moment I left here.

"Did you bring your dog in?" the tech behind the counter asked.

"Not yet. I wanted to talk to Dr. Drammon first. I saw him on TV and thought he had some good ideas about making sure pets didn't suffer. I figured I'd discuss my older dog with him before bringing him in . . . maybe for the last time." I didn't have to work hard to bring tears to my eyes at that. I hated the idea of any animal suffering, but I suffered myself when I had to bring one to a vet for its final visit.

I supposed my emotionalism worked, since my pseudonym was called soon after I returned to my seat.

I was shown into an examination room and took a seat on one of its uncomfortable, well-used wooden chairs. A scratched metal table jutted from the wall, and I imagined lifting a dog up there for the doctor to see. There was another door that I assumed led into the medical area. A few pet magazines were in a hanging rack. I didn't grab one.

The place smelled nauseatingly sweet, or maybe my stomach was just churning like my mind as I thought about what to say.

A knock on the door and its opening happened simultaneously. Dr. Victor Drammon walked in. He looked as I'd seen him on TV and at Miles Frankovick's memorial service: glasses, salt-and-pepper hair, receding hairline. He didn't look like a persecutor of animals, but he hadn't opened his mouth yet, either.

Would he recognize me from the church? I doubted it. We hadn't met each other, nor had we been in the same vicinity very much.

"Hello, Lauren," he said, as if he knew me. Uh-oh. Could I be wrong? He held a chart on which I assumed my name and reason for being there had been written. "Tell me about your senior dog." Good. No indication of recognition, just friendliness.

"I don't want to kill him. Do you?" I stopped and closed my eyes for a second. Why had I let my emotions get the better of me?

The vet had thick brows that hadn't yet turned gray. They drew together as he frowned. "I assume this is somehow related to the interview I gave on television. Do you really have a dog you'd like to discuss, or—"

I drew in a breath to help me grab hold of my temper. Berating him wouldn't help me learn anything. "My name is actually Lauren Vancouver," I told him. "I'm the administrator of HotRescues. I'm also a friend of Bella Frankovick's, and I believe in what she is doing with Save Them All Sanctuary. I just wanted to meet you, to see what kind of veterinarian goes public about wanting to kill special-needs animals. Why would a good vet want to shut down a place that caters to making sure pets survive in a nurturing environment as long as they aren't suffering? Of course, maybe I made false assumptions. Good vet? What kind of vet are you?"

All right. Maybe I did wind up berating him. I didn't attempt to soften my glare.

Instead of getting defensive or angry, as I'd expected, the doctor walked around the jutting examination table toward me. I stiffened.

He sat down on the chair beside the one I occupied. He was taller than me, thin beneath his white jacket. He wore a large watch on his left wrist. "I understand why you're upset on Bella's behalf, Lauren. I said what I had to. The circumstances . . . well, I was all for Bella's founding her new pet sanctuary—at first. But I was afraid that people would start believing they should keep animals alive beyond the times that it made sense to do so. I'd intended to work with Bella to make sure she didn't allow any of her residents to suffer, but . . . like I said, circumstances changed."

"What circumstances?"

"I care—cared—about Bella. She and Miles and my ex-wife and I were really close friends for a while. But our marriages—both couples'—fell apart. I'd liked Bella's attitude about pets at first, but she started becoming so rabid about it. Pushing it. I had hopes that—Well, a lot changed and we both had to move on. That's all. But . . ."

"But what?" I demanded. "Aren't you going to defend your terrible attitude? I mean, there's been no indication that Bella would let any animal suffer. To the contrary, if you'd been the kind of vet she needed, you could have made sure that the sick or injured pets that could be saved were as well cared for as you thought they should be. And that the older ones were living with the best quality of life possible until they really did begin suffering. But you—" Oops. I hadn't meant to start a tirade like that. "Sorry," I finished. "Not for what I said, but for getting so riled. You're going to believe what you want to believe. My opinion won't change that." Especially when Bella's hadn't.

"You're right." His voice sounded sad but resigned. "Maybe . . . if things had been different, I'd have been able to help Bella."

I was through here. Except for one thing. "Since you're dedicated to killing animals when you think they shouldn't be allowed to live anymore, I don't suppose you'd admit to killing Miles, would you?"

He rose so suddenly that his clipboard hit the examination table, startling me.

"What do you mean?" he demanded. "Of course I wouldn't admit to that."

"I didn't think so," I said. I usually maintain control and don't blurt things out without thinking them through. Not this time. But I wasn't sorry. If I antagonized him more, why not? His reaction didn't surprise me.

"That's because I didn't do it," he emphasized as I walked out the examination room door.

I thought about calling Bella when I returned to HotRescues. I'd accomplished a couple of interesting visits on her behalf that day.

But I hadn't learned enough to get either one of us excited.

And I wasn't sure I wanted to stir up anything about her possible love-hate situation with Dr. Vic Drammon.

With Zoey contentedly lying on the rug under my desk, I entered what I could into my computer files. I maneuvered them around to put the Traymores in places of honor on my suspect list, while Vic Drammon stayed near the bottom. But the more I stared at the names and information I'd collected, the less I felt I knew who actually could have killed Miles.

I hate being in that kind of situation. I like to know where I'm going. How I'll get there.

That was one major reason why, when I received a call from Matt, I smiled and happily cast my files aside, at least for now.

The other reason was that I was glad to hear from him, despite our agreement to disagree about my helping Bella. I really liked the guy.

When he suggested that Zoey and I meet with Rex and him for dinner, of course I agreed.

We planned to meet at a nice steakhouse in Northridge with an outside eating area where we could sit with the dogs. Since our usual restaurants were more casual, I wondered if there was something on Matt's mind that he wanted to discuss.

An apology?

Or maybe he intended to press his point even more, try to woo me out of attempting to find Miles's killer.

I'd keep an open mind for now. No sense stoking fury until I knew if it was justified.

Zoey and I arrived first and were shown to a nice table for two with lots of room around it for the dogs. This restaurant would drive them nuts with its wonderful aromas of charcoaled meats, since the grill, though inside, was vented nearby. I didn't usually give dogs table scraps while I was eating, but in a situation like this a little leniency in policy might be called for.

Matt and Rex arrived soon after we did. I stood to greet them, and the kiss I received from Matt was disarming, as nice and hot as the charcoal embers. Which made me worry, as we all took our places, what was really on his mind.

Did he want to come home with me that night? That might be pleasant . . . and more. As long as we didn't start arguing.

We each ordered a cocktail. Mine was fruitier than Matt's. I wasn't extremely hungry and decided on a grilled burger. Matt, unsurprisingly, chose a steak.

"This was a great idea," I told him when our server left with our orders. Matt was dressed in a medium blue button-down shirt that looked good on him. I'd also changed from my HotRescues uniform into a dressy rose knit top over black slacks. This felt like a special occasion, but I wasn't sure why.

"Yeah," he agreed. "I've missed you, Lauren."

"It hasn't been that long since we saw each other," I reminded him.

"But things have been strained between us."

Ah, was he about to apologize?

"I'm sorry about that, but not about the reason. I think you know that I care for you. I understand why you think you have to help Bella, and if there's anything I can do to help *you*, then just tell me."

I heard the "but" in his tone and just waited.

"But—" Here it came. I took a sip of my martini. "Like I said, I'm concerned about your safety. One of the things I love about you is your determination."

That earned a startled glance from me. Love? That had to just be an expression. And he hadn't really professed to love *me*, just things about me.

"When you start something, you follow through," he continued. "I understand and respect that. And like you, I really like the premise of Save Them All Sanctuary. But—"

He stopped as the server brought fresh bread and some interesting toppings—cheese and a tomato-based spread. I took some and passed it to him. My mind was in turmoil. I waited to hear the rest of his sentence after this newest "but."

"Lauren," Matt finally said. "I've been doing some checking. Asking questions. I can't say that what I found is additional proof that Bella killed her ex, but it does show she doesn't let anything stand in her way of reaching a goal."

"Neither do I," I said dryly. "Does that mean I should be a murder suspect again?"

His smile didn't quite light up his gorgeously craggy features as it usually did.

"Not if I can help it. But the thing you should know is that Bella may have attempted to bribe some people to get her permits in order."

Interesting. I'd wondered what Dr. Vic Drammon had meant when he said that Bella had pushed things in her attempt to open Save'Em. Is this what he had been referring to?

"I don't know if she succeeded," Matt continued, "or how she finally got around the issues that stood in her way of opening the sanctuary as quickly as she did, and maybe opening at all. Does that mean she's a killer? Not necessarily. But it also means that she's willing to do things that aren't always legit to get her way—and Miles was jeopardizing her money source."

Chapter 16

Matt came home with me. He stayed the night. I was glad. As always, I enjoyed being with him—and our nighttime activities were delightful.

But when we weren't completely occupied with each other in bed, my mind sailed off on wind-tossed seas of concern and annoyance and planning and worrying.

Lying in the dark, with Matt and the two dogs breathing heavily as they all slept in my room, I considered what he had said about Bella. So what if she'd cut some corners, greased some palms, did what she had to so she could get Save'Em open, running, and saving animals? I may have done the same. I had just been extremely fortunate that I'd been an employee with HotRescues from the start. A damned good one, of course—one who took charge, made sure things ran as smoothly as possible.

But Dante DeFrancisco's name and financial backing had taken care of all the hurdles that Bella had had to overcome herself.

That made her resourceful. Smart. Assertive, and maybe even aggressive. But it didn't make her a killer.

This revelation was not going to change anything I'd already considered.

One issue I hadn't yet figured out was how I could find Clara Traymore and visit her in the hospital. She was apparently a psychiatric as well as medical patient, so even if she stood up and confessed to stabbing Miles it wouldn't prove her guilt. But I wanted to get my own impression of her.

I also needed to talk to Bella about my findings. Soon.

When we all awoke the next morning, Matt and I didn't have to communicate aloud to know what we'd all do next: dogs and humans would run through my neighborhood to practice for the marathon.

It felt easier all the time. I was able to run farther, without getting nearly as out of breath as I had at first.

The neighbors were probably getting just as used to seeing us pass by—at least Zoey and me.

"We're doing great," Matt said as we turned onto the street that led back to my home. He didn't sound winded. He had thrown on workout shorts and a white T-shirt that he kept in his car for the gym. The outfit looked good on him, especially plastered to his muscular body by sweat.

I, too, was dressed for the occasion, in red, loose-knit shorts and a V-neck pink T-shirt. The outfit was a little looser on me than when we had begun our practice runs.

I hadn't needed to lose weight. In fact, I hoped I wasn't losing the few curves I'd had prior to this exercise regimen. But even if I did, it would be worth it to garner whatever additional donations we could for HotRescues and other animal rescue organizations. I was determined to finish this marathon.

"We. Sure. Are." I was out of breath. But I was still going, and my speed, though not breaking any records, hadn't diminished to a crawl.

Even the dogs, leashed at our sides, were panting by then, tongues hanging out. I'd make sure they had plenty of water the instant we got back.

As we reached my front walk, Matt's cell phone rang. He pulled it out of his pocket. I was pleased to hear that he did sound at least slightly winded as he answered.

He listened, nodded, responded, then closed the flap. "I've got to shower and run," he said. "SmART is on a rescue now—a couple of cats are in trouble on a hillside. I told the team I wanted to go on the next mission since I haven't been on one for a while, so I'll go meet up with them."

"You'll have to tell me all about it later."

"I will, but it'll also be on their Facebook page."

Of course. And I was on Facebook, too, thanks to my son, Kevin. I now used it to post information about some of our inhabitants and what good pets they would make. Rather, I usually had Nina do the posting. But I did check out other shelters' pages, too. As well as the Small Animal Rescue Team's.

We walked into the house and I led the dogs into the kitchen for a drink. Then Matt gave me a quick kiss with our damp bodies pressed close.

"What are you up to today?" he asked.

"I'll be at HotRescues." Which wasn't anything new.

"I'll check in with you later." He aimed an inquisitive glance at me with his engaging brown eyes. "Are you planning on doing any more investigating on Bella Frankovick's behalf today?"

"No," I said, meaning it. Although I did intend to do something, it wouldn't be an investigation. Not exactly.

I didn't like being devious. Most of the time I preferred being candid. But as sweet as Matt's worrying about me was, I didn't want him criticizing me, or even trying to protect me.

If it made sense later, I'd let him know what I'd decided to do. But for now, I'd just keep it to myself.

I called Bella before heading toward Save'Em. I'd already been at HotRescues for a couple of hours and left Zoey there with Nina. For now, everything was under control. If potential adopters came in, my staff and our volunteers could get introductions started and make sure applications were filled out. None would go through without my okay and a session with our Dr. Mona, but I didn't need to be there.

Instead, I'd drop in and see how things were going at Save'Em. Have lunch with Bella. I'd casually mention some people I'd been checking out on her behalf, see what her comments were.

A little less casually, I'd learn if she would admit to any of the things Matt accused her of to get Save'Em opened—

and try not to applaud her. I knew what it was like to test the system to accomplish an important goal.

We were kindred spirits. The stuff Matt had referred to only bolstered that. But at the moment I wasn't a murder suspect, and she was. How far she might go to save endangered pets could be relevant to what had happened to her ex.

I hoped not.

I pulled into the front parking lot and walked up the path to the front door with its large overhanging sign. I yanked on the handle. It was unlocked, so I just went in.

"Hi," said Peggy. The volunteer had just come through the far archway. "Glad to see you, Lauren. Bella told me to wait for you and bring you to her in the back."

As we stood there, I was greeted by two little dachshunds this time. Both Ignatz and Durwood trotted up and gave me hello sniffs. I knelt to give them hugs. "Hi, fellows. How are you doing? Are you a pack now?" I stood again and addressed the question to Peggy. "How've they been?"

"Great," she said. "And, yes, they're close friends now. But there's a poor little cocker spaniel mix in our hospital area that Bella wants you to meet. You won't believe what's happened to her."

The dog in question was on Bella's lap in the Save'Em infirmary.

The large room was on the second floor of the area where special-needs pets were housed, toward the rear. It had a gleaming linoleum floor, and its small kennels and large metal examination table in the center looked as if they had just been sanitized. Smelled it, too, since the strong odor of disinfectant accosted my senses as I walked in.

A few plastic chairs were strewn around the edges, and Bella occupied one near the door. The dog she held was small and ginger-colored—where it wasn't bandaged.

"Want me to stay, Bella?" Peggy asked softly. "No one else is in the front now."

"Go on back there," Bella said. "Thank you, Peggy." She looked up toward me. "I'm so glad you're here, Lauren." Her tone was heartfelt but her voice was low, as if she didn't want to disturb the pup, who appeared to be sleeping. "Everyone here has been sympathetic and understanding, but I think you of all people will really understand."

I pulled out one of the chairs and sat down in it, putting my bag on the floor beside me. I wondered if the surface was so sterile that its cleanliness would engulf my purse.

"What's that?" I asked.

"I can't give up my funding for Save'Em," she cried, then let her head drop until her brow touched the cocker's back.

I figured this wasn't necessarily a non sequitur, so I waited for her to continue.

It took a minute, but then she looked up once more. The haunted expression in her blue eyes all but pierced my tranquility, making me feel like crying without understanding why. Her long brown hair hung limply around her face, and as she bent forward it haloed around the dog. She carefully rearranged the pup on her lap, hugging her closer against her Save Them All Sanctuary denim work shirt. That was when I got a better look at the dog's left rear leg—or the area where its left rear leg should be. Instead, there were bandages covering a stump. The part of her leg below what had once been her knee wasn't there any longer.

"This is Soozle," Bella said. "She was hit by a car a couple of days ago. The car didn't stop. Some good Samaritans took poor Soozle to the East Valley Animal Shelter. No chip or other ID was found on her, and they were going to put her down because of her injuries, but fortunately Kip and I happened to be there to check on another dog, a stray we'd brought in but put a first right to pick up if no one claimed or adopted him."

That was something private shelters did whenever possible. We couldn't take in strays under our licenses but instead had to turn them over to the official city shelters. We were allowed, though, to say we'd come back for the ones we brought in instead of having them euthanized for lack of space if their owners didn't claim them.

"We picked up both dogs and immediately ran Soozle to Carlie's vet clinic. They were able to save her—but not her entire leg. It wasn't cheap, though, even with the wonderful discount Carlie gives us, and Soozle will still require ongoing care for a while." She shook her head. "Miles would have had a fit. And if poor Soozle had wound up in Vic Drammon's care—"

"She'd be dead by now," I finished.

Bella nodded. "I hated fighting with Miles about our divorce settlement. But I'd no idea that his brothers would be even worse. They're filing a lawsuit against me now on behalf of Miles's estate. Too bad I didn't protect him from being murdered." Her smile was wan. "Don't look so stricken, Lauren. I didn't kill him, and I didn't know anyone else was going to, either."

"I figured," I said, but I was glad she had once again confirmed it.

"The thing is, I admit I'd started to relax a bit after Miles died. Even though I had nothing to do with his death, I was relying on it to stop the fight over our divorce settlement." She stood carefully, cuddling the dog long enough to carefully place her on my lap.

My turn to hold Soozle. The little spaniel looked up into my face with sad but loving eyes, as though she recognized another human being who would do anything to help her—and who would never, ever hurt her. With a tiny sigh, she settled down. As I held her, I felt around her gently. The bandage over the stump of her leg was stiff. There was an area on her back that had been shaved so a wound from her accident could be stitched.

Would I have taken her in at HotRescues? Almost certainly yes—but I did have to be practical about my rescues. I wanted to save as many pets as I could, but my mandate was to try to get them adopted as soon as possible so I could bring in replacements to love and rehome.

I therefore might have at least considered skipping over a pup as badly injured as Soozle. I'd have been upset with myself for that if I hadn't let my practicality rule my emotions.

But the fact that Bella had saved her, gotten her medical attention, and brought her here made me even more determined to help my new friend.

"I can't lose the funding for Save'Em, Lauren," Bella whispered shakily. "I can't let pets like Soozle die."

I was still holding Soozle a short while later when Kip Schaley came in.

"How's she doing now?" he said to Bella.

"Still a bit groggy from her medication, but we'll keep close watch on her."

"People who hit animals with their cars and then just drive off that way should be shot," Kip said. That earned him a warm smile from Bella. In fact, they were standing so close before I handed Soozle back that my presence felt intrusive, as if I was stopping them from engaging in a nice, warm kiss. Was I reading things into their relationship? It seemed pretty clear what Kip hoped for, but I wasn't so sure about Bella.

Maybe she just wanted a good, solid accountant who kept track of Save'Em's funding—and magically made more appear as needed.

"Are you still snooping into who killed Miles?" Kip asked me when Bella was in the special medical kennel area with Soozle.

I nodded.

"I figured. Look, you don't have to do that. I'm checking into things myself, working with the police. I'll take care of—" Before he could finish, Bella came out and we talked more about Soozle as we walked back to the office area.

On my way back to HotRescues a while later, I thought

again about how the concept of money provided a reason for people to kill.

Notwithstanding Bella's frequent disclaimers and my hopes, her innocence wasn't conclusive. Not at all.

I had managed to ask briefly about how easy it had been for her to get permits to open Save'Em. She'd indicated she had done what she had to but hadn't elaborated. That suggested she'd done as Matt had said and perhaps gone a bit too far, by bribing people.

Even if she had, that didn't mean she had murdered Miles—but it did mean she wouldn't just give up if something was important to her.

To stop their fighting over money, to make sure she retained rights to their real property and didn't have to pay back her half of their cash and stocks, would she have killed?

The money had been needed to save not only dear little Soozle, but all the animals at Save'Em and those to come.

Would Miles's relatives have killed him instead so they could inherit what he had left—and the right to fight with Bella for the rest? If not, they still could have had other reasons.

What about the Traymores? Not only money was involved but revenge, too. Fighting over medical and other expenses could have been part of the reason one of them had killed Miles.

Miles's coworkers at the plastic surgery clinic? Money and emotions could have been involved there as well.

Kip, to help Bella financially and get her ex out of her life once and for all? That would be another reason he'd want me to butt out.

Who else was there—someone I didn't yet know about? Someone I knew of whom I hadn't yet recognized as a list-heading murder suspect?

I didn't know. But I did know that my own determination to figure this out was stronger than ever.

I only hoped I wouldn't come to regret it.

Chapter 17

I entered some notes into my computer files as soon as I got back to my office, to memorialize the things my mind had obsessed over on the ride back here.

Staring almost unseeing at Zoey lying on the rug beside me, I considered the order of suspects. Once again, I thought of what I'd learned from Stefan Garciana when the detective had entered me at the top of his suspect list and let me dangle there for a long time: Be sure to consider those you think least likely to have done it. In his eyes, that hadn't been me—but it was his method of investigating.

What about Miles's family? His brothers and sister-in-law were apparently making more waves now with Bella. I had put them toward the bottom of those I thought likely to have killed Miles—but that was before learning about their pursuit of his money.

I wanted to get together with all of them so I could make a better determination of how they'd felt about their brother—and whether they were happier now that he was gone.

I could have suggested such a gathering to Bella when I'd been at Save'Em before, but I'd been so involved in getting to know Soozle and her situation that I hadn't focused on it.

Now, though, I called Bella and recruited her to invite her ex-in-laws to join us for coffee, today if possible. She in turn was to call them with the excuse of wanting to talk about their current monetary standoff without lawyers involved. Maybe they could make headway on their own. She wasn't to mention I'd be along as an unofficial mediator—and just as unofficial an inquisitor.

They'd agreed as long as we met in a neutral location. Surprisingly, perhaps, they were all available at three that afternoon. Did their prompt agreement mean they were hopeful, too, of reaching some kind of accord?

If they knew of my ulterior motive, they probably wouldn't have been so agreeable.

On the phone once more before I headed out, I asked Bella a few telling questions about her three former relatives, their lifestyles, and how they had all gotten along together—before. Then, I was ready.

By design, Bella and I met there first. The place was a chain coffee shop in Burbank, filled as most of them are with people with expensive drinks either working diligently on computers or having earnest conversations.

Not my lifestyle, but it obviously worked for a lot of folks.

Bella got there before me and commandeered a fair-sized table in a corner. She had donned an obviously expensive gray suit, as if she were confronting the group in a lawyer's office. That went against my suggestion that she dress casually, as I had—a nice cotton shirt and dark slacks. I'd also said she should act casual, too—unless, as we talked, my attitude changed.

I said hi to her, ordered my drink at the counter—brewed coffee, no room for cream—then joined her.

"You ready for this?" I asked.

She nodded, then took a swig from her cup as if it contained something a lot stronger than a mocha latte.

She had already told me none of the Frankovicks was financially strapped or even in any real need of inheriting something from Miles. Apparently the fight was more of a memorial to Miles than a play for money.

"Tell me again where the furniture shop owned by Brewster and Eleanor is located?" The way she had described it, it was well established and popular among residents of its nice Pasadena neighborhood, so it hadn't been affected much by the recent economic downturn. The other brother, Edson, was in marketing at a major film studio and was apparently well paid.

By the time Bella had finished telling me the store's location, we were near the time the Frankovick crowd was due to arrive. "Do they tend to be prompt?" I asked.

"Not always."

"Good. Now tell me about their home lives. Do they

have kids? Pets? Did you get along with them before Miles and you broke up?"

I'd gotten only a smattering of this before when we'd talked on the phone. Some of what Bella said was important, and some of it wasn't.

I also threw out an idea that had been percolating in my mind, and Bella seemed receptive.

The Frankovicks did indeed arrive on time just a few minutes later. They appeared like a military battalion girding for war, with their grim expressions and taut stances as they remained close to one another while ordering their drinks.

They soon joined us. All of them glared from me to Bella, then back again, their question clear: Who the heck was this interloper?

"You may have met my friend Lauren at Miles's memorial," Bella said. "It may seem silly, but I brought her along for moral support since there are three of you and only one of me."

They were all seated by then. None looked especially welcoming, but no one tried to boot me out, either.

"Let's try to be honest," I began. "Do you all hate Bella?"

Four pairs of shocked eyes lit on me—Bella's included.

"If she killed my brother, I do," Edson finally said through gritted teeth. He was the one with light eyes and gaunt features. He had dressed in business casual, with a turtleneck beneath his button-down shirt.

"I didn't, Eddy." Bella's voice was low and sincere.

I looked at the married couple, Brewster and Eleanor, as

they glanced at one another. I couldn't read their expressions, but thought that they were at least listening.

"Assuming that Bella didn't hurt Miles—and I believe that's true," I said, "what do you think of Save Them All Sanctuary?" Bella had already told me that Brewster and Eleanor always kept at least one dog and a couple of cats around their upscale Pasadena home. Edson had a pet allergy and lived alone.

"I think it's a worthwhile cause," Eleanor said at once. She had been the one to snap at Bella at Miles's service, so I found it interesting that she would be supportive now of Bella's undertaking. I recalled likening her to a snake. Today, though, with her light hair loose around her face and her pink vest over a red shirt, she resembled a younger, hipper woman. Maybe that was who she tried to be in their furniture store.

I looked at Brewster. He nodded slightly. I still thought he resembled Miles physically, with his round face and loose skin beneath his chin, but I was willing to overlook that for now. "Do you have any pets?" I asked, knowing the answer—or at least what it had been before, when Bella had been part of the family.

"Yes, a couple of dogs and one cat now," Brewster said. "They were all rescues."

"You knew that Miles wanted Bella to shut down Save Them All Sanctuary?" I made my tone questioning.

Brewster nodded. "Our brother liked animals but thought a shelter like that just wasted money on trying to keep them alive past their time."

"Is that what you think?" I looked from one to the other, not meeting Bella's gaze. I couldn't focus on her now.

"I don't," Eleanor said firmly.

"I heard a friend of yours, Bella—that vet, Vic Drammon—say that your shelter makes animals suffer." Brewster looked steadily toward Bella.

I held my breath while she answered. She had to finesse this—make it sound like it wasn't just her own opinion that what she was doing was worthwhile. "I heard Vic, too. I've talked to him and—well, we disagree with one another. I've checked with other vets including Dr. Carlie Stellan—you know, that really wonderful lady vet who has both an excellent clinic here in L.A. and also stars on the *Pet Fitness* show on the Longevity Vision cable channel?" She looked at the others, clearly trying to gauge if they'd heard of Carlie. All three nodded. "She's filming a show at Save'Em that will demonstrate some of the good we're doing. And—well, if you take up Miles's argument, fight me for money and property that are rightly mine, I may not be able to keep Save'Em going."

"Is that why you killed him?" Edson interjected.

Bella closed her moist blue eyes as if in pain. "I already said, Eddy, that I didn't kill him. I'm sorry if you don't believe me."

"Okay, let's diverge here, since you started it again," I said. "Anyone at this table who killed Miles Frankovick, please raise your hand."

Eleanor tossed an angry scowl toward me. I caught it and lobbed a similar one in her direction.

"Was it you?" I asked her.

"Of course not. You're making it sound like a game."

"No," I said. "I just want us all to get beyond this point." Maybe. I didn't really expect any of Miles's relatives to admit to being a murderer. But on the other hand, I did look from one to the next to observe their expressions.

Not that I'm a lie detection professional or a shrink like Mona, but none appeared to be trying to hide a guilty look.

"So, any admissions here?" I pressed.

Brewster smiled wryly. "I don't think so, Lauren. Bella's already said she didn't do it. Did you?"

"I hardly knew Miles," I said. "I didn't like his attitude about Save'Em, but I didn't kill him, either. Okay, so no one here committed the crime—or at least will admit to it. Next item—who here wants to close down the very worthwhile Save Them All Sanctuary?"

Again no takers. "That isn't our point," Edson said. "We just feel that Miles's last wishes should be upheld."

"Then here's a suggestion: Miles might have wanted to punish Bella for leaving him and taking money from their accounts. He claimed he didn't want the money wasted. But none of you seems to be against Save'Em the way he was. How about working something out so that almost all of the money and property they argued about would go to Save'Em and not to Bella?" I'd already run the idea by Bella. She was fine with it, especially under the terms I was about to toss out for consideration.

I went through my plan. The bulk of the money would be put into a trust for the benefit of the sanctuary, and one of the trustees would either be Carlie or someone she suggested. The idea would be to make sure that the money wasn't wasted but in this case was put to good use caring for special-needs animals. Not exactly what Miles had wanted, true, but the trust would be partly in his name, a memorial to him that would make him look like a good guy. Plus, Save'Em would solicit donations from other sources.

Bella would get a fair salary and benefits as long as she remained chief administrator of Save'Em—which she intended to be forever. She couldn't dip into the rest of the trust money except on behalf of the pets at the sanctuary, and then only if the trustees agreed. That way, she wasn't growing rich from the money that perhaps rightly should have been half hers anyway, but it would at least be dedicated to the cause she loved. Besides, she did have some other money she had inherited from a dead aunt, so she wouldn't starve.

No one completely won but the animals. No one completely lost, either.

"Interesting idea," Eleanor said when I was through. "We'll need to think about it, though. Run it by our lawyers."

"Bella will, too." I'd suggest that she run it not only past her divorce lawyer but also by Kendra Ballantyne, the lawyer—and pet-sitter—who was Dante DeFrancisco's lady friend. She did a lot of pet law, so this might be something right up her alley.

We had all finished our drinks and our conversation.

"We'll get back to you within the next few days and let you know our decision, Bella," Edson said.

Bella scanned their faces, as did I. "Do you think you're likely to agree?"

"Probably," Eleanor said.

"But don't hold us to that till you hear from us," cautioned Brewster.

The three of them left, and I walked Bella out to our cars.

"That was such a wonderful idea, Lauren," she said. "Whatever their answer, I really thank you for coming up with it."

"You're welcome," I said. "Anything to help animals. I've heard of shelters being run this way, although the trusts were established after the main people funding them had passed away. I just hope the Frankovicks are kind and smart enough to go for it."

I was smiling almost the whole way back to HotRescues. Until I got a phone call from Carlie.

I answered on my car's hands-free system. "Hi," I said. "I may have another angle for you to toss into your show on Save'Em."

"Great," she said. "But . . . well, Lauren, we've got a problem. Your guy Pete from HotRescues just brought a dog who'd supposedly been an owner relinquishment to my clinic. But she was actually a dog we were supposed to be treating here at one of the Animal Services shelters. She was stolen this morning. And—Lauren, she most likely has parvo."

Chapter 18

Fortunately, I was close to HotRescues. Otherwise, I might have broken a lot of speed limits to get there.

I soon parked and sprinted inside. Nina was in the welcome area, as usual. Zoey wasn't, but I heard her *woof* from the office. Good. Better that she was there than in the thick of things.

Instead of smiling a greeting, or even saying hi, Nina stood before I could start hammering her with questions. Her brown eyes were teary.

"I think I made a terrible mistake, Lauren," she said. "I couldn't help it, though. The puppy was so cute . . ."

"What happened?" I stayed as calm as possible while wanting to shake the truth out of her. Fast.

"This older man came here," she said. "He had a puppy in his arms—looked like part Basset hound and maybe some Lab. An adorable combination. He told me he had adopted the pup from a high-kill shelter a month ago, just before she was scheduled to be euthanized, but he had a family emergency and had to leave the area. He couldn't take the dog. He said he knew this was a private shelter but seemed to know that we could take in owner relinquishments. If we couldn't accept her, he'd hot to take her back to a public shelter and couldn't bear the thought of having her put down. Couldn't we save her?"

"And you said yes?"

Nina nodded. "We filled out the paperwork. I looked her over, walked with her for a short while—but not long enough. The guy disappeared just about the time the puppy threw up."

I know my eyes widened. "Any diarrhea?"

"Yes. Right afterward. Pete immediately took her to Carlie's clinic. He just called a little while ago. It's what I was afraid of."

"I heard from Carlie," I said. "It's even worse than you thought." I told her how Carlie had related that the dog was stolen from The Fittest Pet Veterinary Clinic just that morning.

"What the hell is going on, Lauren?" she asked as tears poured down her face.

"I don't know," I said grimly. "I'll find out. But not right now."

Grabbing all the cleaning equipment from the storage building at the rear of our original HotRescues property would usually have been Pete's job, but I couldn't wait till he got back.

Parvovirus is a highly contagious disease that can kill dogs, especially puppies. It's one of several illnesses that shelter administrators are worried about occurring in their facilities. It's often fatal. Vaccinations are available, but they don't work well with younger dogs. The best thing is to keep all dogs away from contact with other canines with parvo—and any of their eliminations since the virus can survive for quite a while. Rushing this one to the vet had been the right thing to do.

I didn't go to see Zoey yet. I wouldn't, until everything else had been sterilized, and then I would clean my office.

All of Zoey's shots were up to date. Of course. I wouldn't have allowed otherwise. But I would still have Carlie check her out. Our residents here, too.

First, though, with the help of Ricki and several other volunteers, as well as Nina and even Angie Shayde, I gathered mops and towels and, most important, bleach and other cleaning liquids. We marched toward the front of our shelter to begin our cleaning foray. Nina showed me exactly where the relinquished pup had been—not in areas where any of our residents were, thank heavens.

Even so, I was glad we were always diligent about making sure our residents got all inoculations as soon as they arrived here, as long as they were old enough. Those we had only recently saved from the public shelter had already been to Carlie's clinic and gotten their shots. They should be well protected against this horrible virus.

Most fortunate, as much as I enjoyed bringing puppies here, we currently had no dogs that were too young to have gotten their vaccines against parvo or other diseases.

Even so, I made sure that Angie looked everyone over—

not just the dogs, but any elimination they had deposited in their kennels, from either end.

Fortunately, none had vomited. Nor were there any signs of diarrhea.

I made sure that every place the ill pup could have been was scrubbed down and sanitized with lots of bleach and disinfectant. Then the entire cleaning crew sanitized ourselves, too, by spraying our shoes and using lots of antibacterial hand soap.

I knew we had done a good job of cleaning.

I just hoped that was enough.

"Yes, the poor dog's still alive, even after all that," Carlie told me. I'd phoned her from my office when our cleaning frenzy was done.

Zoey lay stretched out below my chair on the sterilized and gleaming tile floor. The rug that was usually under my desk was now in our washing machine, just in case.

I'd even had Margo, our new groomer, give Zoey a bath.

Yes, maybe that was preferential treatment, but our other dogs, too, would get baths as quickly as could be managed. Their kennel areas had already been cleaned. With their inoculations, I believed they would all be safe.

"Just alive, or likely to stay that way?" I cringed, waiting for her response. I hated the possibility that, after all this, the poor dog might not survive.

"Good chance she'll be fine," Carlie said.

"Nina said that the guy who left her here called her Lassie. Is that right? Did she come from the public shelter with that name?" I'm not a superstitious sort, but I didn't want to call her the same thing as that horrible dog thief had unless it was definitely what she would respond to. But I also didn't want to continue calling her "the dog." That was so cold and impersonal.

And if she healed, I would do all I could to bring her to HotRescues instead of sending her back to where she might wind up being euthanized despite her survival.

"Not Lassie," Carlie said. "In fact . . . no, I've got her paperwork here, and the only name listed is 'Female Dog.' But I've started calling her Miracle."

I rolled that around in my brain. It worked.

"Miracle it is." I hated to put Carlie on the spot, but I had to ask her. "How was she stolen in the first place?"

"Unsure. She was one of several young dogs that Animal Services brought in because of a parvo outbreak, for extra care—and to get them away from the rest of their population. None of them had names, by the way. Maybe no one wanted to name them until it was clear they'd survive. Anyway, Miracle apparently had no symptoms then but had been housed with another young dog that was sick. I gather that she was taken from their van while the others were being brought inside our clinic."

"That's so strange . . . Well, how long will you need to keep her there?"

"Unknown, but I assume you'll want to take her in at HotRescues when she's recuperated."

"Absolutely. As long as I can get the okay from Animal Services—and there's no further possibility of contagion."

"She's in isolation now, but by the time I'll be willing to let her go there'll be no way she could pass this along."

"Gotcha. And . . ."

"And?"

"Thanks, Carlie."

"Don't worry. You'll pay."

Of course HotRescues would pay. She knew that. She also knew that meant Dante DeFrancisco would underwrite it—at least whatever Carlie wasn't able to collect from Animal Services. Even though Miracle had been stolen from outside Carlie's clinic in the first place, she had been brought back there by HotRescues.

Still sitting at my desk, I called Dante on my Black-Berry to let him know what was going on here.

"Everyone there—dogs included—you're all okay?"

"Yes," I said firmly. "And we worked hard to keep it that way."

"No chance of the cats catching this?"

"We scrubbed the cat enclosures, too, just in case. But the feline parvovirus is different from canine, so I don't think so."

"Great. Like always, keep up the good work, Lauren."

"I'm so sorry, Lauren," Nina said for the millionth time. We were back in the welcome area. She looked stricken.

She had been the one to accept the owner relinquishment.

I always had final say over such things, and she knew it. But in this instance, as she described it, the adorable young dog was friendly and looked healthy.

And her life had been in imminent danger. That took precedence over everything.

"Don't blame yourself, Nina. You did the right thing."

With potentially disastrously wrong consequences, but she couldn't have known that at the time. Her feeling guilty wouldn't help the situation. And I didn't really fault her. Not with a dog's life at stake—one who had initially appeared to be fine except for having a monster of an apparent owner.

The guy might not have known Miracle was sick when he'd stolen her from Animal Services—but he'd taken her from outside a veterinary clinic. And then, instead of returning her there when he might have suspected that the poor thing was ill, he'd dropped her off here as a claimed owner relinquishment. Why?

"Here is all the information the guy gave me." I'd already asked Nina to put together the relinquishment application and anything else that was pertinent to the situation.

I wanted to find the cruel jerk and give him a piece of my absolutely furious mind. Then I'd turn him over to Animal Services.

I sat at the table near the window, and Nina joined me. She handed me the paperwork he'd filled out. His handwriting was atrocious, but it appeared that his name was John Russell. He lived in Granada Hills, which was also our location at HotRescues.

I tried calling the phone number he had written down. It belonged to a restaurant in Sherman Oaks.

"Do a little Internet search for me, will you, Nina? I bet there are hundreds of John Russells, if that's even his name. It's so close to Jack Russell, like the terrier, that it could even be a joke. Let's see if there's one at the address he gave. And if there's anything else you remember about him that might lead to figuring out who he is, let's talk about it."

First, though, I had her describe him.

He was a senior citizen who appeared as old as our volunteers Bev and Mamie, maybe older. He was stooped a bit, so his height wasn't clear, but he had been strong enough to carry the puppy. A mixed Basset-Lab at that age wasn't huge, but it was larger than a combo of toy breeds.

"He wore jeans, loafers, and a blue UCLA sweatshirt," Nina continued. "They all looked large on him, like he'd bought them a size or two too big."

"Or he'd shrunken after he bought them," I said. "That sometimes happens with senior citizens."

"Yes, but . . ." Nina's voiced trailed off.

"But what?" I prompted.

She pushed her long brown hair back from her face in a gesture that suggested she was trying to wipe a cloud of haze away from her mind. "You know, I hadn't really thought about it, but when I had Lassie—I mean Miracle—in my arms and John Russell walked out through the door"—she gestured toward the door that led to the parking lot—"he seemed to straighten a bit, like he was relieved of a burden. I noticed that since I thought he seemed just a bit too happy for having to leave a poor, sweet member of his family here, even one that had only been with him a short while."

"We already know he's a jerk," I reminded her.

"But . . . well, he also seemed to walk faster. Like he was escaping, yes, but it was more than that. He'd seemed older, somehow, before that moment, but it was as if he'd shed years along with poor Miracle."

Interesting. "Anything else you remember about him?"

"Well, there was something odd about his voice. It was

high, almost female, but I know that sometimes happens as people get older."

"Okay, let's both do a little Internet searching and see if we can find him. I'll forward any pictures I find of likely candidates to you to look at. When you say he was a senior—"

"He had as many wrinkles as anyone I've ever seen," she explained. "And he had no hair."

Even more interesting.

I spent the next hour or so on my computer, comparing lots of John Russells and where they lived, their ages, their social networking—just in case, although if he really was older he might shy away from such things even more than I did.

No John Russell apparently lived at the address he'd given. I didn't see one anywhere nearby, either.

I checked with Nina often. She checked with me.

I called Brooke to let her know what had gone on here today and told her I'd explain more when she arrived for her overnight stay.

I encouraged her, in the meantime, to check in both with our security company and with Antonio. Not that there was likely to be a rash of people stealing sick dogs and dumping them at shelters, but I hoped to file a report of some kind. It was at least a theft, and a form of animal endangerment.

But after all that searching, all my questioning, there was no indication of who John Russell really was, let alone why he had done such a thing.

I admit that I'm skeptical at times. Even cynical.

I reason things out and jump to conclusions—right or wrong.

Right now, I wasn't merely jumping to conclusions. I was leaping to them, and they were really nasty.

I wondered who this supposed John Russell really was—old or young. I'd seen clips on TV news about crooks wearing some really lifelike masks to fool people, and some of those masks made them look like geezers. If he was young and in disguise, his spryness after giving up Miracle would be highly explainable.

Was he male or female, with his high voice?

I was probably doing more than leaping at offbeat angles now—but I wondered whether it was possible that the relinquishment of the dog with a disease that threatened not only her life but other dogs', too, had actually been fully intentional. Perhaps it had been to get me so busy saving animals at my shelter that I wouldn't have time to try to find Miles Frankovick's killer.

Maybe it was even to teach me a lesson for daring to attempt to help Bella.

Yes, I was reading a lot into this situation without having any specific threat that would cause my mind to veer this way.

But several people hadn't wanted me to help Bella. Three of them—Matt, Brooke, and Antonio—wouldn't have done anything so mean to stop me.

But what about Kip Schaley? He seemed to be enough of an animal lover not to have done this. But what if it was a way to get me off the investigation? Did he want to help Bella to impress her? Or had he already helped her by killing Miles and was afraid I'd find out?

Or was it one of the other people I considered to be major suspects and who knew I was prying into the murder? How about one of Miles's colleagues in the plastic surgery office?

His family members? I'd all but eliminated them as suspects, so I doubted it.

Who, then?

Well, whoever he was, John Russell hadn't gotten me off the investigation of Miles's murder.

Instead, he had threatened the animals who were my charges here at HotRescues.

That only spurred me to look for the truth all the harder.

Chapter 19

I wanted company that night, so I called Matt.

I wouldn't tell him about the way my mind had been churning as soon as I stopped being physically active after helping to scrub down HotRescues. He'd most likely think I was nuts. Paranoid. Both. And weren't paranoid people, by definition, nuts?

We met for dinner at that Mexican restaurant with the outdoor patio that allowed us to bring Zoey and Rex. I warned Matt, of course, about what had happened that day. But as I'd anticipated, Rex was up-to-date on his shots. Plus, after all the scrubbing we'd undertaken, I doubted that Zoey and I could be carrying anything tainted by parvo.

Matt and Rex arrived first and reserved the table for us.

When Zoey and I joined them, I got a delightful kiss hello from Matt and a sweet lick when I petted Rex. We settled down amidst a bunch of other diners. The October night air was a little chilly so the pole heaters had been turned on, making the area too warm. I maneuvered my chair until I felt comfortable. I was also closer to Matt this way, which felt good. The dogs, used to hanging out together outside restaurants and being scolded if they begged for treats, lay on the ground, occasionally staring up at us with long-suffering gazes.

Matt wore a long-sleeved blue T-shirt with a V-neck that revealed his beige Animal Services shirt beneath. I'd left my HotRescues clothes to be run through the shelter's washing machine and had changed into jeans and a light gray sweater that was among various clothes I'd thrown into the back of my car for emergencies like this.

I ordered a kiwi margarita and Matt asked for a regular one. As we began nibbling on tortilla chips and salsa, I didn't meet his eyes at first. I wondered if this had been a good idea.

"Tell me about it, Lauren," he said just loud enough to be heard over conversations at nearby tables. He reached over for my empty hand, squeezing it gently in his larger, warm one.

The caring gesture brought tears to my eyes, damn it. I was stronger than this.

Usually.

I inhaled deeply, refusing to break down. I didn't have to answer. I could smile and make small talk and just have a pleasant evening.

But this was Matt. We'd been seeing each other for a few months, friends with benefits that hovered around a lot more.

He had even been the one who had introduced me to Zoey.

"I did tell you about it," I finally responded, looking him straight in the eye. For a second. Then I looked back down at the chips as if they'd shouted my name.

"You told me how awful things were today at HotRescues because of an owner relinquishment that went bad. I got that. But there's more, isn't there?"

The server came with our margaritas, which gave me time to think before responding. I took a long sip of the fruity drink, almost wishing it was straight tequila.

I could lie to Matt, but he'd see through it. And, hey, why not get sympathy from him?

Only, that wasn't me.

"I've been second-guessing myself," I blurted, again looking at him. Damn. That wasn't me, either. This time when my eyes welled up, a few tears spilled over, and I angrily wiped them away with the back of my index finger.

"What do you mean?"

I glared at him and admitted with fury, "I've been wondering if you were right—Brooke, Antonio, and you."

"About not continuing to look into Miles Frankovick's murder?"

"What else?" I sighed, taking another gulp of margarita. "I know you all had my best interests at heart. You were sweet enough to be worried about me. But I thought I knew better. And I made my decision after Bella asked for help. The thing is . . ." I stopped. I was saying too much.

"Is what?" Matt prodded. There was a caring and sympathetic look on his face that I had to ignore or I'd get all emotional again.

"It's that my stubbornness and determination may have endangered the animals at HotRescues."

Not a good time for our meals to arrive. I had no appetite now anyway. But I had ordered a tostada salad that would have looked delicious any other time, and Matt had gotten a combo plate with tacos, beans, and rice.

As soon as our server finished fussing over us and left, Matt said, "What is it you feel guilty about, Lauren?"

"I don't feel guilty," I snapped back, then amended, "Okay, yes, I do." I explained generally the way my train of thought had gone after our cleanup today, when Nina and I couldn't find anything online or otherwise about the John Russell who'd stolen Miracle, then left her at HotRescues.

I expected Matt to laugh. It even sounded far-fetched to me.

But he didn't. When I was done, he said, "Is Brooke at HotRescues tonight?"

I nodded.

"Good. Call her and tell her to get Antonio there, too. We have things to discuss."

I anticipated another intervention by the three of them, this time telling me I needed psychiatric help. Or, just as likely, a big "I told you so" session, at the end of which they'd tell me again to back off. Let Bella fight by herself or rely only on her lawyer.

But sitting at the conference table upstairs in the main

HotRescues building a while later—dogs, including Brooke's Cheyenne, again at our feet—the humans instead all expressed concern. And agreement.

"Damn. I wish I'd been here when that S.O.B. brought the dog," Brooke said. She sat straight beside Antonio, her black security staff shirt snug against her curves. She'd apparently taken extra care with her makeup before reporting for work tonight, possibly because she knew her guy would be here, too. The highlights in her hair softly glowed under the room's ceiling illumination. "I might have seen what he was up to—or at least I'd have taken enough notice of his car or other identifying features so we could figure him out."

"What happened could have nothing at all to do with Miles Frankovick's death and your nosiness about it." Antonio drummed long fingers on the table in front of us. His scowl made his jutting brow stand out even farther than usual—and stopped me from protesting his characterization of my intense search for answers as nosiness. "But you might be right. We're not likely to find much because you had to clean everything so thoroughly, but let me get some crime scene guys here to check for prints. Maybe they could check out the Animal Services van, too."

"Sounds good to me." Matt was sitting so close that our shoulders could have touched, but I kept away. I was on my own here, ready to fend off these people, who'd been on my case before.

I blinked. "Then you don't think I'm nuts?" Or its subcategory of paranoia?

"I didn't say that." Matt didn't smile despite the joking

nature of his words—or at least that's how I'd chosen to interpret them. "But a crime's been committed, and the thief should be apprehended."

I hung around HotRescues till Antonio got his fingerprint collectors there. So did Matt. Since Brooke was on duty, it was no surprise that she stayed, too.

When I walked around the HotRescues grounds, I had plenty of company—Matt and Brooke, at least. Antonio stayed in the front to wait for the people he'd called.

I wanted to stop at every kennel and ask the dogs how they were feeling.

By the time we returned to the front building, the crime scene techs had arrived.

There wouldn't be any immediate results, I was warned. And even if they identified the horrible person who had stolen Miracle and left her here, there was no link to Miles's killing that anyone else would necessarily glom onto. But I felt relieved and vindicated that these people whom I cared about—and who all knew something about bad guys—might be taking my way-out-there concerns seriously.

Matt and Rex came home with Zoey and me that night. I almost felt schizophrenic in addition to my other psychological self-diagnoses, the way my mood had gone from dark and miserable to lighter and redeemed.

None of that was like me. I hated feeling all those

extreme emotions. I was the kind of person who was always in charge, of everything around me and, most of all, myself.

But having Matt in bed with me that night did a lot to keep my mind from dwelling on the stress.

And in the morning, when we all, dogs included, once more did a marathon rehearsal in my sunlit residential community, I felt at peace again. Myself, renewed.

I had several goals now. I still intended to find out what really happened to Miles Frankovick and exonerate Bella, assuming she wasn't guilty. I knew she hadn't been involved with the theft and relinquishing of Miracle, at least, which convinced me even more of her innocence.

And that was my second goal—finding out who did leave that poor sick pup at HotRescues.

Which all blended and churned into a related goal: determining whether my paranoia was rooted in fact, whether the first two were part of the same batter, all baked into a single felonious cake that combined murder, theft, and animal endangerment.

I would accomplish all of these objectives, along with all the other tasks I'd set for myself, like taking excellent care of all the animals at HotRescues. And if I was right, and the person who'd left Miracle on our doorstep was also the killer, I would have the pleasure of accomplishing something very special for myself in addition to helping Bella.

Matt and Rex went one direction after the humans had showered and eaten a low-effort breakfast of cereal and milk, and Zoey and I went another.

I fed Rex along with Zoey. The kibble I used was good stuff, and Rex enjoyed it, too.

At HotRescues, I arrived early enough to say good-bye to Brooke and to thank her again for her dedication to HotRescues and to helping her boss here—me.

"You're welcome." She smiled impishly. "So . . . when are you going to ask Dante to give me a raise?"

I laughed. "Maybe after I ask for one for myself."

I was kidding. Dante was generous. I couldn't complain about my salary, or the bonuses he gave me when I needed them—like to help finance my kids going to college.

I would keep him up-to-date about all that was going on here, including more about the parvo incident and the fact that the cops would look into it because of the related theft, if nothing else.

I would also suggest a salary increase for Brooke, though I figured she was kidding, too.

"Does Antonio know when we might get fingerprint results?"

"Soon was all he said. I'll keep you up-to-date."

"Thanks. How late did he stay?"

Her usually pink complexion grew rosy. "He—"

"Never mind," I said. "Your look tells me more than I want to know. Everyone here look okay?"

"No indication of anyone being sick," she assured me, clearly relieved by the change in topic.

I did my morning walk-through with Zoey more slowly than usual anyway, checking once again for signs of parvo. Brooke had been right, though. Everyone looked fine.

By the time I returned to the welcome area, Pete was in

the back area getting food together for our inhabitants and Nina had arrived up front.

That meant I was free to start the adventure I'd planned for that day.

Chapter 20

I had phone calls to make first.

I sat at my desk, stacking papers, glancing at the increasingly data-crammed folders on the computer—and planning the order in which I'd make my calls while gathering the numbers.

Plus, I let my mind veer in a lot of related directions.

I am never wishy-washy. But I am realistic.

Even after all I'd gone through discussing the situation with Matt, Brooke, and Antonio, I knew I might be reading a lot of deviousness into the relinquishment of an ill Miracle to HotRescues.

Whoever had stolen her might not have realized she was so ill at the time, then panicked and decided to get rid of her in a manner that could still end with her survival—relinquishing her at a wonderful, caring, no-kill shelter.

It might have been completely unrelated to my looking into Miles Frankovick's murder. I recognized that. I also realized that it gave me a reason to examine each of the suspects all over again, at least in my own mind.

I called Dante first, though, and brought him current, as I'd planned, on the parvo situation. As we discussed it, I told him my latest musing, that the thief might have believed he was acting in the sick dog's best interests by bringing her to HotRescues. He wouldn't have wanted to go back to Carlie's, in case he was caught.

But why not another vet? And why here? My idea sounded too coincidental, even as I suggested it.

I also mentioned my initial belief that the relinquisher could have left the ill dog intentionally.

"And you think that's to distract you from helping to clear your friend Bella from suspicion in her ex's murder?"

My hand tightened on the files I held. If Dante told me to back off, I might have to do it. He'd have a different agenda from Matt, Brooke, and Antonio—and it would involve the best interests of HotRescues even more strongly.

"It seems far-fetched," I said, "but . . . yes."

"Interesting." The word trailed for a few seconds, so I knew he was considering the ramifications. I pulled myself taut, waiting for orders that I might not like but would have to at least consider obeying. "Well, I know you care about HotRescues. Let's talk about some additional ground rules for when staff besides you can accept an owner relinquishment. But as far as this stopping you from doing what you think is right? Let's not go there yet. I'm too interested in hearing who you decide actually killed Miles Frankovick."

"By the way, did you know him?" I'd recalled that Miles, while still alive, once mentioned knowing Dante, and also knew that I ran HotRescues. I never had figured that out, but Miles had made their relationship sound ominous.

"Why—do you think I killed him?" Dante's voice was droll, and I knew he wasn't serious.

"Just looking into all possibilities," I quipped.

"I figured. Actually, he did contact me once to see if I'd buy Save Them All Sanctuary out from under his ex-wife, make her an offer she couldn't refuse. He'd done his homework, knew I fund both HotRescues and HotWildlife. I played along for a conversation or two, described both of those shelters in the most glowing of terms—and their administrators, too. Then I very firmly but kindly told him where to go—and to leave Save'Em alone. That was all."

"Interesting. . . ." It was yet another aspect of what kind of S.O.B. Miles had been, trying to blindside Bella that way.

"Yes, isn't it? Anyhow, keep me informed about how your investigation progresses."

That was that. My boss was a good man, especially for a mega-billionaire. Maybe the fact that his lady friend, Kendra Ballantyne, walked into similar situations by investigating murders captured his fascination. Whatever his reason, I relaxed and let myself breathe again—before I started making the other calls I'd planned.

"Here goes, Zoey." My dog must have recognized the grimness in my tone. She rose from where she had been lying and put her head on my lap. I patted her distractedly as I reached for the next phone number—Dr. Vic Drammon's.

He was a vet. He would know about parvo. And maybe he'd heard rumors about someone stealing sick dogs.

I'd check with Carlie later, too, of course, but this gave me an excuse to chat with Drammon about sick animals. Would he have put Miracle down instead of saving her?

I had to wait about five minutes before his staff put me through to him. He'd probably been with a patient.

"Yes, I've sometimes treated dogs with parvo for L.A. Animal Services," he said in response to my general question. "I know you won't like to hear this, Lauren, but most dogs that catch it are young, and many don't survive. They become too dehydrated too quickly to be saved. I then have to euthanize for health reasons." What a surprise. Only, in those circumstances, he was probably right. "I fortunately haven't seen any cases either through Animal Services or private owners lately. Do you have an outbreak at HotRescues?"

"No, thank heavens," I responded. Notwithstanding the acts of the guy who'd left Miracle here. "I've just heard of some recent cases in the public shelters, though. Have you treated any of their animals lately?" And have any of the dogs been stolen on the way to your clinic? That would be my next question after a positive response.

But I received a negative one. "No, not recently. Are you—Is there an outbreak at Save Them All Sanctuary? Is that why you're calling?"

"No. I was just wondering, though, if you'd heard anything about sick dogs being stolen." Negative or not, I decided I wanted to hear his answer. Might he have done it? Anything was possible. But surely if a vet wanted to do something with a dog with parvo, he'd have access to one without stealing it.

"Stolen from Bella's?" He sounded horrified. And getting his reaction was another reason for my call.

I didn't want to mention Carlie. They were at public odds with one another since her TV ads that contradicted his on-air position about special-needs shelters had started airing. He might love to create a diversion from their underlying issues by criticizing her for something else about her clinic.

"No. I'm in close touch with her, and everything there is fine." Except that we both hated his attitude, but I didn't need to mention that to him again. "But a friend told me about a situation where a dog with parvo was recently taken. It was found, though, and it will survive. No need to put it down." I had to rub that in, wished I could smear it right onto his snotty, pet-euthanizing face.

"How nice that it will be all right." He sounded polite but not convinced. "Was there anything else on your mind?"

"Not really." I thanked him—for nothing—and said good-bye. This call had been pretty useless. I'd learned nothing either favorable about or against Drammon, and no new info about where the parvo might have originated.

Even so, talking to him had only spurred my resolve to hear the reactions of others involved with Bella when I mentioned the parvo incident—starting with those from whom I expected nothing.

My next call would be to the Frankovicks. I considered phoning one of the brothers, Edson or Brewster, but decided on Eleanor. She was the one who'd appeared most support-ive of Save Them All Sanctuary, and I thought she'd be more up front about responding to my questions.

"Hello, this is Eleanor." Her tone was both businesslike and friendly. I gathered she didn't recognize my phone number or otherwise have caller ID. I pictured her in an office at their furniture store, assuming, perhaps, that I was a supplier or prospective customer.

"Hello, Eleanor. This is Lauren Vancouver, Bella Frankovick's friend."

"Oh, yes." The businesslike aspect of her tone remained, but it sounded less amiable. "If you're calling about the settlement you proposed, we're having our lawyer draw up papers that will describe the way we'd agree to it. I think it follows what you suggested, although it also provides for what happens if Bella is unable to continue as head admin-istrator . . . such as if she is arrested."

Interesting. At least it was mostly positive.

"I'm calling not on Bella's behalf this time but my own," I said. "I'm not sure whether I mentioned it but I run a pet shelter, too—HotRescues."

"The one Dante DeFrancisco's affiliated with?" That brisk tone had thawed again. I'd already learned she was an animal lover, so that made sense. Even so, would she respond to what I asked?

"That's right. I'm calling because of an incident that occurred at HotRescues yesterday. I've reason to believe it might be related to my attempt to help clear Bella— assuming she is innocent."

"What's that?" She sounded interested.

I briefly related the story. "There's some question about

whether the person who took, then left, the dog was in disguise and if the situation was intended to warn me off. I know you like animals and wouldn't have done such a thing." Although I'd listen to her tone for any nuance that might indicate she was covering her behind. "But I've been looking into all angles and—well, I really hate to ask this." Not. "But is there any chance your husband or his brother might have been involved somehow in an attempt to stop me from trying to help your former sister-in-law?" Or to hide that they'd killed their brother, but I didn't say that.

Nor did I ask how they might have known where to pick up a sick dog. That aspect made my inquiry sound ludicrous even to me—although I really didn't know them well enough to figure out what they knew about *anything*. But since they apparently viewed the proposed settlement favorably, their trying to distract me from helping Bella made no sense.

Unless one or more of them had killed Miles.

A pause. Then Eleanor seemed to reply through gritted teeth. "If I thought either Brewster or Edson did such a thing or were even capable of it, I'd turn them in myself— maybe after skewering them." She hesitated. "That sounds wrong. In case you're wondering after my poor choice of words, I didn't kill Miles. I know he didn't like Save'Em, but all he was talking about was withdrawing money, not torturing any animals. And though Brewster and Edson aren't as interested in saving animals as I am, I don't see either trying to make pets sick to get back at someone they don't like."

"Then they don't like me?" I felt sure she'd hear the amusement in my tone.

Eleanor laughed, too. "Probably not, since you're trying to get Bella off the hook and, despite what you say, they think she killed Miles. But you're barking up the wrong tree on both the murder and the attempt to hurt your shelter, Lauren, if you come after either of them—or me."

Easy enough for her to say, but I believed her. They all remained near the bottom of my list of suspects.

My next call was to Al Traymore. I'd planned on going through a similar scenario with him, but his initial response caused me to finagle an invitation to his house.

His wife, Clara, was home from the hospital.

I conducted my usual micromanaging by walking through HotRescues before leaving. Twice, this time, although quicker than each tour usually was.

I was still concerned about finding any parvo symptoms in the dogs.

In addition, I felt even more paranoid than usual and had to take special care about looking over our cats, making sure none of them appeared to be ill, either.

When I finally left, I made it clear to Nina that I wanted her to take special care of Zoey, keep her close, watch her every move—and elimination. Just in case.

The Traymores lived in the residential area of Los Angeles just west of the old Farmer's Market and the much newer, adjoining shopping center called The Grove. It was a good central location from the sheriff's station where Al Traymore worked and the Beverly Hills boutique owned partly by Clara.

I had to drive around for a while to find a nearby parking meter instead of leaving my car in an area designated only for residents with permits. Then I walked a few blocks to the small but nice-looking brick house that sat among similar ones on the block.

I strolled up onto the porch and rang the bell. A dog barked. Al Traymore, in a sweatsuit and not his sheriff's uniform, quickly answered, along with a golden retriever mix. "Come in, Lauren," he grumbled. "But make it quick." I figured that if I didn't, he'd start acting deputy-like and kick me out. As it was, I didn't understand why he'd let me come in the first place.

"Who's this?" I asked, bending to pat the dog.

"Chaz." His thick jaw clenched even more than I'd seen it before as he led me down a short hall and into the living room.

The place was dimly lit, with window shades drawn. Oil paintings trooped around the walls, and the scent of incense hovered in the air.

A woman sat on the fluffy red couch that was as antique-looking as the rest of the room's upholstered seating and gleaming woodwork. Clara wore blue-and-white striped pajamas on what appeared to be a frail body. I didn't spend much time looking at her outfit, though. Instead, my attention was quickly riveted to her face.

It was nearly as red as the furniture on which she sat. Her lips were paler than the rest of her skin, though—and so swollen that it appeared she'd been punched there.

A bandage was attached beneath her chin. The skin around her eyes, too, looked puffy.

"Hello, Clara," I said. "I'm Lauren Vancouver. I'm very glad to meet you." I'd decided not to mention my visit to her BHark shop unless it came up in our conversation.

"You're a friend of Al's?" I had to strain to make out her words. They were slow and indistinct.

Chaz lay down protectively at her feet, and Al joined her on the sofa.

"We've met," I said, glancing at him. He regarded me benignly, his expression giving no clue to his thoughts. Had he mentioned to Clara the fictional friend I'd told him about who'd supposedly also received damaging cosmetic surgery from Dr. Miles Frankovick? "When did you get out of the hospital?" I asked.

"Yesterday. Afternoon."

I eliminated her from my list of suspects in the Miracle theft and relinquishment immediately. Even if she had worn a mask, like I believed the guilty person had done, Nina would have noticed a speech pattern—or non-pattern—like this. Plus, she would have had to go straight to Carlie's from the hospital, then to HotRescues—unlikely.

Her husband, though? Just in case, I asked if he had brought her home and if he'd stayed with her.

"Oh, yes," she acknowledged.

"Of course," he confirmed, glaring at me for seeming to doubt how devoted a husband he was.

I decided to be somewhat up-front about what I was here for. I glossed over some of it, telling them briefly about the horrible person who'd stolen a sick dog yesterday then left it at my shelter.

"You thought it was me?" Clara sounded horrified as

her eyes widened. I noticed for the first time that they were hazel.

"I thought it was someone who wanted to warn me away from trying to find out who really killed Miles Frankovick."

Al Traymore was suddenly on his feet, fists clenched. Chaz rose, too, as if ready to attack me if his master did. "That's enough," Al said. "I shouldn't have let you come, but since I did you had better not—"

"My intent wasn't to upset Clara," I said quickly, noticing tears in her eyes before she dropped her head to stare at the floor. "I'm so sorry."

She looked back up at me. "I didn't kill him," she said. "Al didn't, either. He was with me at the hospital the night I heard that S.O.B. was finally disposed of. He deserved it, though. He did this to me, and my doctors now say that, though I'll heal, I'll never be completely the same. You can be sure, Lauren, that I'd never try to hurt the animals at either your shelter or even that butcher's ex-wife's. I love animals. It's why I have a shop that caters to them. And why we have our own sweet Chaz. And you can be sure of one other thing, too."

"What's that?" I asked gently, sharing a quick look with Al.

"That I hope whoever did kill him never gets caught. Better yet, gets an award for it. Miles Frankovick deserved to die."

I walked back to the front door with Al Traymore and Chaz.

"Being in law enforcement," Al said, "I hate to hear her say that, even though we both feel it. Look, Lauren. I have to admit that I jumped at the idea of your coming here when you asked, mostly because I thought my wife needed some distractions from her medical issues—only I should have thought it through. The things you talked about aren't the kinds of distraction she needs."

"I understand. And I hope you understand why I felt I had to ask."

"You're trying to help your friend who was also disfigured by that S.O.B—maybe trying to prove that whoever she is, she didn't kill the jerk. Unofficially, I don't regret the murder of Frankovick any more than Clara does. But if to help a friend you feel like you have to point fingers at everyone else the bastard knew, don't even think of dragging us into it. Like Clara said, we're fans of whoever did it. But it wasn't us."

I didn't mention that the person I was trying to clear wasn't another patient of Frankovick's, nor that someone else had pointed fingers toward them first—a doctor in Miles's medical practice. It didn't matter any longer, at least not to me. I'd be kicking these two to the bottom of my suspect list.

I wasn't far from Beverly Hills, so I decided to stop there, too, at BHark once again. They knew dogs. They sold high-end accessories.

Would they know how to find one accessorized with parvo that could be used as a weapon?

Clara's partner, Mercedes, was speaking with a customer when I walked in. Someone I hadn't met came up and asked to help me—a slim woman of Asian background in a skirt and blouse. Her nametag announced her name as Lu.

"Thanks," I said. I'd need to talk to Mercedes, but if Lu had been here for a while she might also be helpful. "I just spoke with Clara Traymore. She's home now, you know."

She did know. "But I don't think she'll be back here for a while."

What I'd said, though, made her act even friendlier toward me. Even so, I didn't really connect with her, since she seemed much more interested in accessorizing pure-bred dogs and cats from recognized breeders than discussing anything having to do with the Traymores.

When Mercedes was through with the customer, I excused myself to join her. Lu walked off as someone else came through the door.

"Hi," I said. "I'm Lauren Vancouver. I spoke with you here at BHark a while ago. I'm an acquaintance of Clara Traymore's, and I run HotRescues, a pet shelter in the San Fernando Valley. I—"

"I just got a call from Clara," Mercedes interrupted. "I gather you were one of her first visitors."

I nodded.

"She called because she was upset. She told me the terrible thing about HotRescues and someone bringing in a dog with parvo. She said you're trying to find whoever stole it—and that you have some kind of far-fetched idea that it's connected with whoever killed the butcher doctor who hurt poor Clara."

Far-fetched? Maybe, but it could be true.

"That's right," I said. "At least I'm trying to rule that out. I don't suppose you have any ideas about the source of the parvo, do you?"

"Well, since both that veterinary clinic and HotRescues are in the Valley I doubt that my putting out feelers to people I know at the city shelters is likely to be helpful, but I'd be glad to try to find out who might have known about parvo-infected dogs. I hated what that doctor did to Clara, but if the real killer isn't his ex-wife, I'd rather the truth be figured out—so, like Clara said, we can all thank whoever it was. For her sake. Although . . ."

"Although?" I prompted.

"My assumption was that Clara and Al would be able to sue the pants off that damned Frankovick. Now that he's gone, it'll be all the harder. His death actually makes things worse for them if you think about it."

So with two suspects knocked completely off my list, even if what I suspected was true about Miracle's relinquishment being linked to Miles's murder, no one was admitting it or giving me any new leads I could use.

At least not yet.

I had hoped to go to Save'Em next, but a call from Dr. Mona stopped that. There was a couple at HotRescues who'd been there before, back to adopt two cats. I had okayed their application, and now our part-time shrink had also approved them.

The couple was eager. As always, I was pleased that

more animals were going home. But I needed to go back so the adoption could be finalized today.

That meant visiting Bella again at Save'Em would have to wait.

Chapter 21

The cat adoption went through as well as if I'd programmed each of the people and animals involved to behave exactly the way I wanted them to.

The husband and wife who were potential adopters had waited for me to get back to HotRescues by spending time in our cat enclosure, getting to know their impending new family members better.

One was a golden tabby with green eyes and attitude. The other was all black except for her two front paws, which were white. She was friendlier and talked a lot more than her cohort. They'd both been in the same cat room for several months so I knew they got along fine.

I met with all four in my office, sitting in the conversation area so we'd be friendly and at ease—despite the litany of commands I was about to issue. I first asked some questions while the cats prowled along my desk and shelves and around us on the furniture. I'd left Zoey out in the welcome room with Nina so as not to be a distraction.

I gave my usual rundown of adoption information and instructions and warnings as far as making sure that the earnest and clearly thrilled pair facing me on my couch never turned these about-to-be-former residents into outdoor cats. Too much danger there.

I had them sign papers where they vowed to do as I instructed. I wouldn't necessarily know if they didn't, but one of the many things they agreed to was my right to visit their home to check on the cats.

They also received information on the microchips embedded in the cats for identification purposes, in case they did get out and lost somehow. The adopters received veterinary records, too. In addition, I gave them some food to start with—from HotPets, of course.

Then they were good to go—once the kitties were placed into their new crates for transportation home. Their new family would be able to use the crates again for vet checkups or any other time they needed to ride in a car.

When the group left, I was smiling and teary-eyed and happy for all of them—my usual reaction when an adoption was finalized.

Nina walked with them to their car, so I was alone in the welcome area when the phone rang. I walked behind the leopard-print counter to the table and answered. "HotRescues, this is Lauren. How can I help you?"

"Hi, Lauren," said a female voice. "Glad I caught you. This is Corina Carey."

I almost hung up, but curiosity made me remain on the

line. I sat down on the stiff desk chair. Or was it me who was stiff? In either case, I was more comfortable sitting than standing. No use feeling physically uncomfortable as well as mentally.

"Hi," I said with no warmth in my voice. I never liked talking to media people. In fact, I hated it.

I didn't consider Carlie among those vultures, since she had an excellent show with the wonderful purpose of helping animals. Corina Carey, though, was a paparazzo of the most despicable kind. She was a reporter for *National News-Shakers*. I'd met her a while back when she did a story related to the puppy mill rescue that had so affected me.

I hadn't heard from her for a while and realized I should feel delighted that I hadn't been interesting enough to attract her attention.

Why now?

"I wanted to get your statement," she said, almost as if she had read my thoughts. I couldn't wait to hear what she sought my opinion about. And in case you're wondering, yes, that was sarcasm. "I heard that someone stole a sick cat from Animal Services at a veterinary clinic yesterday or the day before, then dropped it off at HotRescues. It was rumored to be a warning to you, to keep you from looking any further into the murder of Miles Frankovick. Is this true?"

I felt stunned. Bad enough that the situation with Miracle happened, but for it to have gotten into the crosshairs of the media—and for someone else to have connected it to my actions in trying to help Bella . . .

"Where did you hear that?" I demanded.

"A confidential source," she said so quickly that I

figured it was her standard response to the question no matter where her information came from. "Can you tell me if it's true?"

"No," I said. "It's not. We did have an unfortunate situation yesterday where a sick dog—not cat—was brought in. The dog will be fine, and so will all the other animals at HotRescues." I was positive she was recording all I said and wanted to make sure that nothing reflected badly on my wonderful shelter—nor on Carlie's veterinary clinic. I didn't even confirm that the dog had been stolen. "It was an owner relinquishment." Supposedly. I wasn't about to tell her that she had reiterated my suspicions. "And as for the rest—it's not correct either." At least, I couldn't prove it if it was. "I admire Bella Frankovick and her new shelter, Save Them All Sanctuary. I heard about what happened to her ex-husband, of course, and—"

"Didn't you find his body?"

I let my head sink forward while I took a couple of deep breaths. What would be the worst that could happen if I hung up?

She could say publicly that I didn't cooperate with her, but so what? I could always claim that the connection died.

But would whatever she said reflect badly on HotRescues? What would Dante think?

I suspected he would be amused and would back me. But why take the chance?

"I was one of the people who found him, yes," I said carefully. That wasn't a real admission, since it had already appeared in news stories after the police interrogated me. Details weren't revealed, though—as limited as they were.

"I understand that you're not a suspect, but that his ex is.

I know you've been asking questions to help get her off the hook. Can you give me a comment about that?"

"No," I said, "I can't. In case you're not aware of it, I'm an animal shelter director, not a police officer or private investigator or anything like that. And before you ask, yes, when I had an incident that affected me here at HotRescues, I did help to figure out what had really happened." I chose not to mention my second murder investigation, where I had helped to clear Mamie. Of course the media had been on that one, too, but I hadn't been quizzed by Corina Carey then.

I wished I wasn't now.

"Then you say you're not looking into the Miles Frankovick murder?"

"I say I'd really like to know how you heard about the health problem of the animal dropped off at HotRescues yesterday." That question had lassoed an edge of my mind and was twirling around ceaselessly. Yes, I'd talked about it to several people while attempting to pare down my suspect list—and assuming, rightly or not, that the nasty relinquishment had something to do with warning me away from the murder. But stealing a sick animal, then leaving it at a shelter wasn't the kind of event that should spark a *National NewsShaker*'s interest. Unless her "anonymous source" had an ulterior motive about revealing it. Publicly.

Was that person still trying to get me to back off? If something private but chillingly dangerous didn't do it, maybe horrible publicity would.

"Apparently my source wasn't entirely correct—or truthful." That admission into my ear made my eyes pop open in amazement. Did reporters ever own up to such things? Maybe Corina Carey wasn't as terrible a person as I assumed.

Or she believed that feigning genuineness might scrape out my cooperation.

"You know, I am interested in what the media have to say about the Frankovick killing," I lied. "I'm not involved, and neither is HotRescues, but since I admire Bella for her founding such a wonderful shelter as Save Them All Sanctuary, I'm very concerned about the situation and making sure she's treated fairly. I think that, in any story you do, you need to be sure to stress what a kind, caring person Bella is, and how Save'Em is a fantastic sanctuary for older and special-needs animals."

"There are other opinions about that," Corina said. "In any event, thank you for your time, Lauren. I hope you don't mind, but I may be in touch again."

Oh, yes, I minded. But she had already hung up before I was able to tell her so.

Before I left HotRescues that night, I called Carlie. "How's our little Miracle?" I asked.

"Doing amazingly well," she replied. "No more dehydration or any major problems. We'll probably be ready to let her come home to you in a few days."

"Without being contagious?"

"Without being contagious," she confirmed. "By the way, I'm gathering a crew together to film some more at Save'Em soon. Have you talked to Bella recently?"

"No, but I'm heading her way tomorrow. We can talk about who her favorite pups and kitties are to be immortalized on *Pet Fitness*, and I'll let you know her suggestions."

"Excellent."

I waited for Brooke to arrive before departing from HotRescues. "I don't suppose you've been blabbing to the media about our ill, stolen dog who became a pet relinquishment," I said. "And accidentally said it was a cat?"

"What are you talking about?"

Nina and most of the staff had left, so we sat at the table in the welcome area and I filled Brooke in on my conversation with Corina Carey.

"Very odd," she said when I was done. "I'll talk to Antonio and we'll do some checking around about that as well as the rest. I'd love to know where it came from."

"Me, too."

That night at home, I called both my kids.

Having spoken with the media, however unwillingly, I was concerned that I'd be quoted, either accurately or not. My children had at various times seen postings on the Internet that included me on YouTube and elsewhere. If they happened on to whatever Corina Carey said about me, I wanted to warn them first about why I'd sort of cooperated, and how I didn't expect the report would be truthful.

Sitting in my living room after eating my take-out Hawaiian barbecue, with Zoey beside me on the sofa, the TV off, and a glass of wine in my hand, I called my daughter, Tracy.

"Mom! Hi. Are you okay? I was going to call you. I heard from Kevin that HotRescues was in the news because of some nasty dog illness being dumped there by a nutcase who wanted revenge."

I sighed. It was exactly what I didn't want. Now I might have to allow myself to be interviewed again to counter it.

"That was all an exaggeration. There was a sick dog, but she's going to be fine, and none of the other animals got it. No need to worry about me, or them. How's life at Stanford?"

She started telling me about a course she just loved, and how she couldn't wait till she could come home at Christmas break in a couple of months, and other things that relaxed me and warmed my heart.

My discussion with Kevin was similar, but he said he'd forwarded the Web link to me of the TV news show where Corina Carey talked about the HotRescues–Save Them All Sanctuary link: me. And the sick dog and how that might be related, tenuously, to the investigation into whether Bella killed her ex.

I watched it. I also saw how other news shows were picking up on it. People enjoyed hearing about pet rescue organizations. They apparently liked it even more if there was scandal and intrigue involved. Or at least the media appeared to think so.

Much too real. Much too scary.

It was bad enough that it had happened. But who was talking about it in public?

And how did they know so much?

Chapter 22

I hugged Zoey and left her at HotRescues when I headed toward Save'Em around eleven the next morning.

Everything was fine at my shelter. I'd felt confident about that after taking two walk-throughs and speaking with everyone present before I left.

I'd also talked to a group of schoolkids who were there getting community service credit for learning how to volunteer, plus a group of three college students who were at HotRescues looking for a cat to adopt. I'd already sifted through their application and gotten them to agree which one would be chief adopter. Roommates tended to change a lot during college years, and I wanted them all to know up front that they'd not be allowed to take a cat home from our shelter without a commitment by one of them to love and care for the adopted pet forever.

Now I was free to concentrate on what I'd look for at Save'Em, and ask Bella.

Everything looked the same when I arrived. Volunteer Daya let me into the front of the main building. I remembered her uneven teeth as she smiled, and I smiled back.

"I'll show you where Bella is," she said. "There's this cool new resident she's working with."

Both Ignatz and Durwood pranced at her feet on their short dachshund legs. She shut them into Bella's office, then led me through the main building.

That cool new resident turned out to be a gorgeous Norwegian elkhound, apparently a purebred, who was twelve years old according to Daya. Bella was with him in the backyard area near the rear of the main building. Looking as lovely and poised as always in her Save Them All denim work shirt, her long brown hair mussed about her face, Bella was running the dog through some tricks. Kip stood nearby, watching silently, as did some shelter volunteers. None of us said anything as the dog sat on the grass and gave Bella his paw on command, then stood and danced on his hind legs. He wasn't especially fast, but he seemed eager to comply with what she told him to do. She handed him a small treat each time, but I had the sense that the dog would have done it all just to please her—for the warm attention.

"Hi, Lauren," Bella eventually said in her delightful British accent. "This is Spruce. Spruce, say hi to Lauren. Speak."

He obeyed, then wriggled over to me as I laughed and held out my hand. His coat was well brushed, and I could see a lot of silver on his muzzle and the rest of his face. He was twelve? Definitely becoming a senior dog, but he didn't seem to know it.

"He's a charmer," I said. "What's his story?"

Bella told one of the volunteers to put a leash on Spruce and take him for a short walk around the yard, starting with the paved path. Then she joined me, with Kip, on the nearby bench beneath a lemon tree. It wasn't a very long bench, and I noticed how Kip stayed close to Bella, perhaps even touching her thighs with his own. The thin, grinning guy was wearing a similar Save'Em work shirt that day. It was one of the few times I didn't see the spectacled accountant toting paperwork.

I wished I could read his mind.

As logically as the accounting he conducted, he had become one of my primary suspects as so many others fell to the nether end of my list. He could have killed Miles for Bella's sake—and his own. He had been to Carlie's veterinary hospital. I wasn't sure how he might have known when sick dogs were being brought there. Maybe it was a crime of opportunity. But he certainly could have taken advantage of it, thrown on a disguise, and "relinquished" the stolen dog at HotRescues to warn me to back off looking for whoever had murdered Miles.

He had, after all, already told me to butt out.

Now would be a good time to look into whether any of the rest of my surmises could be true.

"He's an owner relinquishment," Bella began. "Can you believe it? The awful excuse for a human being decided she couldn't deal with the fact that poor Spruce was getting old and she would lose him someday. She had decided to replace him with a puppy and had heard about Save'Em on

TV—the interviews with Vic Drammon." She spoke his name in a clipped, emotional tone, then sighed. "I suppose that woman and Vic are two of a kind in the terrible department. She inquired whether he was right, and shouldn't I make sure that Spruce was put down soon so he wouldn't suffer? I wanted to . . ." Her hand went to her mouth. "Sorry. I was about to say something terrible that could let people think I really was capable of murder. Anyway, I pretended to be friendly until she filled out the paperwork and I'd had Spruce taken to our area to await a visit with Carlie and her vet clinic. Then I told her what I really thought of her. Spruce is fine, by the way. We'll keep him in quarantine as we must, but I believe he has several more good years here. Or maybe we'll even find him a new, loving home. I hope so."

It was a perfect opening for my line of questioning.

"I'm glad this relinquishment had a good result for poor Spruce," I said. "If she'd taken him to a city shelter and he didn't get adopted, which wouldn't have been likely . . . Well, you know. The latest relinquishment at HotRescues will have a happy ending, too." I smiled innocently at both Kip and Bella, attempting to read their thoughts from their reactions.

"What relinquishment was that?" Kip asked, his tone as noncommittal as my feigned ingenuousness.

"The dog with parvo?" Bella said. "That was so awful. I did hear about it on the news after you told me about it."

"You didn't hear, then, Kip?" I asked, watching him carefully.

He shook his head. "You said a happy ending. Is the dog okay?"

"She's back at Carlie's clinic, recuperating. She'll be fine. We had to scrub down HotRescues just in case, but all our dogs there are fine, too. No thanks to our false relinquisher—or at least I think he was false. Would you know anything about that, Kip?"

That direct an accusation might be uncalled for, but I hadn't gotten any reaction yet and wanted to see what he would do.

"What do you mean?" His tone was shrill—a sign of guilt or just being upset at what I'd asked?

"You can't seriously believe that Kip had anything to do with it." Bella had risen suddenly. She now glared down at me with blue eyes as frigid as the Arctic Sea.

"I just want to eliminate him from my suspect list," I said, also standing. "You know, the one I've developed since you asked for help."

"That doesn't mean you have the right to accuse perfectly innocent people."

"How else can I make sure they're innocent?" I peered down at Kip, who watched with a shocked expression behind his glasses. Real, or feigned? "Did you happen to be at Carlie's clinic and see that some dogs with parvo were being brought in?" I asked. "Did that trigger this nefarious plan to keep me from digging further? Maybe you killed Miles to help Bella, then decided it was better that the police suspect her than you. When I kept investigating, you decided it would be better to scare me off, in case I got too close."

"No!" He leaped to his feet, and his rage caused him to ball his hands into fists. He surely wasn't going to slug me—not in front of his beloved Bella.

Unless he thought she wanted it, too.

"Now, look." I backed away from the bench toward the path. Fortunately, the young volunteer walking Spruce was getting close again. There were other volunteers and staff members around, too. He wouldn't attack me in public, would he? "Maybe I should have been more discreet in my questions, but—"

His shoulders crumpled and his hands relaxed. "I get it, Lauren. And, yes, I'd do anything to help Bella, especially since I know she couldn't have killed Miles." He raised his hands in a gesture that suggested he was trying to shape my interpretation of what he said. "Don't take that wrong. I didn't kill him, either. I just trust her and know her well enough to understand that, even though she sometimes says things that might imply she'd do something awful, that's not her."

"Oh, Kip, you're such a dear," Bella said.

They shared a smile that told me that their friendship might actually be turning into a romantic relationship.

"Tell me how I can help you find who really did leave that sick dog at HotRescues. It definitely wasn't me." Kip had stepped around Bella and now stood looking down at me. He wasn't much taller than me—nor was he much taller than Bella. He didn't look very strong.

But he had undoubtedly wished Miles dead. That might have lent him the strength and cunning to become a murderer. Besides, the large, general-purpose kitchen knife Miles had been killed with had probably been sharp enough for nearly anyone to use.

And getting me to back off, letting him take the lead in the unofficial investigation, could keep anyone from taking him too seriously as a possible killer.

"Got it," I said as if I believed him. "And I apologize—sort of. I think I got the information I was looking for here, and that means eliminating you from my suspect list, Kip."

Yes, I lie when it makes sense to do so.

I still couldn't prove it was him. Nor could I prove it was—or, better yet, wasn't—Bella.

"How does tomorrow look for you for Carlie to visit here again?" I asked Bella a short while later.

She'd retrieved her dog, Sammy, from her house, and accompanied me into the part of the main building reserved for special-needs dogs. She had sent Kip back to his office to work on some accounting info she'd claimed to need finalized.

More likely, she wanted to separate Kip from me so I couldn't accuse him of anything else. Of course I'd finished doing that. For now.

We took Soozle from her kennel and let the now three-legged spaniel, who'd been healing well from her hit-and-run car accident, hobble gamely around the central area with Sammy and us.

"It's a Saturday," I continued as we meandered slowly. A number of volunteers were there, too, inside the kennels petting and hugging the dogs who inhabited them. "We're usually pretty busy at HotRescues since people who work during the week either volunteer or come in to consider adoptions. Is that the case here, too?"

"Not really. As you know, with our special-needs pets we don't have nearly as many adoptions as you. Tomorrow would be all right, but I would actually prefer Sunday."

"I'll check with Carlie," I told her. "I know she's eager to film Soozle, not only as a prime example of one of the animals you take care of here but also to demonstrate other special help that's available. She intends to finish the show on Save'Em as quickly as possible so she can air it soon."

Which would be a good idea. Maybe it would capture more attention than the dog theft and parvo relinquishment at HotRescues, which had become a minor media event.

Who had first suggested that to some reporter? That was something I really wanted to know. It might be the key to the whole thing.

Did Kip Schaley have media contacts?

"Do check with Carlie about Sunday," Bella said. "If that works for her, it will work for us as well. Won't it, Soozle?" She bent down and carefully hugged the three-legged dog, who wagged her stubby tail.

Oh, yes, Soozle would make an excellent doggy star on Carlie's *Pet Fitness* show.

Chapter 23

Carlie was pleased about filming on Sunday. She said so when I called her from my HotRescues office late that Friday afternoon. Zoey fell right to sleep at my feet. Nina had already told me that one of the newest volunteers was nuts about my dog and was permitted to take her on walks—but only on the HotRescues grounds. And then only after staff and other volunteers were notified.

Everyone remained on high alert after the parvo incident.

"I have some things to set up first," Carlie said, "so I'll call Bella, maybe go visit her tomorrow, but I'll make sure it all comes together the next day."

"Great," I said. "How's Miracle, and when can we pick her up?" I'd worked things out with Matt and Animal Services so she could become a HotRescues rescue.

"She's doing really well. I'd say you can bring her to HotRescues on Monday. Even before might be all right, but I'd rather have my colleagues stay in charge of watching her for the weekend, okay?"

"That's fine. I'm so glad she's okay." I said good-bye then. Another call was coming in on my phone—Matt.

"I'd hoped to ask you out to dinner tonight," he said, "but the North Central Shelter put out an alert. They're overcrowded and will have to start euthanizing a bunch of otherwise healthy animals tomorrow unless someone picks them up in the morning."

"Why did they wait till the last minute?"

"It wasn't intentional. Sounds as if they got deluged over the last few days by some relinquishments, plus they'd gotten in a bunch of strays before that weren't claimed, and—"

"Business as usual," I muttered.

"Exactly."

I knew what I'd be doing tomorrow. After some great adoptions this week, I did have kennel room available, as well as some openings in our cat enclosures.

But I gathered that the need was for more space than I had. I posted on the Southern California Rescuers Web site that it was an emergency. And even though I knew that the Pet Shelters Together group monitored the site, I sent a personal e-mail to its current chief administrator, Cricket Borley.

By the time I was ready to leave for home that night, I felt reasonably certain that all the endangered pets would have someplace to go.

I was exhausted. I was also keyed up with happiness.

Tomorrow was going to be a big day for rescuing pets.

. . .

Sometimes people—like my kids, or my parents and brother in Arizona—ask if I'm a slave to my job. If I was hired to work seven days a week. If I ever aspire to having a real life outside HotRescues.

My answer is yes to all those questions, and more.

I admit that I'm an addict of sorts—to situations when I can pick up dogs and cats that are otherwise going to die if not rescued, then bring them to a new, temporary home while they await wonderful futures.

That's what made my voyage to the city care center that Saturday so poignant. It was the kind of event I live for these days.

Plus, I got to share it with administrators of other shelters. Nearly a dozen showed up, some good friends of mine, others acquaintances, all participants in the SoCal Rescuers Web site and quite a few members of Pet Shelters Together, an affiliated group of shelters that had been the crux of my second murder investigation when its chief administrator had been killed. Her successor, Cricket, seemed more . . . well, human. And definitely involved in saving as many endangered pets as she could, too.

Matt was there. It wasn't part of his job with Animal Services to pay attention to this kind of situation, but he did. Often. That was one of the things I especially liked about him. That, and the fact that he had let me know so I could put out the word.

I owed him. Plus, I was so happy that I wanted to celebrate. He and I made a date for dinner that night.

That was my answer to the last of those questions:

wanting another life outside pet rescue. I'd socialize with people I liked or cared for—but of course they had to love animals, too.

The shelter administrators like me were met by some of the city care center staff, who took us to the area where they had put the animals in most critical need of saving. Sad-faced dogs seemed to know things were different around here and looked at us with hope as we looked back at them.

Pete attended this rescue with me. We'd brought the large HotRescues van. It was filled with four cats and a half-dozen dogs when we left.

And both of us were smiling.

I was still smiling the next day. Yes, I admit I wasn't always aware of my expression over the last twenty hours or so, but I know I felt gratified as Pete and I took the animals to Carlie's veterinary clinic to have them checked out. Carlie was around and said hi, then got her staff busy, and Pete and I left.

The prognosis later in the day was that all our new prospective residents were healthy, except for a few fleas, some mange, and other minor kinds of issues that could be resolved with medicines and determination. I'd send a crew to pick them up on Monday so they could remain under observation for a couple of days.

Then there was my evening with Matt. Rather, Zoey's and my evening, and night, with Rex and Matt. We ran, practicing for the marathon. We ordered in pizza so our bodies wouldn't assume we were fully turning over a new leaf in our attempts to be fit. Matt and Rex stayed the night, and that definitely inspired me to smile, too. Our increasingly athletic bodies made for some interesting exercises together.

Matt had Sunday off. I theoretically did, too. Instead, I popped in at HotRescues after sending Matt and Rex on their way. And then it was time to head to Save'Em to watch Carlie in action.

"Soozle, you're one sweet spaniel." Carlie was in the Save'Em infirmary's examination room with her film crew hovering around, probably making sure that all angles possible were captured. "You remind me of my Max." Max was also a cocker spaniel, the first dog ever to be adopted from HotRescues. That was how Carlie and I had originally become friends.

Carlie, in a white veterinary jacket, her blond hair arranged carefully around her face, stood by the gleaming metal table in the center of the room. Soozle, the ginger-colored cocker mix, was on it, standing on her three legs and turning this way and that to lick Carlie's face.

I'd shoehorned my way into a corner—a dark one, out of the way. I didn't want to be filmed for Carlie's show. I just wanted to watch what she was doing. Some of the Save'Em volunteers and staff hovered in the background with me, including Peggy, Daya, and Neddie.

Bella, though, stood right beside Carlie, clad proudly in her Save Them All Sanctuary work shirt and wearing tasteful but exaggerated makeup. She was a minor star of this show, after host Carlie and the animals she would feature on *Pet Fitness*. Today's filming was all about Soozle.

Kip was with us, too. He observed mostly from outside the infirmary. I figured he was even less eager to get captured on camera than me.

I saw the admiring, caring look on his face, though. The guy definitely had it bad for Bella. So bad he would kill—and menace a great shelter like HotRescues with parvo?

Yes, he still headlined my list, notwithstanding his denial and Bella's siding with him.

Especially when, after joining us briefly, he edged over to me and got in a dig. "So . . . it's been a while since this all started. Have you cleared Bella yet?"

"Working on it," I responded.

"Maybe I'd better take over your investigation after all."

I just shrugged and continued watching what was going on. He once again moved out of the infirmary.

"Here's what we'll do," Carlie said from the middle of the room. "I'm going to take all sorts of measurements. Can you see us?"

That last question was directed to a laptop computer that was sitting on the examination table, its cover open and against the wall. On its screen were a couple of youthful, earnest guys in white coats—people from the company ProsthaPetics whom Carlie had interviewed a while back on her show featuring animal orthotics and prosthetics. One was Paul, the guy who had come here about a week ago to help fit Nifty, the Basset hound mix, with a wheelchair.

"Yes, Carlie." The voice sounded nearly as good as if the pair were in the room with us instead of talking from the screen. "We're ready to write down the parameters as you tell them to us."

Soozle was about to be fitted with a bionic leg.

I wished whoever had hit her with a car and just left her there to die knew about it. Could see that, instead of the poor dog just dying because of the S.O.B. driver's actions and failure to try to help her, she would be a TV star. An example of renewed dog mobility, filmed for posterity.

Much more important than her tormenter would ever be.

Once Carlie got all the measurements and gave answers to each of the questions posed by Paul and his colleague, the three of them bantered over the Internet for a few minutes. Bella joined in about how wonderful the situation was, how pleased she was that they were all involved in helping Soozle not only just survive, but thrive with a new leg up on life.

When the chatting ended, so did the filming. Before shutting off the screen, though, Carlie obtained a confirmation from Paul and his buddy that the device they were putting together for Soozle would be finished within a couple of days and shipped by overnight delivery. Carlie would then arrange to come back to Save'Em and fit the gadget onto Soozle here, on camera. Afterward, she'd send a vet tech or two to work with Soozle, make sure the dog acclimated to the device without hurting herself.

"I'm hoping to have someone else here with me, too," she told Bella, Kip, and me as we started walking toward the front of the main building. The camera guys were left behind for a while to take location shots for the show.

"Who's that?" I asked. We were just meandering along the first floor of the two-story housing area for senior dogs, and I'd been peering into the kennels. As I'd seen each time I was here, there were a lot of volunteers giving each one individual attention.

"You remember that veterinarian Dr. Victor Drammon, who was so against what Bella was doing here at Save Them All?"

Bella drew in her breath so sharply that I turned toward her. "You . . . you invited Vic?" Her voice was tiny and shrill.

Kip planted himself beside her. He looked uncertain. I saw his arm rise as if he wanted to put it around her, but he dropped it again.

"Sure," Carlie said. "I'm going to interview him here on camera for the show on Save'Em. His earlier interview was pretty nasty. I want to film what his reaction is when he sees how the animals here are thriving, that none is suffering and ready to keel over in pain because of your keeping them alive past their prime. Right, sweetie?"

We were passing a kennel in which an Afghan hound with more gray hair than black was standing, watching us go by. Carlie reached in through the wire gate and stroked him. If he'd been a cat, I suspected he'd have purred. Instead, he rubbed his long, thin muzzle against Carlie's hand.

"I . . . I don't think that's a good idea," Bella said. She had stopped walking and faced Carlie.

"Of course it is. We'll show him, for all the world to see, just how wrong he was about your place here, Bella."

I'd recognized before that Carlie loved to take on controversial subjects regarding animal health. Sometimes I thought she went too far.

Was this one of them?

"I've left him a phone message, which he's ignored. I'll try again. Maybe even drop in on him," Carlie continued.

I recalled my own visit to his Beverly Hills–adjacent

veterinary clinic. How I'd left still angry about his explanation of why he had chosen to be so nasty on-camera about Save'Em. He hadn't given me any useful information when I'd called him after the parvo dump, but I'd admitted to myself later that my questions hadn't been particularly incisive. This would give me another chance to interrogate him if I could come up with the right angle.

"I like this idea," I said, planting myself right between Bella and Carlie. Kip remained behind Bella, but I didn't need to address him. "It'll probably reflect even better on Save'Em. The guy can't help but look really dumb on camera faced with all the great stuff you're doing here, Bella. Carlie's show will make you famous anyway." I looked toward Carlie, who beamed. "But having the person who criticized you so publicly reamed in front of an even bigger audience should be amazing, don't you think?"

"Maybe." Bella sounded unsure, though. Her face was pale beneath her makeup.

"The guy's a miserable bastard." Kip inserted himself into the middle of the three of us. "He was even supposed to be the shelter's main vet until he started acting that way. Bella was afraid he'd hurt the animals to make his point. Right, Bella?"

"Well . . . I didn't think so, but—"

"Not that I'm glad he made threats," Carlie said, "but I have to admit that I'm happy he ruined his chances of working with you guys. His Santa Beverly Animal Hospital has a great reputation in the veterinary community. I know one of his partners, and I've heard how successful they are. They've been around for years and are still a reputable practice. I can't say I'm sorry he shot himself in the foot, though. I'm thrilled that my Fittest Pet Veterinary Clinic is your vet. And to be able to help special-needs animals this way . . . fantastic!"

I grinned at her enthusiasm. Even Bella managed a tiny smile, though she still didn't look happy.

"Imagine how wonderful it'll feel to make sure the guy gets his comeuppance in front of thousands of viewers," Carlie added.

"It may not be a bad idea," Kip said tentatively to Bella. "If you can stand seeing him again."

For an instant, an almost grieving expression passed over Bella's face. "Maybe you all are right," she finally said, sounding brave. "I'd love to see Vic eat his words about Save'Em." Her pursed lips turned into a hint of a smile. "I'll be surprised, though, Carlie, if he agrees to come here and take you on like that. But . . . go for it!"

Chapter 24

There wasn't a lot of traffic on the freeway on my way back to HotRescues, usually a good thing. A truck passed by even faster than I was going, and I inhaled its noxious fumes. Ugh. That was worse than the kennels at my shelter before we cleaned them each day.

I slowed down so I could vent the smell out of my car.

I realized then that something was niggling at my mind, and it wasn't a hallucination due to breathing in something potentially toxic.

No, it was a scratching on the edges of my conscious-ness, from things that had been said while I was at Save'Em.

I needed to get back to my computer files and type in my thoughts. See if putting them in a semi-tangible form gave them more sense than the whirling haze constituting my unfettered brain waves.

But when I pulled into the parking lot and ran into the welcome area at HotRescues, I was greeted by a tearful Mamie. The senior citizen volunteer who'd once been my mentor loved to come in on weekends and see all the extra activity when even more people came in and met animals they might want to take home with them.

Small, red-haired Mamie had some psychological issues— the ones that had turned her into an animal hoarder. But she was usually happy at HotRescues.

"What's wrong?" I asked her.

She sat behind our leopard-print welcome desk as our greeters usually did. I assumed she had also been answering phones, and her reply confirmed it.

"There was a call," she gulped out. "It was terrible."

"On the answering machine?" I could only hope, since I wanted to hear it.

"No. I answered. The person on the other end . . ." Tears rolled down her wrinkled, papery cheeks. I almost hated to prompt her to go on.

But I did. "Did they say who they were?"

"No. And I couldn't tell if it was a lady or a man. But whoever it was threatened you, Lauren. And HotRescues."

I froze. "Mamie, tell me exactly what you remember the person said."

"Something like you're too nosy for your own good, and also for the good of the HotRescues animals. Parvo's not the only thing that can go wrong. You should watch your back."

I called Brooke right away from my office, knowing she would contact not only Antonio, but also EverySecurity, the outfit that was supposed to be handling all HotRescues safety issues.

"I'll have them drive by more often, both during the day and at night," Brooke assured me. "But you'll need to be careful, Lauren. Maybe hold a short meeting with everyone there, warn them to be careful, too, not accept any relinquishments or take anyone into the shelter area without your okay. And then you—"

"Will do like the creep said," I finished. "Watch my back."

Though I felt somewhat unnerved, I also had a sense that what my mind had been circling around as I drove had more substance now. I could be getting nearer to zeroing in on, and proving, who had killed Miles Frankovick.

I also felt more vindicated that the situation with Miracle being left here with parvo had something to do with the murder.

I sat at my computer, the files I had created with separate pages for everyone whom I remotely suspected of killing Miles in front of me.

I'd indexed them at the front, listed by name, from most to least likely.

I went over what I'd heard today at Save'Em. Sweet, loving, newly sarcastic and dedicated—too dedicated?—Kip remained at the forefront. I just couldn't bring myself to move him farther down despite the conversations I'd had with him and with Bella. Too many factors pointed to him to shuffle him lower in my complicated and unstable deck of cards.

Bella, too—as much as I wanted to clear her and believed in her innocence, the authorities might still be correct in thinking she was the most likely suspect. Her asking me to help could have been a way of obfuscating the truth. Maybe she'd put me in front of her to trip the detectives and earn their rage rather than doing it herself. But how would the parvo situation fit in?

Then there were those I hadn't yet discarded, thanks to my glomming onto Detective Stefan Garciana's precept of thinking about the least likely suspects: Al or Clara Traymore. Miles's relatives. Dr. Victor Drammon.

Also . . . I still felt I was right about linking the parvo incident to the killing—and the person who'd dropped Miracle off at HotRescues had obviously been in disguise. Who better than a cosmetic surgeon to know how to do that well? Dr. Abe Renteen? Maybe. With her medical connections, Dr. Serena Santoval might have been able to find an ill dog when she needed to. Plus, she had apparently been Bella's successor in Miles's love life. A jilted or unhappy lover was always a good suspect.

On the other hand, how would she, or anyone else from Miles's medical practice, know that dogs with parvo were being dropped off at Carlie's, let alone decide to steal one and leave it at HotRescues as a warning?

Then there was Miles's young assistant Keara, who might also have considered herself a jilted lover. But the dog connection? And could she really have killed him? I doubted it.

Still too many questions, and not enough answers—or evidence—for me to zero in on a suspect.

And until I figured it out, yes, I would be watching my back.

• • •

I was nearly ready to go home that Sunday night. I took my last walk-through around HotRescues with Zoey. Brooke and Cheyenne were with us, too.

We walked out the door and into the shelter area, where dogs in kennels on both sides of our paths came to the gates, some leaping, others barking; hardly any were nice and calm. Despite our encouragement of good behavior, dogs would be dogs.

"I've been in close touch with the EverySecurity guys," Brooke said above the din, pulling her cell phone out of her jeans pocket. "All I need to do is call and they'll storm in here. Do you want me to have them do the same thing at your home?"

"No." I patted my thigh to get Zoey's attention on me and away from one of the enclosed dogs who was asserting alpha-ness. "I just wish Bella had something like that for Save'Em. Someone may be threatening HotRescues and me, but the reason appears to be making sure that Bella remains the primary suspect in her ex's murder."

When we'd checked in on all the dogs and cats and found everyone looking healthy and ready to find new homes, I left Brooke at the middle building and returned to my office.

Yes, it was late. But I went through my files yet again. Did some further online research. Stretched my fingers on the computer and my thoughts on everyone I'd been considering a suspect. Rearranged their order again. Or at least some of them.

Eventually, Zoey and I left for home. But I didn't sleep well.

I wanted answers—especially since HotRescues and I had been threatened again. I realized I should tell Matt about that sometime soon. Tomorrow, maybe.

But so far, I was still as much in the dark about who killed Miles as I was while lying there sleepless in bed.

I called not Matt but Carlie almost as soon as I arrived at HotRescues the next morning—even before Zoey and I took our first walk-through. I sat at my desk, ignoring the computer . . . for now. I didn't want to add anything from last night's near all-nighter.

"How's Miracle?" I asked first thing, hoping for the most favorable response.

I got it. "She's fine. Ready for someone from HotRescues to come pick her up today, in fact."

"I'll do it," I said immediately. "Can we grab lunch together first? I've got something I want to run by you."

I'd gotten an idea how she could use her filming tomorrow to either prove, or disprove, the culpability of one of my primary suspects: Kip Schaley.

If I was wrong, there'd be no harm, no foul. And I'd be able to lower him down on my suspect list.

We met for a quick bite at a sandwich shop not far from Carlie's Fittest Pet veterinary clinic.

"What's up?" she asked as soon as we'd placed our orders at the counter. I liked the place's turkey, sprouts, and cheese sandwich and had the self-control to order low-fat chips and a bottle of flavored water to drink.

I led the way to a booth. We both carried our drinks— Carlie had ordered iced tea—and metal sign holders with numbers showing so a server could bring our food when it was ready. Then I answered.

"A couple of the people who'll be at your filming tomorrow could be Miles's killer." I'd pondered whether to let her know, too, about the latest threat that included me personally and decided I'd better. She might be adding herself to the list of those in the killer's crosshairs, so to speak—if she wasn't already.

"Who?" she asked immediately, leaning over the table with her eyes large and her expression excited.

"I'll tell you when it's over," I said, then told her about the call. "Right now, let's finish eating so I can follow you to your clinic and pick up Miracle."

Chapter 25

When I take a position, it's because I've reasoned it out first.

Kip had had the motive, means, and opportunity to kill Miles. He'd wanted to protect Bella—and possibly position himself to be in a romantic relationship with her. He was always around Save'Em, and he, like hundreds of other people, could have bought the knife anonymously from one of the kitchen supply stores.

Plus, he had been to Carlie's veterinary clinic. It was still a bit problematic to figure out how he happened to be there when some parvo-infected dogs were being brought in, but he knew that Carlie and I were friends and could simply have been watching the place for an opportunity to take an animal that he could then drop at HotRescues in warning.

Since the person who'd claimed to be relinquishing the sick dog at my shelter was probably wearing a mask, that, too, could be anyone—including Kip.

He had already asked me—more than once—to stop investigating Miles's death. He claimed to be the one who'd wanted to help Bella that way. But what if he had, instead, wanted to make sure I didn't find any other viable suspects? Maybe he had become frightened and decided to allow Bella to take the blame after all.

We would see his reaction today.

"What are you thinking about?" Carlie demanded. We were at the gate of Save Them All Sanctuary. I had arranged to get here at the same time she was due to arrive with her camera folks.

One of the veterinary technicians from her clinic stood behind us, a hulking guy who carried a large box from ProsthaPetics.

"Just getting psyched for watching your show being filmed," I said with a grin as the gate opened and Peggy appeared, beaming, the two shelter dachshund mascots at her feet.

"Yeah, and the other stuff you've set up has nothing to do with it."

I merely batted my eyes a few times in an expression of innocence, which Carlie knew was feigned. She chuckled and waved for her troops to follow us.

I wasn't about to tell her that my goal today was to, at last, solve Miles's murder—if my thought processes had been on the right track.

I'd even dared to run some of my thoughts by Antonio in a phone call earlier, then met up with him briefly.

Now I took a quick look around outside. Not seeing what I was hoping to, I rejoined the group.

Bella met us right inside, along with Ignatz and Durwood. I knelt to pet the adorable and friendly senior dogs, admiring the new pack they had formed together.

Bella shut them into her office for now. Then we all strode under the arch and through the senior dog area, halting at the center of the area reserved for special-needs animals. Kip was there with some of the Save'Em volunteers and staff, Daya and Neddie among them. They formed an irregular circle around Soozle.

Nifty was there, too, receiving attention from other humans as he seemed to get along just great on his attached wheelchair. When we arrived, Bella requested that he be put into his kennel. Soozle was the dog of the moment.

I made myself forbear from staring at Kip. I didn't want him to know in advance that I was gunning for him—so to speak.

Carlie looked around. "I gather that Dr. Drammon isn't here yet," she said to Bella, who shook her head in the negative.

"I told my staff to let me know when he arrives," she said. "Other audience members, too. A few are here already touring the place."

"Maybe Drammon chickened out." Carlie looked at me. "He wasn't thrilled about my invitation when I called him a few days ago. Not everyone likes to have their opinions ridiculed on national television."

She had already told me how much fun she planned to have rubbing the euthanasia-loving vet's nose in the scenario she was going to be filming—helping a disabled dog walk once more on four legs.

"Come on, gang," she continued. "Let's get to work helping Soozle."

Before she'd done more than removing the contraption of a plastic limb combined with metal tubing and vinyl straps from its large box, I saw two people enter through the door from the senior dog area. One strode in first, followed by the other in a volunteer shirt who immediately skirted around him and dashed up to Bella. She was kneeling beside Carlie, holding and examining the prosthetic device.

I again stayed in the background so I wouldn't be filmed, but I heard the volunteer apologize to Bella. "I was going to tell you he was here, but he didn't wait."

"That's okay," Bella told the young girl as she stood to greet the newcomer.

I watched Kip's reaction. He had moved to stand near me, and his stiff body and expressionless face spoke volumes. He despised Drammon, too—but not necessarily for the same reason that I did. The vet had apparently had a fledgling relationship with Bella that he'd ruined by his position on killing special-needs animals. Was Kip jealous of him anyway?

If Kip had in fact killed Miles, he'd have been better off framing Dr. Drammon than allowing suspicion to become an Atlas-like weight impacting Bella's much smaller shoulders.

Dr. Victor Drammon wore a suit as funereal as the one he'd had on at Miles's memorial service. He appeared sad as he looked down at Bella through his thick glasses. "We're both entitled to our opinions, you know. I understand yours. I really do. I hate this—disagreeing in public, making a spectacle of ourselves."

Bella appeared sad, too, and upset. "Then why did you criticize Save'Em—and me—that way, Vic?"

I moved closer to listen, and so did Carlie. She also motioned for her camera guys to move in. She, too, had worn a suit to show her professionalism, but hers was an attractive deep rose. She'd taken off the coat, though, and replaced it with a white veterinary jacket. "Have you had a change of heart, Dr. Drammon? Why don't you come over here and watch what I do? Feel free to help—or if I misunderstood, you can always comment on how I'm torturing this poor dog. We will be taping this for my show, of course."

"I didn't agree to be filmed." His voice was tight.

"By coming here, you did. This is on the order of a news show, and by participating in an interview yourself you've made yourself a public figure. You won't find suing me easy." Carlie's grin was snide, and I could tell her crew was lapping it up, filming her and the other vet from all angles. "Come on into the infirmary, gang."

I watched Vic Drammon exchange another look with Bella, as if asking for her help. She seemed to hesitate, then shrugged and followed Carlie. Me, too.

Once inside the smaller room, Carlie stooped to put Soozle up on the metal table in the center. The same guy who'd been toting the box before had it in his arms, and at Carlie's nod he extracted the prosthetic device from it.

"The fact that Soozle still has a stump of leg makes this a bit easier," Carlie said to the camera. "There are ways of attaching devices to a pet's bones, but this way we can just strap it on and see how it works out. It's less intrusive as well as less painful. If we can't keep it on her adequately but the concept works for her, we can always do surgery to attach a permanent device later." She looked at Vic Drammon, who now stood along the edge of the room across from me. "Isn't that right, Dr. Drammon?"

Again the cameras panned in his direction. He nodded his head slightly. "This way is certainly preferable, if it works."

"It works," Carlie said. "Although we'll keep an eye on Soozle, and if there are any problems we'll come up with an alternative solution. Now, watch as I put it on." She did so skillfully, fastening the straps. "This device has some hinges that help to absorb stress and make it easier to walk. It's one of my favorites. But it might not wind up being Soozle's. We'll see."

When she was done, she again lifted Soozle. She walked outside the infirmary room and back into the center of the special-needs area, putting the dog back down where staff, volunteers, and visitors could watch. "Okay, girl, give it a try."

Soozle looked confused, which I was sure was picked up by the cameras. She sniffed the device on her rear leg, lifted her leg a bit, then put it down on the floor. Carlie took a treat from a bag she'd brought and waved it in front of the dog's nose. That got Soozle's attention, and Carlie gave the treat to her. She moved the next treat farther away. Soozle took a few hobbling steps forward to get it.

"Good girl!" Carlie hugged the dog gently, then lured her again. And again.

After a few minutes, Soozle seemed almost at ease with

her new prosthetic device—at least when it came to seeking treats.

I ached to work with her, too. Hug her to help ease her confusion and to encourage her amazingly brave efforts.

But this was Carlie's show. And Bella's.

I watched Kip watching them, too. He was smiling so proudly.

Dr. Drammon? His expression was unreadable. Skeptical? Unhappy? Or just the opposite? But its intensity drew some oddly irregular thoughts onto the surface of my mind.

Or maybe it was more than that . . . like the way my prior musings were now etching ideas in different directions than they'd been skewing before.

"You and your staff will need to work with her, of course," Carlie told Bella and gave some general, then more specific, instructions while being filmed. She watched as Bella similarly lured, then treated, the pup, who seemed to know she was the center of attention—and that she had been given a new leash on life. Or at least a new prosthetic.

As Bella continued training herself, her staff, and Soozle, Carlie approached Dr. Drammon, waving one of her camera folks to join her.

"So what do you think, Dr. Drammon? Am I torturing Soozle?"

"It appears that she might acclimate herself to her new device," he said formally.

"And she's not suffering? Not in immediate need of being euthanized?"

"Not immediate," he said. "It remains to be seen how she'll do long-term."

"Do you see anything to indicate that she won't now be able to live out her full life span as a result of her infirmity?"

"It remains to be seen," he repeated. His breathing seemed a little more rapid, but otherwise his professional demeanor didn't change.

"Then doesn't this indicate that your prior interviews about Save Them All Sanctuary, and your blanket statements on how all injured dogs should immediately be euthanized to keep them from suffering—might they have been incorrect?" Carlie stood there with her arms crossed. I stayed off camera and silent, but I wanted to applaud her.

"It depends on the animal," he said. "That was always my position. But a place like this is likely to see a lot more that might be worse off being kept alive than being put to death humanely. That's all."

"That's all?" This came from Bella. She'd left her staff to work with Soozle and joined Carlie in her inquisition.

"Yes. Of course." The look he shot at Bella seemed pained and then he once more faced Carlie. "You invited me here to see this. I came. I don't need to be attacked on camera for voicing my opinion. I still believe that dogs should not be kept alive while suffering."

"And what about if they have a chance at survival? A new life, like Soozle? Or love for a senior dog or cat?" Carlie kept pressing him.

"Whatever," he practically shouted. More quietly, he repeated, "Whatever," then turned slowly and with dignity.

Once he was off camera, it was my turn.

I didn't suggest that Kip take a walk with me now, as I'd

originally planned, so I could casually ask some very important, if disguised, questions.

Instead, leaving Kip to congratulate Bella, Carlie, and Soozle, I followed Dr. Victor Drammon.

He made it easy to confront him alone, since he immediately headed out of the area for special-needs pets toward the front of the building. I caught up with him in the large first-floor room comprising part of the area where senior dogs were kenneled. A lot of them started barking. I just smiled.

"This place holds such mixed memories for me," I told him over the din. "Were you aware that I found Miles's body?"

He looked down at me through his glasses. His expression looked both bleak and guarded. "Yes, I'd heard that."

"In the parking lot. Maybe you even parked in the spot where he died." I didn't distinguish between the two lots. Because of the way Drammon had been shown in, I figured he had parked in the front one—and I'd found Miles in the back.

"I don't . . . That's a gruesome thing to say."

I wished he'd finished his first sentence. What he'd said was too inconclusive—although it sounded as if it had started out as a denial.

Even so, it wouldn't have been much use as evidence. The news had undoubtedly described where Miles's body was found.

"You were friends with him." I didn't make it a question. "Both of you were against Save'Em, but for different reasons. Did that add to your friendship?"

"I suppose you could say that."

"Then you must have known he was visiting Bella here a lot."

"I knew he had come here to see her, yes."

"But the night he died—before that, he'd confronted her, given her a hard time, yet that night he hadn't even let her know he was there. She heard him—or the killer—but she didn't see either of them. I wonder why."

He just shrugged and started walking again.

"Carlie's putting together such a wonderful show," I said, catching up with him. I'd decided to aim my comments in a different direction. "Featuring Save Them All Sanctuary—it'll attract a huge number of viewers. But the way she interviewed you . . . Maybe she should have let you speak on the show without immediate contradiction. Not that I agree with what you said, especially in your earlier interviews, but you had the right to say it."

"I'm surprised to hear that from you, Lauren." He stopped and looked down at me again, this time both startled and pleased. And maybe off guard.

"Of course, speaking is a far cry from killing," I said. "Euthanizing animals that don't need to be killed—well, I, of course, disagree with that. That's why I run a no-kill shelter."

"But your animals are healthier than the ones here."

"Right. And they're theoretically more adoptable. But I know you're quite comfortable with killing, aren't you?"

He sighed, rubbing what was left of his salt-and-pepper hair in apparent exasperation. "I'm a veterinarian. I do what needs to be done."

"I don't mean just animals," I said. I knew my tiny smile looked snide. And angry. "As far as I know, Dr. Miles

Frankovick wasn't that old. Nor was he ill. Why did you . . . euthanize him, Dr. Drammon?"

His eyes widened behind his glasses in apparent horror. "That's—Why on earth would you ask me that?"

"Because I think you murdered him."

I watched for something on his face, in his rigid posture, his demeanor, to give him away. He just shook his head as his mouth pursed. "And I think you're nuts, Lauren. Do you think that by accusing me you'll somehow help Bella get off the hook, so she can help extend the lives of the poor, suffering animals here? That's really stretching things."

With a final glare, he hurried out of the room toward the front exit, while a lot of dogs in their kennels at the perimeter started barking again. They, too, seemed to voice their anger at Drammon's opinions, which had now been proven wrong for posterity, on camera, at least in some cases.

But our disagreement now hadn't gotten me the results I'd wanted.

Maybe I hadn't asked the question right. Maybe—

This couldn't be over.

I didn't often change my mind. But my focus was no longer on Kip, at least not for the moment.

I followed Drammon.

But I couldn't catch up with him. Once out of range of the camera and my inquiry, he all but ran to the front door, ignoring the greeters who watched him, careful only not to step on Ignatz and Durwood.

By the time I got to the exit, he was gone.

I sighed, heading back toward the filming. I'd been pleased to see Drammon get a dressing-down in public. He deserved it, after the position he'd taken against Save'Em, and against saving elderly or infirm pets that weren't suffering.

But I hadn't considered him seriously as a murder suspect. Until now.

I had been focusing on Kip, believed he had killed Miles to help Bella.

But what if he—and maybe Bella, too—were being framed instead by Vic Drammon, to keep scrutiny off himself?

Had Drammon killed Miles? If so, I didn't yet know his motive.

He had denied it. Of course. I didn't really expect him to admit guilt.

But his attitude hadn't seemed to be that of a guilty man.

He'd admitted to me, when I'd called to ask him about parvo, that he sometimes treated sick pets from Animal Services. He might, therefore, have somehow learned when a few with parvo were being taken to Carlie's. He might have wanted me not to keep digging into suspects to help Bella, so he could have then relinquished poor Miracle at HotRescues to distract me—and warn me off. And whoever did that had to be the person who'd made the threatening call to HotRescues.

I lifted my chin in an expression of indifference as I went back to where Carlie continued recording background scenery at Save'Em.

She was going to interview Bella some more, too. Kip was watching, and so were a lot of the volunteers and staff, plus some shelter visitors.

Was Kip in fact a victim and not a killer?

My goal today was to figure out a suspect and either exonerate him or prove he was guilty, maybe even get a confession. I could try that with Vic Drammon first.

I kept up my nonchalant demeanor as I soon left, heading toward my car. Good thing I hadn't been very specific about what I'd been trying to accomplish here today.

If I had, Antonio, Brooke, and Matt would all share a laugh at my expense. Very soon.

There were a lot of cars in the front parking lot, partly because of all the vehicles driven here by Carlie and her film crew. As a result, I'd parked toward the back of Save'Em, nearer Bella's house—and the area where I had found Miles's body.

I was by myself as I crunched over the gravel in the athletic shoes I wore as part of my HotRescues uniform. I hadn't dressed up to come here, since I had no intention of getting on camera.

My mood was partly bleak. I was thrilled for Soozle getting the new gadget attached that would help her walk more easily.

I was thrilled for Bella, since she and Save'Em would be featured on Carlie's show—which would undoubtedly garner a lot of publicity. And with publicity should come donations.

And I was thrilled for Carlie. Her shows were always good. This one would be great.

But I was not thrilled for me. Where did I go now in trying to help Bella get out of her position as top murder suspect in Miles's death? I'd neither proved, nor disproved, that it was Vic Drammon—or Kip, for that matter.

I pulled my key from my tote bag and pressed the button to unlock my Venza's door. I opened it, planning to thrust the bag across to the passenger seat.

But before I could, I was grabbed from behind.

"How did you know?" demanded Dr. Victor Drammon.

Chapter 26

I turned carefully, despite how his grip hurt my arms. Fortunately, he loosened it a bit. I supposed he didn't intend to kill me from behind.

Maybe that was a good thing.

I wasn't about to tell him that, until a short while ago, he'd been fairly far down on my suspect list—until my subconscious mind had veered way ahead of my conscious ideas.

"I just guessed." I kept my voice as friendly as if we discussed the nice October weather in L.A. "Not too many people would consider an owner relinquishment of an ill dog at a shelter—*my* shelter—as a warning to back off. Where did you get that mask?"

"At one of those temporary Halloween stores. They're

popping up all over now since it's October. I paid cash. No way to ID anyone that way."

"Smart." I attempted to feign an admiring tone. "You were mad that I was trying to clear Bella, learn who really killed Miles, and you wanted me to stop, so you did the thing that you knew would get my attention."

"You should have heeded the warning," he said in a harsh growl. "It was a mild one. No other animal had to be hurt. Your dogs were all vaccinated, weren't they?"

"We could have had puppies around that were too young to be inoculated," I spat back at him, then made myself breathe. Showing my own anger might not be in my best interests. "I assume that you also called to threaten both me and my animals at HotRescues when you realized the parvo incident hadn't warned me off." I tried to smile, but I realized it must look like an angry grimace. I kept my voice calm, though, as I said, "It's one thing to threaten me, but two warnings against my animals? Two too many. I'm really upset about everything you've done, Vic. I'm sure you understand why. But maybe we can work things out. Any suggestions?"

"Are you asking me to pay you so you'll keep quiet?" he demanded. "That's what the bastard Miles did. After his blackmail . . ." He trailed off, staring at me. "Did you guess that, too?"

"Some of it," I lied. "But I'd like to hear your version." Interesting. I'd just wanted him to keep talking, to make his own proposal about how we both could just walk away from here. Not that it would happen for him, of course.

He'd made his own assumption, based on experience.

And by doing so, he'd given me another piece of the puzzle: his motive. But I needed some elaboration.

"I figured you'd get it," he continued. "And, you know, if I told you everything, you might even sympathize. It's why I had to go against Bella and what I really thought about what she was doing here." He gestured toward the inside of Save'Em. "But you'll just have to die not knowing." Oops. That wasn't a negotiation for us both to walk away. "Yes, I killed Miles, so what's one more? When the cops ask, I'll say you attacked me here and I acted in self-defense."

He lunged with his hands out as though he planned to strangle me. I carefully pulled my hand from where it had dipped into my tote bag and pulled out a can of pepper spray. Very calmly, I pushed the button and sprayed it into his eyes—just as Detective Antonio Bautrel dashed from the back of the Save'Em main building, along with a couple of uniformed cops.

"You're under arrest," Antonio told him, "for the murder of Dr. Miles Frankovick."

"And for animal cruelty at HotRescues," I added.

The next few hours were almost as chaotic as when I found Miles Frankovick's body in his car here at Save'Em.

A bunch more cops arrived, including the lead detective on this murder investigation, my onetime adversary and current uneasy ally Stefan Garciana.

Antonio had cuffed Drammon and kept watch over him in an empty office near Bella's. I would rather have seen him in a remote, smelly, stark concrete kennel. He deserved to be there more than any sweet dog did.

Although the kennels here at Save'Em, like those at HotRescues, were actually fairly nice. Not as good as a wonderful home with loving humans around, but okay. More than Drammon was worthy of.

A pit in hell was more like it. One where its hounds could laugh at him.

I hung around to answer questions. Again. I was a witness once more, and I'd also helped to bring in evidence to convict Dr. Victor Drammon.

I'd played the game well this time. Good thing I had a cop-friend. This had been Antonio's day off, and he'd been willing to participate in my scheme.

Maybe "willing" was too strong a word. I'd let him in on the fact I was attempting something regarding the case without specifying exactly what. He hadn't been happy but he knew that forbidding me would be to no avail. Plus, he knew about the threat that had been phoned in to HotRescues, and had expressed his concern about me to Brooke.

Consequently, he had come to Save'Em in case I was right and put myself in more danger. It never hurt to have official help nearby. He had been one of the visitors in the background wearing casual clothes instead of a suit, watching the filming. Apparently he'd also had backup on standby.

Antonio had fitted me with a wire. All Drammon said had been recorded, including his confession.

Of course the suspect I'd reeled in wasn't the one I'd anticipated tossing bait to. But it really made sense, now that I had more time to consider Drammon as the murderer.

He had known Miles Frankovick. But Bella had appeared to think that with her ex out of the picture she might have had some kind of relationship with Vic. Of course, the way she had intended Miles to go was simply through divorce, not death.

But instead of being on her side, Vic had publicly chastised her for her laudable work with special-needs animals. She'd thought it out of character, but he had refused to discuss it with her. Instead, he had become even more of a buddy to Miles—or so it had appeared. He had even admitted to it.

I still couldn't shout out triumphantly to the authorities that I knew, and understood, it all. I was still unclear about all facets of his motive. What was Miles blackmailing him about? And why was it so important that it caused Vic to kill him?

I hoped to learn more. Soon.

I didn't have to wait long, as it turned out. Just till later that evening.

I'd left Bella in Kip's hovering care. Was that good for her? I wasn't sure how I felt about Kip now, after holding him in my mind near the top of the suspect list for so long and even planning on outing him today—till the truth had implanted itself in my mind like some alien force in a sci-fi movie that wouldn't let go.

Plus, he acted so clingy. But it was her life. And maybe she needed a lot of extra attention and TLC right now, after all that had happened.

I had returned to HotRescues, exhausted and talked out. I felt as if I'd been a contestant on some bizarre reality TV show where the idea was to extract every ounce of knowledge from the foolish soul who'd agreed to participate, leaving her an oozing puddle of emptiness lying senseless on the ground.

Maybe it got worse each time I was interrogated by the cops, or maybe I just imagined it. Either way, I'd driven back to my shelter slowly and carefully, no doubt making other freeway drivers crazy.

I'd walked slowly with Zoey through HotRescues, too, earning me a lot of sympathetic and even pitying comments from everyone I met along the way, even sad-eyed gazes from quiet, attentive dogs. I couldn't help it. I needed some TLC as well, so I ducked into some of the kennels to give hugs and receive licks. Zoey, of course, was my main supporter, staying close by my feet and kissing my face each time I bent to pet her.

The cats? They, too, paid attention to me—at least most of them did. I hugged those who allowed me to, stroked others till they purred. I dragged my feet even more in their enclosures, trying to lure as many as possible into my arms.

It wasn't like me to be so sluggish. I hated it.

But I perked up with Brooke's call after I returned to my office. Antonio wanted us all to meet for dinner, including Matt.

Matt. He'd called me earlier. Chewed me out for doing what I'd done—and for not telling him about it. The media had gotten wind of it when more LAPD officers and detectives besides Antonio arrived at Save'Em, so the news was full of the arrest. Matt had known right away that I had to be involved.

"I'm fine," I'd told him.

"Good. Then you'll be in great shape for me to give you a good spanking the next time we're together." I doubted he meant that in a sexual sense, but I grinned anyway.

"Guess I'll have to avoid you, then." We had nevertheless made plans to meet for dinner that night so I could tell him what I knew—which, unfortunately, wasn't everything.

I'd also had to call my kids since they were aware I was friends with the director at Save'Em. So far I hadn't seen my name mentioned in any stories, thank heavens. But my kids were smart like their mom. They'd make assumptions about my involvement, so I'd wanted to reassure them before they had any opportunity to worry.

That was when Brooke had called. Antonio wanted to fill us in over dinner about some additional information the authorities had gotten from, and on, Vic Drammon. And, yes, Matt was welcome to join us, too.

We planned to meet at a quiet Italian restaurant on Devonshire, south of HotRescues' location on Rinaldi. I could hardly wait.

Brooke came to HotRescues first, though, to leave Cheyenne while we ate. Glad that Zoey would have company, I left her there, too, in the second-floor apartment in the center building where Cheyenne would hang out.

Brooke pulled a light blue sweatshirt on over her black HotRescues security uniform for our outing. Her amber eyes glowed as if she had had something to do with the arrest of the person who'd committed murder and had been tormenting HotRescues. In fact, she did have something to do with it. She was the one dating an LAPD detective who had potentially risked his job to help catch this murderer.

Hanging out with a potentially ditzy woman trying to do a cop's job probably wasn't in his best professional interest, especially if I'd been wrong.

But I wasn't—exactly. Even if we'd caught a different suspect than I'd originally thought, Antonio had helped to nab the real killer.

I felt vindicated, too. More like my ever-confident self.

If Antonio had told Brooke anything in advance, though, she wasn't about to relate it to me. "I don't know much more than you do." She sounded exasperated as I continued to press her for answers while she drove us to the restaurant. "Antonio will tell all of us everything."

Matt got there first, reserving us a table. He was wearing a nice shirt and slacks, not his Animal Services uniform, as if this was a social event, a double date. In a way it was—though it would provide most of us some potentially interesting information.

The guy looked good. I liked the way he kept glaring at me, too, with those hot, toasty eyes. It reminded me of the spanking comment. On the other hand, I figured he still wanted to shake some of what he considered sense into me. Too bad. I had plenty of it. I'd come out of this situation just fine, hadn't I?

We sat down and ordered a bottle of the house Chianti. Brooke had promised not to drink much. Though her health had improved, she was the security person on duty at HotRescues that night so she had to be alert. She didn't know whether Antonio would still be on duty, so the group might have to rely on Matt and me to drink most of the wine.

Fine by me.

Antonio soon arrived. He'd apparently put on a suit

once more but the jacket was off, and he had rolled up the sleeves of his blue shirt. He gave Brooke a quick kiss, then sat down. He seemed pleased to get a glass of wine immediately, although he soon ordered his own beer. He obviously was not on duty now.

When crusty rolls and a creamy Parmesan cheese spread were brought to the table after we ordered, Antonio finally got down to business, telling us what he had learned about the continuing investigation into Drammon.

"You understand, of course, that this can go no further. We're still collecting evidence and some of this is speculation based on what the guy has said. He's lawyered up now and not talking any more, but taking what he said before with what we'd learned from others, plus some preliminary checking into what he'd revealed—"

"Yeah, we got it," Matt interrupted. "We won't talk about this except among ourselves. Right, ladies?"

Brooke and I looked at each other. "Yes, sir," she said.

"Ditto," came from me.

"So some of this you know." Antonio leaned forward conspiratorially. "It started with Dr. Victor Drammon skimming profits from his veterinary clinic and hiding it from his partners."

Intriguing. This might be the reason that the facility looked so run-down—not enough funds available to keep it looking as spiffy as a near–Beverly Hills veterinary hospital should be.

"The guy was in love with Bella Frankovick. He was in love with gambling even more. He visited the Hustler Casino in Gardena with almost as much frequency as he did his veterinary clinic."

Antonio continued his narrative. Unsurprisingly, the casino got more money out of the relationship than Vic did. To fund his gambling addiction, Vic stole from his clinic. One night he was out drinking with Miles, hearing how awful the soon-to-be divorced guy felt about the still unresolved financial issues in ending his marriage. Miles claimed Bella had stolen from him and would continue to forever. They'd both over-imbibed and Vic admitted to his own problem.

Miles decided to use it against him. Went gambling with him but instead of losing big, gained even bigger by taking photos of Vic at the tables.

"Even though they were buddies, Vic eventually became furious that Miles kept giving Bella a hard time and came to confront him," Antonio continued. "Instead, Miles confronted *him*. Told him he had pictures of him gambling away his clinic's profits. He blackmailed Vic into doing those interviews dissing what Save Them All Sanctuary was all about. And then, when Vic said he'd done it and they were even, Miles demanded more, including money that Vic didn't have. Otherwise, Vic's partners would learn why their clinic wasn't earning them all the proceeds they thought they were bringing in."

"And that didn't make Vic happy," Brooke interrupted.

Antonio's rough features lightened into a fond smile as he continued, "That's an understatement. He was furious."

And desperate, Antonio continued. He had actually loved Bella and now knew that would be impossible to follow up on. That was Miles's fault. So was the peril hanging over his ongoing relationship with his veterinary partners. In his mind, it had to stop.

With a knife in Miles's chest. Vic hadn't necessarily wanted to pin it on Bella, but he held out no hope that they'd ever get together, and it was better that she be blamed than him.

He knew Miles had gone to Save'Em a few times before and lured him there that night with a promise he would show him something he could use against Bella in his quest to take back his money.

"Amazing," I said. "It's all so close to what I suspected." At least what I ultimately suspected, after I'd decided to confront Vic earlier that day. Not that I knew about the gambling problem. But I figured Vic would have had some reason, logical or not.

"You've gotten all this from him in—what?" Matt looked at his watch. "Eight, nine hours?"

"Like I said, it's a lot of speculation," Antonio said.

"Based on facts and reality," I said, defending him.

"And your nosiness," Matt grumbled, but I tossed him a huge, smug grin.

"And my shrewdness and perseverance," I countered. "And love for animals. And—"

"We got it." Matt was the one to smile now. A sexy enough smile to tell me he just might want to pick up Rex and spend the night at my place.

"Now all you and your gang have to do," Brooke said to Antonio, "is gather all the evidence you need to convict the jerk."

"No problem," he said. Was that sarcasm I heard in his tone? "One thing, though." He looked at me. "We did find his contact in Animal Services—with some help." He nodded sideways toward Matt, who grinned and shrugged.

"Meaning?" I asked

"Meaning Drammon learned about the outbreak of parvo at one of the public shelters from someone who'd used his veterinary services before, but he said he was too busy to help—and recommended Carlie's clinic."

I sat up straighter. "Then he knew when the sick pups would be dropped off so he could steal one, then relinquish it at HotRescues as a warning to me."

"You got it," Antonio said.

I certainly did.

Chapter 27

I imagined that a lot of storefront business owners along Santa Monica Boulevard in West Hollywood were peeved.

It was the day of the HotPets marathon, and about six miles of it were closed to road traffic.

On the other hand, there were a lot of people on the sidewalks, ready to watch the runners and their leashed dogs attempt to make it to the finish line. They had probably brought money for food and even clothing if they got bored waiting for the race to begin.

Reaching the finish line was my only aspiration. I didn't need to win. I just needed to complete the race. That way, Dante would make good on his pledge to endow HotRescues with even more funds than his already generous donations.

The marathon had been Dante's idea, to call attention to

homeless animals and the shelters that saved them. Everyone running had been required to solicit donations for the animal shelter of their choice. Dante himself had made a pledge to help Save Them All Sanctuary and other shelters he'd discussed with me, as long as the people who had signed up as their team members finished, too.

Plus, I'd gotten other donors to make pledges—thanks to contacts at the Southern California Rescuers Web site. A few other shelter administrators were also running. We'd all shared info about who might provide donations, so all was good.

And, yes, it was also about me. I had taken on this challenge, a different one for me. But when I decided to accept any challenge, I met it.

Like finding Miles Frankovick's killer.

Right now, I stood at the corner of Santa Monica and La Cienega at seven thirty in the morning with hundreds of other people, most of whom had also brought their dogs. This was, after all, a marathon to benefit pet rescue, to encourage spaying and neutering, the works. The crowd sounds were loud and enthusiastic, including the barking of some of the dog entrants.

The dogs were of all sizes, from Chihuahuas to Great Danes, and those in between like my Zoey and Matt's Rex. Fortunately, the canines seemed to get along okay—maybe unlike their rowdy, competitive owners. I figured the smallest dogs' owners would carry them through some of the race, but maybe some were hardy enough to tough it out. And everyone was advised to drop out if their dogs got too tired to continue.

"You look good," Matt told me. I'd donned a running

outfit of loose blue shorts and a tank top. The number 47 hung around my neck, and he wore a 48 over his yellow T-shirt, which did a great job of hugging his muscles.

"You, too."

To my surprise, Brooke and Antonio were also participating. Brooke had designated one of her security-staff employees to keep an eye on HotRescues last night so she could sleep. She had brought Cheyenne, of course.

Antonio still wasn't owned by a dog, at least not yet. I suspected that Brooke and he would unite into even more of an item soon, so he'd become part of that family. Just in case, though, I'd suggested that Brooke start working on him to adopt from HotRescues. He lived in the bottom floor of a town house in the Valley and had a yard. On the other hand, his job came with a lot of time pressures, and leaving a dog alone for long periods wasn't a good idea. Two dogs, so they'd have a pack? That depended. We'd just have to see how things worked out.

Both had dressed appropriately. Brooke was very thin in her light clothing, but that was the sole indication she'd had health issues. She would run only as long as she comfortably could but wouldn't push herself to finish.

Antonio the cop was in almost as great physical condition as Matt. His number and Brooke's were both in the eighties.

We'd all be exhausted when this was over. Even so, Zoey and I would spend the afternoon at HotRescues— probably just vegging out in my office. Maybe even napping. Later? Well, Matt and I planned to have dinner together, and others would join us, including Carlie and her guy Liam. Then we would go to my place to watch the episode of Carlie's *Pet Fitness* on TV that featured Save Them All Sanctuary: "Hug'Em at Save'Em." I couldn't wait!

Half an hour till the race began. I'd been given periodic updates into what was happening after Dr. Vic Drammon's arrest, but this was a good opportunity to jab for more.

"So, Antonio." I squinted up into his face despite the bright Southern California sun over his shoulder.

He held up his hand. "Before you ask about the Miles Frankovick murder investigation—"

"Aw, come on. Anything new?" At the unyielding expression on his craggy face, I glanced my plea toward Brooke.

She took his hand with the one of hers not grasping Cheyenne's leash. She looked up and batted her eyelashes in an exaggerated flirtation that wasn't intended to get Antonio's testosterone going—or at least I didn't think so.

But it was enough to make him smile. And give in.

He waved for us to join him nearer the closest store, one that appropriately sold athletic shoes. Not as many people stood there, so he could talk with less possibility of eavesdropping.

"Everything I told you before?" he began. "Consider it nearly engraved in stone. We're still working on evidence but think it's just a matter of time."

The cops had used a warrant to check out Vic Drammon's home and veterinary clinic. Although it wasn't conclusive, there were knives in both from the same manufacturer as the murder weapon—and some of Vic's hospital subordinates indicated he'd brought them in.

Plus, they'd been talking more with Drammon's Animal

Services contact about what they'd discussed regarding the parvo outbreak and taking the sick dogs to Carlie's clinic.

Not much, perhaps, but the investigation was still ongoing.

A two-minute warning sounded. Antonio stopped talking and we returned to the crowd to take up our starting positions.

I didn't stop pondering what he'd said, though.

"So did he admit to any of it?" I asked as we stood waiting. I knelt to hug Zoey, who was clearly eager to move. I patted Rex, too, then stood again. "Like stealing Miracle from Carlie and dumping her at HotRescues—and otherwise threatening me?"

"Not exactly. He's got a good lawyer. But we'll get him."

The gunshot sounded—a recorded, blank but loud sound—and we all started running.

Not too fast. As I said, I just wanted to finish. There were younger, fitter runners than me in this race who could win it with my blessings, get all the kudos they wanted.

Speaking of kudos, though . . . After a mile, I was still rarin' to go. The men and dogs were, too. Brooke had slowed a little, and Antonio remained at her side. So did Cheyenne.

"See you at the finish line," I called.

In another mile, we passed a small shopping center where I'd left those who wanted to cheer me on.

Yes, both my kids had come home from school. Tracy and Kevin stood there waving, cheering. I couldn't hear them but felt sure they were yelling "Go, Mom!"

With them were folks from HotRescues who had gotten my permission to be here today. Not Pete. I needed him on duty. But Dr. Mona, our shrink; Gavin Mamo, our trainer; Margo, our groomer; and my right hand, Nina, were there. So were some volunteers. Davie Tarbet had driven Mamie there, nice kid that he was.

Carlie was also in that area, with Liam. So were Bella and Kip, and Bella's dog, Sammy. Even Dante was there, and he had brought Kendra Ballantyne. Their dogs, too—Dante's German shepherd, Wagner, and Kendra's Cavalier King Charles spaniel, Lexie. Why weren't they running? They were both younger than me. But this was my choice. My race.

Dante's idea, though. His HotPets stores would get a lot of publicity out of it.

The crowd around us continued to surge forward. Would they lift me, carry me to the end? No. Matt wouldn't, either. He didn't look nearly as out of breath as me. Still, he was sweating. His breathing was heavier.

Three miles. Helicopters overhead—the media? Was that paparazzo Corina Carey out there somewhere, dogging me? She'd put in one of her stories covering the parvo incident that she had an anonymous source within Animal Services, so that had apparently been how she had learned what was going on.

Zoey and Rex were both panting. I waved to Matt. We stopped at a stand set up at the side of the race and we all got drinks, dogs included. Then we started off again.

By mile four, I wondered how productive the training I had done in my neighborhood had been. Yes, I knew that six miles was hardly forever. But this was my first marathon.

I stopped jogging at mile five and started walking briskly. Could I make it to the end?

Yes. I never quit.

I was hot despite the cooling October air as we got nearer to the ocean. I was tired. I was an automaton, no brain to hinder me.

I kept going, Zoey at my side, Matt and Rex, too. Lots of people surging with us. Lots of people watching.

I had helped a friend. I had solved yet another murder. I had discovered who had threatened HotRescues, and he would be punished. I could do this.

And then, there it was. The end.

I heard a roar from the watching crowd.

I slowed a little to pet Zoey and take Matt's hand.

Then I crossed the finish line.

Matt and I shared a huge, enthusiastic kiss. A promise of things to come? I was jazzed enough then to think so. Hope so.

I smiled into the cheering crowd, pretending their enthusiasm was for me. Why not? I'd met this challenge. Of course. I'd earned more funding for HotRescues and helped other needy shelters.

I was ready for many more pet rescue challenges. Just watch me!

"Gutsy Lauren Vancouver easily wins over the hearts of
animals in need—as well as readers."
—Rebecca M. Hale, *New York Times* bestselling author

FROM
LINDA O. JOHNSTON

The More the Terrier

A PET RESCUE MYSTERY

When shelter manager Lauren Vancouver finds out that
her old mentor, Mamie Spelling, is an animal hoarder,
no one is more shocked, and she jumps in to help
rehome the cramped critters. But Mamie's troubles
don't end there. She's accused of murder when the
CEO of a pet shelter network is found dead. And Lauren's dogged determination to clear her former friend
of murder may put a killer on her tail.

PRAISE FOR THE PET RESCUE MYSTERIES

"Animal lovers will delight in a new series filled
with rescued dogs and cats needing loving homes.
Lauren Vancouver is a determined heroine."
—Leann Sweeney

facebook.com/TheCrimeSceneBooks
LindaOJohnston.com
penguin.com

M998T1011

The first book in a new series from

LINDA O. JOHNSTON

A PET RESCUE MYSTERY

At a particularly nasty puppy mill, Lauren helps rescue four adorable beagle puppies that were dumped down a drainpipe, and she's pretty sure she knows who is responsible. Efram Kiley, one of the mill's employees, has a history of dog abuse. And it seems he has a bone to pick with Lauren, because he soon shows up at HotRescues and stirs up trouble by threatening her. When Efram is found dead at the shelter, Lauren becomes the prime suspect, and she'll have to sniff out the real killer to keep herself out of a cage—for life . . .

penguin.com

M898T0511

From the author of *Pug Hill*
ALISON PACE

A Pug's Tale

Hope McNeill has worked at the Metropolitan Museum of Art for years, but this is the first time she's been able to bring along her pug, Max. Officially, at least. Up until now she's had to smuggle him in inside her tote bag.

The occasion: a special "Pug Night" party in honor of a deep-pocketed donor. Max and his friends are having a ball stalking the hors d'oeuvres and getting rambunctious—making Hope wonder if this is also the last time she gets to bring Max to the museum.

But when a valuable painting goes missing, the Met needs Hope's—and Max's—help. In her quest for the culprit, Hope is aided by an enigmatic detective, a larger-than-life society heiress, a lady with a shih tzu in a stroller, and her own arguably intuitive canine—and keeps the heist a secret from her lawyer boyfriend, Ben. With luck, she'll find some inspiration on her trips to Pug Hill before the investigation starts going downhill...

"A world-famous museum—a darling heist—
and pugs! Pure fun."
—Lauren Willig, author of *The Orchid Affair*

"I loved this smart, fun mystery with Alison Pace's
wistful, wonderful voice . . . and one brainy pug."
—Melissa Senate, author of
The Love Goddess' Cooking School

penguin.com

Penguin Group (USA) Inc. proudly joins the fight against animal cruelty by encouraging our readers to "Read Humane.®"

This May we are pleased to offer six of our bestselling mass-market titles featuring our furry friends. Participating authors include Jill Shalvis, Linda O. Johnston, Miranda James, Leann Sweeney, Judi McCoy, and Ali Brandon. These special editions carry a distinctive **Read Humane** seal with a graphic-rendered paw print, conveying our support for this compassionate cause.

Penguin Group (USA) Inc. is proud to grant a $25,000 donation (regardless of sales) to The Humane Society of the United States to support the work of its Animal Rescue Team. According to The Humane Society of the United States, its Animal Rescue Team rescues thousands of animals from puppy mills, animal fighting operations, hoarders, and other situations where animals suffer from life-threatening cruelty. They also provide expert animal rescue response during natural disasters.

The Humane Society of the United States is the nation's largest animal protection organization, and was voted by GuideStar's Philanthropedia experts as the #1 high-impact animal protection group.

Join us in the fight against animal cruelty by making your own tax-deductible donation today. To make a donation online, and to find out more about the work of The Humane Society of the United States, please visit **www.humanesociety.org**.

You can also call their toll-free number, 1-866-720-2676.

Visit **www.penguin.com/readhumane** for more details.

Read Humane® today and help save lives!

Read Humane is a trademark and service mark of Penguin Group (USA) Inc.

M1248G0113